KING
of the
Trailer Park

KING

of the

Trailer Park

TIMOTHY BENSON

iUniverse

KING OF THE TRAILER PARK

iUniverse books may be ordered through booksellers or by contacting:

iUniverse
1663 Liberty Drive
Bloomington, IN 47403
www.iuniverse.com
1-800-Authors (1-800-288-4677)

ISBN: 978-1-4917-7782-4 (sc)
ISBN: 978-1-4917-7781-7 (e)

Library of Congress Control Number: 2015915392

Print information available on the last page.

iUniverse rev. date: 10/09/2015

Dedication

To Pat Merz, my sister, editorial consultant and
tour guide through the publishing world.

1

And the Winner is ...

Gambling has been part of the history of nearly every civilization in every part of the world. It doesn't take long to poke through a library before you find numerous examples of the long standing and infectious appeal of all kinds of gaming. The origins of poker go back to the Minoan civilization of three thousand years ago. There are references to gambling and risk games in the works of Homer and other Greek writers. In medieval England King Richard the Third outlawed dice games because his military was spending too much time playing backgammon, and in Colonial America public lotteries often led good, pious men into financial ruin.

Today it's the lure of Las Vegas, sports bookies and countless Indian casinos that have introduced a new generation to the seduction of games of chance. Those games have made a few people rich but more often than not they have emptied someone's wallet or shattered someone's dreams.

Despite that history and all that came before me I have never had much interest in gambling. To me it's a fool's game, a way to quickly lose what took so long to earn. So of course it felt particularly strange for me to be in that situation at that particular moment. The white and red Powerball tickets were neatly spread across my kitchen counter in five rows of two tickets each; little paper pieces of fantasy that I had purchased only a handful of times in my life. It was an easy way to take a small risk now and again when the spirit moved me. I never feared risk as long as it involved something where the odds were at least somewhat under my control but gambling didn't fit that description. But somehow spending a couple of bucks on the lottery didn't seem to be much of a stretch and it didn't really feel like serious gambling. So there I was, standing at the counter with the Sunday morning newspaper folded back to page two, showing the winning numbers for the long list of games available to the masses of people whose hopes and dreams rose and fell with the results.

It was almost as if I was in some kind of fog. I couldn't figure out if what I was feeling was shock or euphoria or just plain old disbelief. I laid down the yellow highlighter, picked it up and then laid it back down. How many times did I need to check and re-check the numbers? After about a dozen finger touches on the newspaper followed by highlighting the numbers on the tickets followed by writing them down on a legal pad and circling the Powerball number the results were the same. The numbers said I had won three hundred and thirty-five million dollars, assuming that I was the only person with the winning numbers. Three hundred thirty-five freaking million dollars!

"Okay, let's run through it one more time." I said to myself, still unwilling or unable to believe. I picked up the highlighted ticket from the array on the counter, held it close to my face and spoke the numbers aloud and very slowly, as if hearing them would finally validate their genuineness. "15 … 21 … 24 … 37 … and … 54, and the Powerball number is … 29." Then I performed the same ritual reading from the numbers in the newspaper. "Okay," I thought, "better check out the Powerball website." Like most people, I relied on the internet for so much, maybe too much, to verify the facts in my life. I walked into the spare bedroom that served as my home office, fired up my laptop and logged on to *Powerball.com*. I held my ticket against the screen and, one by one, compared the numbers. Finally, my disbelief turned into a palpable shiver down my back. There was no mistake and no doubt. For an investment of just twenty bucks I had totally changed my life.

Money, especially large amounts it, has the power to mess with people and usually not in a good way. How many previous lottery winners had gone bankrupt or squandered their winnings on silly things? How many had invested poorly and lost it all? And here I was, on a rainy Sunday morning, sitting in my sweat suit and wondering if I would end up like those other winners who became losers. It reminded me of a study I had read about Alzheimer's disease. The study said that the disease often enhanced and reinforced people's existing personality traits. If a person was quiet and gentle, with Alzheimer's they became even more docile. If a person was argumentative and negative the disease made them unbearable to be around. I couldn't help but wonder if sudden wealth had that same effect on a person.

"No, not me," I thought. "I'm too smart for that to happen to me. I own a good, solid ad agency and I get great financial advice from the best in the business. I make a nice living and I don't need this money to maintain my lifestyle." Just hearing those words in my head helped me to stay calm and focused on the things I needed to do next. I walked back to the kitchen counter, fished a ballpoint pen out of the junk drawer, picked up the legal pad and tore off the page I'd been using to verify my luck. Then I started to create a list of the things I had to do next.

The first order of business would be to get together with Jeff Norris, my accountant and financial advisor, to discuss the issues I would probably face with the IRS and Arizona state taxes. From what I had read about past winners I knew I had 180 days to decide on how I wanted the payout made. The full amount could only be paid out as an annuity over twenty-nine years. Here I was, a forty-eight year old man who'd be a seventy-seven year old curmudgeon before the last check arrived. All things considered it wasn't a very appealing option. Lottery winnings were always taxed at the highest rate of thirty-five percent so I did a quick mental calculation and figured if I took the quick cash-out it would leave me with about two hundred and eighteen million dollars, give or take a million. Any outrage I might have felt at being forced to give the government a hundred and seventeen million dollars only lasted for a few seconds. "Holy shit," I thought, "two hundred and eighteen million dollars deposited in the bank account of Lincoln Alan Carr sounds pretty damned good." And I knew that once that deposit hit my account Jeff would help me navigate my way through the totally new and unfamiliar financial waters.

The second thing on my list would be to call Jon Aiken, my attorney and golfing buddy. Besides handling my divorce Jon had helped me twelve years earlier when I first decided to leave Pacific Media and start my own ad firm in Phoenix. He played as big of a role in the birth of Carr Creative as I had, even to the point of connecting me with two large and very lucrative clients. My firm had made a solid name for itself in print advertising and television commercial production and we were considered one of the Southwest's cutting edge firms in creating commercial content for the internet. Jon had been with me every step of the way to share in the success.

When I got to the third and last item on my list I wrote down two names and drew a big circle around them: Ozzie and Delilah. Ozzie Hanson was my business partner and best friend and Delilah Samuels was the woman I planned to marry. Each was a huge part of my life and I never liked to make any kind of major decision without the advice of one or both of them. As important as the legalities of the lottery or the taxes or the paperwork might be, it was the feelings of those two people that mattered most to me.

I picked up the winning ticket and stared at it. Suddenly that little thing felt incredibly precious and fragile, like something that needed to be protected. It had only been minutes since I actually realized I was a millionaire and I was already worrying about stuff like the little piece of paper that had become the biggest thing in my life. I wasn't used to having so much to worry about or so much on the line. I wondered if that was the way things would be from now on.

After I cleaned up the clutter of the losing tickets from the kitchen counter I walked back down the hall to the office, opened the bottom desk drawer and found a very large manila envelope to hold the very small lottery ticket. Strangely, I looked around the room and felt the need to have a wall safe or some other impenetrable place to store the little ticket that was worth so much. It made me feel vulnerable. I carefully positioned the manila envelope under my computer keyboard, trying to make it look like just another piece of the mess that was a permanent part of my desk top, something that wouldn't draw anyone's attention to it. Somehow that felt silly. "Okay, man, calm down." I thought to myself, "Nobody's gonna kick in the door and steal your damned ticket."

After a longer than usual shower where I found it hard to focus on simple things like getting the water temperature just right and the cap of the shampoo bottle back on correctly, I dried off and threw on a pair of jeans and my favorite black tee shirt. The man looking back at me in the mirror looked like the same middle-aged guy that I saw there every morning; the thinning salt and pepper hair cut short, the tall, lanky frame with a small paunch and a face with deepening wrinkles that I preferred to call laugh lines. It was the same guy with the high cholesterol and the troublesome heart rhythm. I thought to myself, "There is nothing in that reflection that tells me I'm looking at a very rich man." That was the way I wanted to keep it.

I went back into my office and for a few minutes I sat at my desk in a daze. The big manila envelope sat there, almost calling to me, so I opened it and stared at the little lottery ticket again. "How does a person handle something like this?" I wondered. "How do you keep your head on straight?" Then I thought, "Hell, I'm not the first winner who's had to deal with this." I swiveled my laptop toward me, took my mouse in hand, went online and Googled "Winning a Lottery." Not surprisingly a long list of sites popped up in response to my search. "Gotta love Google," I thought to myself.

A quick scan of the online advice told me I was right on target as far as what to do but with one exception. Three different sites listed the top piece of advice as: "Except for a lawyer don't tell anyone. Keep a low profile until you have the money in hand." I read it again and thought, "How can I keep something like this from the people I care most about?" Delilah and I were in love. She was going to move in with me in a matter of weeks and we planned to marry within the year. Ozzie had been my best friend since our college days. We played the role of Best Man at each other's weddings and helped each other get through our respective divorces. I was happy to make him my business partner when I founded Carr Creative. To keep my winnings a secret from either of them was unthinkable.

The unexpected spring rainstorm outside was unusual for Arizona and it was starting to make its presence felt. Rolling thunder boomed loud enough to make my cat, Otto, seek shelter under the coffee table, his long, gray tail twisting nervously with the sounds outside. A steady rain pelted the tile roof while the wind sprayed it against the windows. "Strange," I thought, knowing full well I was gloating, "my major stroke of good luck should be enough to stop the rain, part the heavens and send sunbeams and rainbows down upon me."

It was a few minutes past noon, my weekend benchmark for an acceptable time to start drinking so I grabbed a beer from the refrigerator and went back into the living room. My frenetic activity with the lottery tickets had occupied much of my morning so I didn't get to watch most of the rounds of politicians whining on the Sunday talk shows. All things considered that was probably a blessing. I took my politics very seriously and more likely than not some tired, old Republican gasbag would have already knocked the big chip from my shoulder and set my teeth grinding for the rest of the day. I was glad that nothing had happened so far to dampen my spirits.

The leather sofa felt like a big, fat, welcoming friend as I nestled into it, cellphone in hand, and I called Oz and Delilah. I asked them to come over at two o'clock for what I told them was a drinks and strategy session for a little joke that Ozzie had wanted to play on an obnoxious neighbor. I was careful not to reveal anything beyond that although it was hard to hide my excitement when I talked to them. I couldn't help but wonder if they had heard anything different in my voice. It was impossible to get the lottery out of my head. I must have sounded reasonably normal because neither of them seemed to be surprised at my request to get together and Delilah always spent Sundays with me anyway.

It would be a lazy and, I hoped, fun afternoon because they both had started to share my love of dreaming up new and better stunts to play on people. I was the one who created the jokes and wrote the scripts for the players. Ozzie's role was to help me find the actors and arrange for the venue where things played out. Delilah was great at refining my ideas and fine-tuning the details to make them more realistic. She was also a semi-regular part of the little group of actors who brought the pranks to life.

Ozzie had been a part of my practical jokes since our college days and, as each successive joke had become more elaborate and complex, he started to refer to them as cons. I didn't consider myself to be a con-man but I had to admit some of my jokes had been small masterpieces of innocent deception. Delilah had a wonderfully inventive mind and a gift for seeing what made people do the things they do. She could always be counted on to come up with an insight or a little twist to make the joke better.

The talking heads of a cable news show were droning on the TV in the background and knowing that the bickering usually had me screaming at the screen before the second commercial I turned it off. With my cellphone on the coffee table and my nervous cat still under it, I closed my eyes and thought back to a joke we had pulled off a couple of years back. We had named it *Operation Budweiser*. It came about totally by accident after I had arranged an outing to take my entire office staff to a Sunday baseball game. The Arizona Diamondbacks had a long home stand against the hated division-rival Los Angeles Dodgers and we had a good turnout for the game. I had purchased a season pass to a VIP box along the third base line and usually just made it available to clients. That particular day was a chance for me to show my staff how much I enjoyed their company and appreciated their hard work. It was a beautiful afternoon, the Diamondbacks were up by two runs and everyone seemed to be relaxed and having fun. During the seventh inning stretch Jason Webb, a young graphic designer who had been with the company for less than two months went to the concession stand for a beer. As he was climbing back up the steps to get to our box he slipped and most of his 32-ounce beer drenched the concrete landing. Jason was embarrassed and we all reacted with a mix of laughter and sympathy but for some reason I saw the potential to turn the incident into something much more. I liked Jason a lot and I saw him as a future star in the company. Any time I had played one of my jokes on someone it was for a reason, either because I liked the person or because I didn't.

The next day at the office I got together with Ozzie and we came up with the framework of my little scheme. It was a plan to convince Jason that he was being sued for damages in a personal injury lawsuit. We made up a story that, after we had all left the stadium an elderly fan had slipped on the landing where the beer had been spilled, fell against a handrail and injured his back. A security guard who saw the man fall told him that a young man sitting with the group in our box, Box B23, had spilled the beer and didn't make any attempt to clean it up or call the stadium staff for assistance. Now both Ozzie and I knew that beer gets spilled numerous times at every game in every stadium in America and nothing ever comes of it. But we also knew that we live in a litigious culture where too many people want to cash in at someone else's expense. The number of TV commercials for personal injury law firms, many of which we had been asked to produce but turned down, would help us make our fake lawsuit come as no surprise to Jason or anyone else.

"Okay, Linc, I get what this is all about," Ozzie said the next day when we sat in my office, "but are you sure Jason won't be scared shitless when we break the news to him? After all, the kid's right out of college and this could really unravel him if we don't handle it right."

"That's the key right there," I answered. "We have to lay the groundwork of the litigation and put it out in front of him. We'll tell him the lawsuit is against him because he spilled the beer, the firm because we rented the box and also the stadium authority because that's where it all happened. That way he won't feel overwhelmed or think that it's just his ass on the line."

Ozzie was smiling ear to ear. "Okay, I like it. He'll feel like he has some cover with other people on the list with him. But how do we make sure he sweats enough to make the con worthwhile? You always say that there has to be enough of a laugh or pain factor to justify the effort."

"Well, stop and think about his position," I replied, still working out the details in my head. "He's brand new to the company. He's young, ambitious and wants to make a good impression on everyone. Then he goes to a ballgame with his boss and coworkers and just happens to spill some beer. A simple thing that happens all the time, no big deal except that it gets his boss dragged into a lawsuit. He's gotta be thinking, "Holy shit, I really screwed up.""

Ozzie nodded, still smiling. "And he sees you looking very worried, very upset and thinks to himself, "I got the boss in trouble and now it's really gonna' hit the fan.""

"Yeah, that's the direction he'll probably go and we'll have to watch him carefully to make sure he doesn't go off the deep end. That's always the risk. You know me, Oz, I wouldn't do this if I didn't like the kid." My words were no sooner out of my mouth before they sounded strange even to me.

Over the next three days, with the help of our talented in-house co-conspirators and our friends at Apex Casting, who helped us find actors for our television and online commercials, Oz and I concocted the details of *Operation Budweiser*. We created the identity of the plaintiff, a seventy-five year old man from Phoenix who would claim that he had slipped on the puddle of beer left by Jason, wrenched his back while trying to break his fall on the concrete steps and did serious damage to his third, fourth and fifth vertebrae. The man's complaint was presented to the defendants, including Mr. Jason Adam Webb, Carr Creative, LLC and the Chase Field Stadium Authority on the letterhead of the fake firm of Yale and Roth, Attorneys at Law, from Phoenix.

Somehow, between meetings and doing all of the work required to keep the agency humming along, Ozzie and I managed to put together the final plan. On Monday morning at precisely 10:00 AM, three people entered the lobby of Carr Creative and were led into our conference room. They included a tall, slender, button-downed looking man playing the role of our corporate attorney, Robert Maywin, a burly looking man with bushy eyebrows, a five o'clock shadow and a particularly malevolent look on his face playing the role of Anthony Greesi, attorney for the plaintiff, and finally a frail looking, elderly man with unruly white hair and wire-framed glasses, hunched over in a wheelchair and playing the injured party, Mortimer Falsdoun. I was hoping the surnames of the players in my little charade wouldn't be too obvious to Jason.

When the three men were seated in the conference room I did a quick run-through of the joke with them and we all worked out our parts and the overall plan, which was basically to instill more than a little fear into our new, young designer. When we felt that everything was in place I asked Ozzie to walk down the hallway to the graphics studio and ask Jason to join a meeting that was getting ready to start. When Jason asked Ozzie what the meeting was about Ozzie gave him his best worried face and said, "I think it's best if Linc fills you in."

Jason trailed behind as he and a silent Ozzie entered the room and the stone-like expressions of everyone at the table were not lost on the nervous young man. He took a seat beside mine and looked around at the three strangers across from him, then leaned over and quietly asked me, "What's up, Linc?"

I maintained a stiff, serious expression, leaned toward him and simply replied, "We have a big problem." I paused a moment then turned to the men across the table and said, "Mr. Greesi, we received your letter, now would you please tell us why you were so eager for this meeting?" With that I handed Jason a copy of the fake letter as the fake attorney responded.

"Well, Mr. Carr, as we stated in our letter, we are representing Mr. Falsdoun here in this civil action against you. We have written testimony from a stadium security guard who saw your employee, Mr. Webb, spill a large amount of beer on the intermediate stair landing in Section 23. And are you that employee, sir?" he asked, looking at Jason.

Jason looked up from reading the letter. His face had turned white as a ghost and he stammered, "Yes, uh, yes sir, uh, that was me."

Greesi maintained his cold, all business demeanor and continued. "The security guard showed us a copy of the guest sign-in book in your company's private box and that's how we obtained your name, Mr. Webb. The guard also told us that he observed you and your colleagues laughing after the incident and also that you made no attempt to clean up the spill or report it."

Ozzie chimed in, trying hard to look like the buttoned-down businessman that he clearly wasn't, his voice tinged with fake anger, "Now wait a minute, it was an accident not an incident, and since when is a fan required to clean up the stadium?"

Greesi glared at Ozzie, then at Jason and snapped, "There is no requirement to clean the stadium, sir, but it stands to reason that any act that creates a potential hazard to the public should be reported immediately."

Our fake attorney, Mr. Maywin interrupted. "Mr. Greesi, I checked with the stadium authority and there are no posted regulations anywhere in Chase Field that state anything whatsoever about reporting hazards. His air quotes around the words "reporting hazards" were almost comical. "Specifically," he continued, "what is your suit based upon?"

Greesi turned to look at the scrawny, tattered looking old man beside him and said, "It is based upon the fact that Mr. Falsdoun here is in a great deal of pain because Mr. Webb was consuming a large quantity of alcohol at your company party and he was careless when he spilled it all over the stairs and the landing where other fans walk."

"What," Maywin responded, "is that all you have?"

"Greesi grinned, leaned toward Maywin and answered, "Counselor, in a jury trial that's all I'll need."

"And," Maywin continued, "I suppose you wanted to have this little meeting to discuss a settlement that will keep things from going to that jury."

The smarmy grin on Greesi's face never wavered. "Well, yes. I'm sure Mr. Carr and Mr. Webb are reasonable men who can see a way out of this situation."

Of course at that point I couldn't pass up my own chance to be an actor so I glared at Greesi and barked, "You slimy son of a bitch. You don't give a rat's ass about Mr. Falsdoun's back or his pain or anything except your damn thirty-percent of whatever award you can squeeze out of Jason and me."

Greesi's smile faded quickly as he spat out his response, "Mr. Carr, your opinion of me is of no concern in this matter. I am here to see that Mr. Falsdoun gets every penny he deserves. Now, are you gentlemen ready to discuss an amount?"

I looked over at Jason. He was still pale and a look of panic was frozen on his face. He ran the back of his hand over his forehead, beaded in sweat. His whole body seemed to be trembling as he stared at the letter in front of him, his head shaking back and forth. He was obviously on the edge of panic and I noticed that Ozzie was looking at him too. All things considered it seemed like it was time to pull the plug on our charade.

I let out an audible sigh as if I was worried. I sat quietly to let the tension hang in the air for a few more seconds and then nodded to the three men, then to Ozzie. As we had arranged in advance, frail, old Mr. Falsdoun, as if he was in great pain, slowly rose from his wheelchair and appeared to struggle as he pushed it aside. He took a wobbly step backward, looked straight at Jason and then began doing jumping jacks. The fake lawyers started chuckling and Jason's eyes bugged out as he watched the old man with the three injured vertebrae perform the exercise like he was a teenager.

I waited a moment and when Jason turned to look at me I smiled and said, "Gotcha!"

Jason's surprise and confusion turned quickly into an awareness that he had been set up. He stared at me and then turned toward Ozzie. Our smiles were all he needed to finally exhale loudly and smile.

"Jason, my man," Ozzie announced, "you have just been on the receiving end of another one of Lincoln Carr's practical jokes. Welcome to the fraternity."

Thinking back to that little scam always brought a smile to my face. I got up and walked into the kitchen, still thinking about how well we had pulled it off. It had been one of the easier and more straightforward schemes I had come up with but it was just as much fun to pull off as the bigger ones. And the small ones involved the same things as the more elaborate ones: a plausible story that usually included some kind of misdirection, a clear understanding of the target, or the mark as Ozzie liked to say, a specific goal and good performances by everyone involved. Call them practical jokes, charades or cons, they all worked pretty much the same way. And they all carried some degree of risk. Whenever I came up with an idea for a joke the same image popped into my head; the classic symbol of the theater; the mask of comedy beside the mask of tragedy. The link between good and bad is very real and I knew that when you try for one you just might get the other.

Just after two o'clock, with the television back on and low in the background, the rain and wind finally letting up and Otto venturing out again from under the coffee table, Delilah and Ozzie arrived within minutes of each other. I was in the kitchen and a quick check of my refrigerator showed it was in its usual state of being more of a wine and beer chiller than a food repository. As I met them at the front door and then walked with them into the living room I was hoping they wouldn't see any signs of the nervousness I was trying so hard to conceal.

Before I could organize the little gathering or even collect my thoughts Ozzie turned and walked into the kitchen. A moment later he called out 'Hey, I'm getting a beer, do you guys want anything?"

I looked at Delilah. "You want anything, babe?"

"Sure, I'll have one too. It seems like a beer kind of day."

All I could think was, "No, it's a champagne kind of day," but I yelled back to Ozzie, "Yeah, how about bringing us the two IPAs from the bottom shelf?"

There was a moment of silence in the kitchen and then Oz yelled back, "Uh, sorry, man, I already sucked on one of them. How about one of you has this pale ale?"

I smiled at Delilah, shrugged and answered back, "Okay, whatever."

Ozzie walked back into the room and handed us our bottles. "No glasses?" I asked.

"They're already in glass, man, tough it out." He plopped down on my well-worn recliner while Delilah snuggled next to me on the sofa.

As usual, Otto jumped up and found her lap and it seemed like the perfect time to get right to the point. Trying to act calm and in control I said, "Okay, guys, please turn off your phones, take a deep breath and pay attention. I'm glad you're sitting down because this is just about the strangest thing I've ever had to say to anyone." They both looked at me with the same curious expression and I hesitated, trying to prolong the anticipation of saying words that I knew I would never forget. I took a long breath and announced, "I am happy, no, make that fucking ecstatic to announce to you that I am the lucky winner of all or some of last night's Powerball drawing."

There was total silence and I waited for a moment, watching as their expressions turned from curiosity to flat-out wide eyed amazement. Ozzie stammered, "What, what the fuck, man, is this another one of your little cons?"

I grinned and looked at Delilah, who seemed to be speechless. "No, Oz, it's not a con. Here, check this out," I handed him the winning ticket and the newspaper to look over.

He studied the numbers, looked at me like he was in shock and as he handed the ticket and newspaper to Delilah he said, "Oh my God man, I can't believe it!' He looked at Delilah who was studying the ticket the same way he had just done, and then said, "You've always been such a cynic about gambling and the lottery.

You call it a game for the mathematically challenged and here you are playing it. When did you buy the ticket?"

"I pick up a few every now and then, usually when I'm getting gas at Circle-K. I just do it to feel like I'm a gambler, you know, someone who takes chances." The conversation and my ear to ear grin were enough to drive the reality home for Delilah.

Still clutching the winning ticket she took Otto and hurriedly laid him on the cushion beside her and then turned and threw her arms around me and in the process nearly knocked my glasses off my face. I could feel her trembling and then she began to cry. "Tears of joy" I thought to myself and then I felt a few of my own filling my eyes.

We clung to each other in silence, neither of us yet fully able to comprehend how the news would affect our lives. Ozzie was shaking his head looking stunned and then, as if feeling left out he got up from his chair, dropped to his knees in front of us and joined in the best and happiest group hug anyone could ask for. It was the strangest mix of emotions I had ever experienced. A huge amount of elation swirling around me combined with a healthy fear of what might lie ahead.

We held that strange and awkward three-way hug for a few more moments before Ozzie pulled away and stood up, his tall, lanky frame looming over Delilah and me. "Man, this is just too damn much to take in," he said. A wisp of his dark hair hung down his forehead, his eyes were wet and he was still shaking his head as he dropped back into his chair.

Delilah relaxed her grasp of me and wiped her tears with the backs of her hands. "You aren't kidding, Oz," she replied in a shaky voice. She was still holding the Powerball ticket and I took it from her hand and said, "Careful babe, your tears might make the ink run and then we wouldn't be able to read the numbers and cash it in."

She smiled, leaned forward and kissed me, and said, "I hope you're just kidding because I'll cry if I want to." Then she kissed me again.

"Geez, maybe he isn't kidding." Ozzie said, smirking and looking straight at Delilah, "He sure was in a hurry to grab that ticket from you."

I knew that both of them, with their feelings for me coming from different directions, understood my usual need to maintain my self- control. Over the years I had been told many times that I had the stone face of a gambler but masking my feelings never meant that I wasn't feeling them and they both knew that. I also knew that they understood my intention would be to stay as normal as possible. Since they were such an important part of my life I told them they would be in charge of keeping me sane, focused and reasonably down to earth. Delilah managed to put it all into a perfect context when she said, "Honey, we promise we won't let you become a squirrel.

And in his own style Ozzie added, "Yeah, or an asshole."

Now that I had shared my big news with them I felt more comfortable about making it an all-out celebration. A bottle of very rare and very expensive bourbon that a client had given me as a Christmas gift but that I never opened seemed like the perfect lubrication for such a situation. It took Delilah and me way too long to fetch the bottle, ice and glasses because we couldn't seem to go ten seconds without stopping to hug and kiss each other but after some very enjoyable effort we finally made it back to the living room.

The three of us talked a while longer and when I made it clear that I intended for each of them to receive a share of the winnings, Ozzie started shaking his head. "No way man, that's your money. You don't owe me a thing."

"I didn't ask you if you wanted it, pal, I'm telling you that I'm going to give it to you." I was trying to keep my tone firm but light-hearted. "As far as I'm concerned it's a done deal." I looked over at Delilah and I could tell the conversation had rattled her a little. "What's the matter, babe?" I asked, "Are you okay with all of this?"

I knew that she realized when she and I got married she'd be a part of everything I owned anyway. "Oh, I'm okay with it I guess," she said, almost sighing. "It's all just too much to process right now."

I let that comment sort of float in the air for a moment. When the emotional part of the announcement finally seemed to have sunk in and things were beginning to feel calmer it seemed like the appropriate time to lay down what I considered to be some ground rules.

"Okay, now that we've all had a minute to absorb the news I want to tell you how I want to handle things, and there's no negotiating or wiggling on this." Both Oz and Delilah were totally still and silent. "First of all, I don't want anyone to know about my winnings other than the two of you and my lawyer, for at least six months to a year if possible. I want to sit on the money, minus a little bit for the three of us to enjoy and just let the company ride on its current book of business. No spending activity that will attract attention, no questionable postings on Facebook or Twitter and no lifestyle changes that will arouse anyone's curiosity." From the nodding of their heads my approach seemed to make sense to them. After a few seconds I continued. "I'm sure you both understand the consequences if word gets out about my new-found wealth. If people know I suddenly came into a kajillion bucks there will be a whole slew of problems that I don't want to even think about and the way people will view me is at the top of the list."

"Agreed," Delilah said as she looked over at Ozzie.

"Yep," he offered, his head nodding in an exaggerated motion, "I totally get it."

His words were no sooner out of his mouth when the news came over the television that the winning Powerball ticket, and the only one, had been purchased at a northeast Phoenix convenience store. It was official, the winning amount was mine and mine alone. It was good news but it only made me feel even more worried and anxious about what laid ahead. The news led to another enthusiastic three way hug.

Despite the time it took to wade through the details of the lottery winnings, the celebration and all of the issues attached to my new financial situation, I eventually managed to find a break in the conversation where I could steer things toward my idea for another one of my little capers. I had reached a point where I wanted and needed to talk about something, anything but the lottery.

"Okay guys, let's catch our breath for a minute," I said, hoping that we could actually stop thinking about my winnings and conduct a normal conversation for a few minutes. "I told you both on the phone that I have another little caper I'd like to try and it will involve both of you."

Delilah set her drink on the table in front of her and said, "I must admit I've been expecting something like this. You haven't played a joke on anyone in what, a whole month?"

Ozzie laughed. "You know back in college Linc couldn't go three freaking days without pulling something on someone. It was like his addiction."

"Well," I replied, "in my defense I was just an immature college kid with an overactive imagination."

"Yeah," Oz answered, "and now you're an immature adult with an overactive imagination."

"Ooh, you never told me about any of the stuff you pulled in your younger days," Delilah said, grinning and grabbing my thigh. "Tell me more!" The playful smile on her face and the glint in her eyes made me a little nervous.

"Oh, your future hubby was quite the prankster," Ozzie said with just a little too much enthusiasm. "For a business major he sure had a creative and twisted mind." He turned and looked at me and said, "You know, now that I think about it, it might have been all those drama and theater classes you were taking your junior and senior years. That was around the time you really got cranked up with the cons."

Delilah looked surprised. "Honey, you never told me about your acting. Were you any good?"

Of course Ozzie had to interrupt. "Good, he was great! I remember the stuff they said about him after he had this minor role in some play. The critic for the school paper said something like, "Carr's portrayal of the cruel younger brother sent shivers all the way to the back row of the theater."

"Alright, that was years ago and besides it wasn't the drama classes It was the fact I minored in Psychology that helped me with the pranks because I knew the basics of how people's minds work and how to tap into them. So how about we get back on track here," I said, trying to send Ozzie a facial signal to not go any further in that direction.

My signal didn't work. "Oh yeah, he was full of schemes. My favorite was his idea for a fake beauty pageant, the "Miss Beaver" contest."

Delilah's head spun toward me so fast it was afraid she had whiplash. Her jaw dropped and she stammered, "The what contest, Miss Beaver, what the hell?"

I never replied to a comment so fast in my whole life. "Babe, I know you're not a sports fan but you know that Oz and I went to Oregon State University and the mascot and the students are the Beavers."

Her expression immediately changed to a twisted little smile and I could hear her exhale in relief. "Oh, okay, I get it but why a fake beauty pageant?

I was desperately trying to find a way to change the subject but Ozzie chimed in, "It was a plan to get all of the best looking girls on campus in one place, under controlled conditions, so he could find a girlfriend."

This time my glaring expression got through to him and he quickly added, "Actually, it was so both Linc and I, well actually all of us in the apartment could find girlfriends. Linc put the whole thing together and charged each of us fifty bucks to cover his expenses, and fifty bucks to find a hot girlfriend seemed totally reasonable to all of us hormone-fueled college-age males."

Much to my relief Delilah's smile had returned and she asked somewhat sarcastically, "So how did it turn out, the fake pageant, was it a success? Did you find a pretty beaver?"

Ozzie gestured for me to answer her and I said, "Well, it's a matter of perspective. Oz and I both met girls and dated them and they turned into relationships and today you know them as our ex-wives."

Delilah started laughing and Ozzie and I both smiled, certain that the irony wasn't lost on her. A few minutes later when she got up to use the bathroom Oz and I went into the kitchen to pour us all another drink. "Geez, man, did you really have to bring up Miss Beaver? I don't want my future wife to think I'm some kind of a stalker"

"Sorry," Oz answered, "I thought you probably told her about that already."

Delilah came back into the room obviously still amused with the subject of the Miss Beaver Contest. She sat down on the sofa again and asked, "So how did you get away with staging a fake contest and charging people money? That sounds like something that could have gotten you into trouble."

Before I could say a word to brush off her question and change the subject Oz answered, "You're right, it wasn't exactly the kind of thing the school administration would have sanctioned and the charging of the fifty dollar fee was kept very low key."

I looked at Ozzie, amazed at his willingness to run off at the mouth about something I preferred to keep in the past. "Okay," I said emphatically, "I think we've said everything about this subject with that needs to be said."

Delilah knew I was squirming with discomfort but with a mischievous smile she asked, "So if you knew you could get in trouble why did you still go through with it?"

Hoping to put an end to the whole subject I answered, "Well, if you really must know it was because I've always believed in trying to find the balance between risk and reward."

I was hoping Ozzie would finally understand why I wanted him to just shut up and then Delilah asked, "So was the risk worth the reward?"

Ozzie chimed in with what I thought was a perfect answer. "Yeah, it was worth it if the reward is only supposed to last a few years."

Delilah looked at me with the same little smile and said, "So I'm engaged to a risk taker, very interesting."

My willingness to take risks didn't seem like the right topic to pursue at the moment. I was eager to get the conversation turned away from my past activities and refocused on my idea for the new con. "Okay, kids, enough about our college years. Let's move on to my next little plan. I think you're going to like it."

This little scheme was one that had a sharper edge to it and it was actually something that Ozzie had wanted to do for quite a while. His next door neighbor was a married, middle-aged lothario who liked to quietly and sometimes not so quietly brag about the women he picked up during his business travels. Oz said every conversation with the guy turned into a "nudge-nudge, wink-wink story" about a sexual conquest. At times he even pursued women locally and when he bragged to Ozzie about a particular young woman he had recently talked into a hotel bed Oz decided it was time to shut the guy up once and for all. Given my reputation for playing elaborate practical jokes he knew I would be more than willing to help him.

Ozzie found out that the woman who his neighbor had taken advantage of was someone Oz had met a few years back at a business networking event and he had helped her get a job with a friend of his. He had kept in touch with her off and on since then so he knew how to make contact. Half an hour later we had created the basic concept for *The New Daddy Caper*, a plan to convince Ozzie's neighbor that his recent covert conquest was pregnant, that she had evidence that he was the baby's father and that she was demanding serious financial restitution. Ozzie was particularly eager to set the con in motion and I said I would get started on the script. Delilah offered to add a few ideas that were already percolating in her inventive mind including a way to get the "not so pregnant" woman involved without making her feel guilty or ashamed about what she had done at the hotel. As usual she had an accurate take on the emotional side of things. We had the details roughed out but as enthusiastic as I was about the scam we all agreed that my lottery arrangements were all I could deal with for now. We agreed to put off another meeting to discuss things for another few weeks.

After a final celebratory sip of bourbon Ozzie said he had to leave and stop on his way home to pick up his two sons at soccer practice. He figured that by now they'd both be covered with mud and grass stains from practicing on a wet field and would be more than ready for him to pick them up and grab a pizza on the way home. Despite the nastiness of his divorce and the years of custodial bickering he had been able to maintain a close relationship with his teenage boys. He and his ex-wife had waited a long time to start their family and, given his busy career, he never really had much time to be just a husband and father. But his boys were the center of his universe and I admired him for it. When I had gotten married about two years after graduation my wife, Chloe, and I decided to postpone starting a family. One thing led to another and somehow we just never got around to it. I wasn't sure if I regretted it or not. But now, in a strange vicarious way I was glad that sharing my good fortune with Ozzie would benefit his boys as well. Oz and I walked to the front door, exchanged another man-hug and said our goodbyes and then he ran to his car in the light but still steady rainfall.

Delilah knew that I didn't want her to leave and she said she wanted to spend the night. She took her cellphone from her purse and called her neighbor and asked if she would feed Bowser, Delilah's new puppy and my other future roommate. With or without Bowser in tow Delilah usually hung out at my house on the weekends and we joked that her wardrobe and feminine essentials had slowly migrated to my closet and bathroom to a point where she was already halfway moved in. Sharing my house with someone was going to be a huge adjustment for me. I grew up as an only child. I had always been comfortable being alone even when I was married and that was something that Chloe had never understood about me. She wanted me to need her more, to be with her constantly but I could never make that work. I liked being alone and I had my work and my practical jokes to keep me occupied. When she announced that she was leaving me it wasn't exactly a surprise.

After the split I told myself I'd concentrate on the business and avoid any personal entanglements for a while. I managed to stick to my plan for over four years until a beautiful young woman with short brown hair and a Bohemian air about her came to our company golf outing with one of my administrative assistants. Delilah Samuels made an instant impression on me. Slender and stylish in a sexy, artistic way, she had an energy and enthusiasm that captivated me. There was something about her that reminded me of a beautiful hippy flower child from the seventies. She was a landscape architect and my love of gardening gave me a way to carry on a reasonably good opening conversation with her. About a week later we went on our first date and things happened quickly after that. Now we were both excited about our pending cohabitation, our plans for a wedding somewhere down the road and after that a long life together.

We spent the rest of our Sunday trying hard not to dwell on the subject of money but we didn't seem to last for more than ten or fifteen minutes at a stretch without one of us blurting out an idea for how to promote some charity or use the winnings to fix some problem. Delilah shared my feeling that every person should find something that makes the world a better place and then get involved in it. She was a huge backer of environmental and animal causes and I devoted my time to finding ways to fund the arts and promote social and political causes that I believed in.

Like everyone else who has ever played a lottery or gambled in any way, I had fantasized about the things enormous wealth could bring me, everything from financial freedom to adventure to power. That last option was the one that made me the most nervous. In our culture money is power. On any given day the newspapers and television were full of stories of how wealthy people were using and abusing the power that came with their fortunes. I liked to think that I was a grounded, moral person who would always be able to recognize the difference between use and abuse of my new wealth. Yes, I liked to think that.

2

Business as Usual, Sort of

The Monday morning traffic was the usual mix of commuters, school buses and an occasional stop at a light-rail train crossing. After a year of trying there didn't seem to be an easy route between my house and my office even though I had experimented with many combinations of freeways and surface streets, so once again I just settled in with my coffee and a local news station and slowly made my way downtown.

Somehow I was able to dive into my routine with surprising ease. My mind wandered to the lottery from time to time but I guess all the years of running the business had somehow taught me to stay focused on what needed to be done in the here and now. Even though the *Powerball* news continued to float at or near the front of my thoughts I was able to get a fair amount of work done. I had even scheduled an afternoon meeting with Jon Aiken to lay the groundwork of the plan to protect my identity and keep the lottery winnings a secret. Some additional online research that I had done before I left the house suggested that it was best to see a lawyer first, not an accountant.

The importance of secrecy couldn't be overstated. Carr Creative was a very good place to work, with an "open door, talk to me" kind of environment, but I knew that any word of my winning a fortune would change the way my team viewed me and

I couldn't let that happen. Money has a way of changing people's perception of everything. There was a lot going on and every person in the office' had a lot on his or her plate and that's what I wanted them to see as their first priority. Our long-term and biggest client, ProInsure, had just signed our contract to produce a major new national television, internet and print campaign and, as usual, the deadlines were unreasonably tight. I had nearly a third of my creative team assigned to work on the campaign and that left some of our other commitments understaffed.

Our internet studio was cranking full speed on new online advertisements for a diverse mix of companies and I knew that bunch of strange and gifted people couldn't handle another task for the time being. We also were getting started on work for two major pharmaceutical companies pitching pills that they viewed as being essential to life. Their one minute commercials consisted of twenty seconds of content and forty seconds of lawyer-speak. When you got finished hearing the long list of health warnings and legal disclaimers you had to wonder why anyone would risk taking their dangerous little pills. Our job was to create commercials that cleared those hurdles without misleading the viewer and it proved to be no small task.

My schedule also included my regular monthly meeting with Wayne Hartzell, our Creative Director. Our agenda usually consisted of just one item, the same item we discussed at every monthly meeting; what concepts did his team have in mind for the various accounts and what were the creative issues and costs involved in producing them? Our mission and all of our efforts were based upon understanding our clients' shifting goals as we helped them chase an ever-changing customer profile. Wayne's creative team was as good as any in the business but I knew they were all becoming increasingly frustrated. They had an ongoing struggle to create innovative, substantive advertising that could connect with a customer base that was becoming less and less educated and less and less interested in most of what was going on around them. To many people the dumbing down of America was just an expression but to us it was a painful reality. For several years we had been seeing evidence that the public was also becoming almost oblivious to the social and political currents that were shaping their world and their lives. I definitely shared Wayne's frustration on both a personal and professional level.

The late morning sun filtered in through the window blinds making it hard to see my computer screen but I managed to answer a long list of e-mails in spite of it. In many ways the daily sunshine was a nuisance but I never wanted to live anywhere that the situation was different. I had spent so many years living in the rainy, foggy Northwest that the desert sun had now become an essential part of my daily routine. I sat at my desk, coffee in my left hand and mouse in my right, squinting as I scrolled through a very long and very detailed summary of our current creative activity broken down by fiscal quarter, client and media type. Along with Wayne's notes about creative content Ozzie's financial staff had added comments on production costs and billable hours that made the report almost too much to absorb.

Beside trying to see where we stood from a business perspective I was looking for, and eventually found, more evidence of something I'd noticed a few years back; a growing trend that we were dumbing down our content to respond to the dumbing down of the marketplace. The shift from advertising in print media to online content was astounding. All trends indicated that very few people read newspapers or magazines anymore and even network television ad revenue had slipped. We were entering a time when our client's messages had to be available on a tablet or smartphone or they wouldn't be seen. That meant the messages had to be brief, overly simple and more visual than verbal. Don't feed people a lot of information, just make it look sexy and colorful and make sure there was a good music line playing behind the beautiful people on the screen. It was a whole new approach for us but we were working hard at it because those short, simple messages were very profitable.

I was still trying to juggle all of the information when Wayne walked in. His broad shoulders and ample girth made him look like he had been poured into his jeans and blue oxford shirt. He seemed to fill the doorway, his long, curly gray hair and beard in their usual state of hirsute chaos. His near-constant grin always lifted my mood. "You ready for me, boss man?" he chirped as he dumped a small mountain of paperwork on my table.

I leaned back to stretch my arms and then motioned toward the small kitchenette in the corner and said, "Grab some coffee and then let's get things going." I always looked forward to my meetings with Wayne. He was an artist at heart and had little time for the numbers and calculations of the business but he grudgingly helped me interpret them. He reminded me of the way I was a long time ago, before I became an owner and had to give the bottom line a much bigger piece of my time than I cared to. Wayne was still able to be free-wheeling, artsy and totally blunt. I respected and enjoyed him for that. The truth be told, I was sort of jealous.

When he was finally ready we sat down at my conference table and I heard Wayne's chair squeak its discomfort. Our omnipresent tablet computers sat in front of us like glowing extensions of our own appendages. We each pulled up the information on our screens and Wayne started things off. "I assume you've had a chance to look over the last quarter, boss. Does anythin' jump out at you from that pile of words and numbers?"

I looked over a list of notes that I'd scrawled during my earlier review of the figures. "Well, mainly I see the same stuff I've been seeing for the last few years or so, the shift away from print and into electronic media and internet is driving up production costs, television, as always, is steady and online is booming. Hell, print has all but disappeared."

"Yep," Wayne sighed, "Mommy and Daddy are still glued to the boob-tube or a laptop, the kids are even more addicted to their smart phones and the newspaper is linin' Fido's cage." He waited a moment for me to comment further and when I didn't he added, "And the read between-the-lines message in all of this stuff is that most of what all three of our studios are working on is a dumb and dumber version of what we were doin' just a few years ago." He sipped his coffee and tapped his finger on the table in a steady, almost clock-like way. "Hear that, boss?" he asked, and before I could respond he said, "That's the clock tickin' on the advertisin' world as we know it.

I knew exactly what he meant and answered, "Yeah, it's getting to be a real balancing act isn't it? Doing smart work to please the client but make it dumb enough for the customer to understand.

"I gotta tell ya', Linc, the meetins' with my team are gettin' really weird. We go around the table and brainstorm concepts and we come up with some amazin' shit. But every fuckin' time we think we have a real diamond, someone speaks up and asks the new question of the day, "Will they understand it in the trailer park? Man, we're all gettin' tired of polishin' turds."

His comment brought a smile to my face. The term "trailer park" had become a regular part of our office lexicon. It was a term we used to describe the domain of the new, average, under-achieving American citizen and consumer. Is this ad going to work in the trailer park? What will the trailer park think? Should we make it simpler so they'll get it in the trailer park? We also used the terms "Walmarter," "Cletus" and "Jethro" when we talked about an ever-increasing number of people we were trying to reach. I constantly wrestled with the thought that we were being condescending or insulting to people we didn't even know. After all, it takes all kinds of folks to make a country or an economy. But there was no denying the fact that America was on the decline in so many ways and it was our ever frustrating job to reach those declining, under-achieving people with our client's message. Just getting their attention was a major task all by itself.

Everything Wayne said was true. It was all tied to so many things I had been reading and hearing in the news and it all just added to my normal negativism about modern life in America. In most ways we were a country on the downslope of things. By any meaningful measure our school kids were way behind kids in the rest of the world. American students could text and take selfies and download useless crap on their smartphones faster than you could follow their flying fingers but they couldn't write an intelligent sentence if their life depended on it. Math and science were what the kids in other countries excelled in and where they were focused, but not our kids. And it all started at home. American Dad, if he was even part of the family unit, was obsessed with sports to a point beyond all understanding and American Mom was frantically chasing her youth while she kept track of the Hollywood gossip.

"You know, Wayne," I said slowly, trying to form a response that wouldn't sound totally insensitive, "I understand and agree with everything you say. I see the ads on TV and online that other agencies do and I think to myself, "Geez, how can people crank out that kind of mindless shit, but I know that mindless shit is probably right on message with the audience. They are who they are."

Wayne sipped his coffee and nodded. "Yeah, I know they are, but it's really tough to deal with some times. I have the best people in the business trying to create advertisin' artistry while the competition is puttin' out stuff that's cringe-worthy."

"Is it possible to have it both ways, I mean are we underestimating people?" I had a pretty good idea what his answer would be.

"Well, I used to think so and so did most of my team but it's almost impossible to keep thinkin' we can make art for morons." After another long sip of coffee he ran his hand over his beard and said, "It's like it's impossible to underestimate Jethro."

I nodded, knowing exactly what he meant. "So, for example, where do we stand on the new ProInsure online stuff?" I asked cautiously, "Is there a way to explain their new incremental homeowners reward program to make it clear enough for Jethro to grasp?"

Wayne smirked and nodded, his chair squeaking with his every movement. "Oh, man, it has been one major pain in the ass to come up with somethin' that's easy to understand in a thirty or sixty-second spot. The overall campaign has a small print component and a few online stills. But since Jethro watches so much television it's all goin' to be tied to the TV campaign so we get maximum coverage in that demographic. I have Stacey workin'

on the copy and I told her, nothin' more than two syllable words."
He grinned as he continued. "So here it is. It's a 3D animated piece.
Picture a rotund bear wearin' a plaid shirt and baseball cap drivin'
a pick-up truck down a little road lined with neat, closely-packed
mobile homes."

At this point I had to study Wayne's face to see if he was joking
or playing it straight and I couldn't tell. He seemed to have a knack
for that kind of thing.

"There's a country band playin' in the background while a
drawlin' male voice-over describes the new policy rewards plan
for people who don't file any damage claims over a period of two
years. It's called the "Care for your Castle Plan.""

I leaned back again in my chair, trying to picture the concept.
Wayne's face still wasn't giving me the slightest clue about whether
the campaign idea was real or he was just messing with me. "You
have more than a few stereotypes packed into that ad," I said, "and
I think we better be careful about offending someone."

"We have a separate ad for the urban and suburban folks. In
that one it's an animated poodle drivin' a mini-van down a street
lined with McMansions, an alt-rock vibe in the background while
a soccer mom type does the voice-over."

Still with no clue as to Wayne's level of seriousness I felt that
a comment was in order. "Okay," so we have two campaigns, one
for each of the targeted demographic groups. The urban-suburban
one seems pretty safe but I gotta tell you that the rural one seems
like it's on the edge of being condescending. The plaid shirt, the
pick-up truck and even the bear I guess I can buy, but why is it set
in a trailer park?"

Wayne's expression finally softened into a grin and he replied,
"Linc, the term trailer park isn't just some kind of inside joke here
in the office. We did our homework on this one. We wound up
with a mountain of research to put this together, and when you
have some time and want to get depressed give it a read."

"What do you mean, why would I get depressed?"

Wayne leaned forward in his chair. "Man, this is definitely not
the kind of target or campaign we're used to doin' around here.

It's like I said, we have a ton of research and studies and all kinds of shit about our target audience for this campaign. I read it cover to cover and I made my team read it too and they couldn't believe some of the stuff in it. We all tried to understand, no, make that relate to the audience we were after. So when we all finished it we did a little exercise. I wanted to know their quick impressions of the people we were reaching out to so I told each person to bark out a single word to describe their take on the audience."

"Oh, God, I can just imagine what you got back," I said, "I'm almost afraid to hear it."

Wayne smiled and said, "Well, I don't remember them all but I heard "distracted," I heard "clueless" and even "stupid." There was "lazy" and "oblivious" and one guy who shall remain anonymous referred to them as "fucked up.""

"Okay, I get it but I just gotta' know what your word was," I said.

"Well, my word was the one that we all finally agreed best summed up the folks in the trailer park, "gullible.""

I couldn't help but laugh. "Gee, a gullible target for an ad campaign. That's my definition of advertising heaven."

Wayne nodded and shared my laugh. "I agree, boss, but let me get back to the research because it really surprised the hell out of me. Did you know there are an estimated ten million mobile homes in the United States? Ten million trailers means between thirty or forty million people livin' in them, and the numbers are growin' like crazy. That's a whole lot of folks that *ProInsure* wants to reach. And the pitch will also reach out to people outside the actual trailer park, the distracted under-achievers and those gullible folks who are just mindlessly coastin' along. The term trailer park is just the perfect metaphor for all of them."

Somehow it was settling in on me that the trailer park that had been kind of a vague concept around the office had morphed into something much more. It was a real, measurable population group and whether they actually lived in a mobile home or not, it was its own substantial and growing demographic. No matter what any of us thought about it personally we had to reach this group on behalf of our clients. I leaned forward, put my right hand on the table and mimicked the tapping sound that Wayne had made earlier. "The clock is ticking on the advertising world as we know it and I'm not sure I'm happy about it."

Wayne laughed. "Relax, boss man," he bellowed, "before long Carr Creative will be the freakin' voice of the folks in the trailer park, the face of Jethro and the connection to Walmarters throughout the land!"

His rolling laughter came from deep inside his belly and I couldn't resist joining in. After a moment I said, "Okay, let's finish the rough cut and see what it all feels like." I paused, then added, "But be careful. We can't appear to be looking down our noses at anyone even if we are."

Wayne winked and said, "Gotcha, boss."

I got through the rest of my morning then stopped by Ozzie's office on my way out the door. I took a step inside, closed the door behind me and said quietly, "I'm heading downtown to meet with Jon Aiken to get things moving on the blind trust and I'm guessing it's going to kill the rest of my day."

Ozzie nodded. "Good luck. It sounds like you're doing everything by the book, just let me know if there's anything I can do to help." He hoisted his hand and gave me a thumbs-up.

"Thanks, man, I will," I said, I turned to leave but stopped and asked, "How about meeting me for a beer later so I can bring you up to date on the big secret."

An odd, almost blushing look came over Ozzie's face. "Uh, thanks but no thanks. I kind of have a date." I knew Oz could see my surprised look and he added, "Now don't start asking a lot of questions just yet, it's just a woman I found on an internet dating site and we agreed to meet for a glass of wine to see how things go."

"A glass of wine," I said, "I think you should be honest with her from the start and tell her you're a beer guy and you avoid wine like it's poison."

"Well, if you must know I've been working on my attitude towards a lot of things, wine included. I'm trying to loosen up a little, you know, get back to being more adventurous and crazy like I used to be."

I smiled, not only because of his comment, since I had always thought Ozzie was as loose as a goose, but also because I was happy that my best friend was finally venturing back out into the world of dating. Between his nasty divorce and the wounding of pride that always goes with that kind of thing, he'd had a tough time getting his bearings when it came to finding a new relationship. "Good for you," I said. "Good luck and I want a full download tomorrow morning."

Oz smiled, nodded and said, "Yeah, sure, just don't be expecting too much, of a download I mean."

I lifted my hand and returned his thumbs up and then headed down the hallway to the elevator.

Lawyer's offices seem to have a dull sameness to them; dark wood everywhere, walls full of legal books, leather upholstery on the chairs and almost always a location on an upper floor of a prestigious building. I wondered if they learned that in Pretentiousness 101 in law school. The offices of Brace & Miller were no exception. Even the elevator was over-the-top luxurious to the point of being off-putting. I decided years ago to overlook that kind of thing because Jon was an excellent lawyer and a loyal friend. He could do his office in Liberace style if he wanted to as long as he continued to take care of me the way he had since we'd first gotten together.

It was a slow elevator ride to the top floor and the doors opened directly into the lobby of the firm. I walked across the travertine floor to a large mahogany and black marble reception desk. The attractive, young brunette woman behind the desk asked me in a very practiced tone, "Yes sir, how may I help you?"

A small, brass nameplate on the counter told me her name was Misty McCormick. "Hi Misty, my name is Lincoln Carr and I have a one o'clock appointment with Jon Aiken."

She gave me a businesslike smile and said, "Please have a seat over there," pointing to a grouping of plush green and beige lounge chairs, and then added, "Can I get you water or coffee?"

"No thanks, I'm good," I answered. I laid my folio book and tablet computer on a large, round table and barely had time to warm the seat cushion before Jon Aiken's booming voice called out, "Hey, I gotta tell you, it's nice to see you in work clothes for a change."

I smiled as I stood up and reached to shake Jon's hand. "Yeah, well, golf is fun but we all have to work to pay the club dues."

I followed Jon down the corridor to his office. From the fifteenth floor he had a beautiful view of South Mountain and a good part of the downtown area. I had been to his office many times but it was the kind of panoramic view that impressed me every time I saw it. He closed the door behind us and then picked up his laptop from his desk. We sat in two plush, leather club chairs with a small limestone topped table separating us.

"Okay," Jon started, "tell me what the big secret is that you couldn't tell me over the phone." He paused and then added, "I hope it's not a pre-nup for you and Delilah." His smile told me he wasn't serious."

"Nah, you don't have to worry about anything like that." But then I paused, for the first time wondering about that very idea, and I said, "You know, now that you mention it, when I tell you the news you just might think I need one." Jon cocked his head, a puzzled look on his face, and I said, "Well, I guess I should just lay the whole thing out in front of you."

I opened my folio and pulled out the large manila envelope that had not been more than a few feet from me since Sunday morning. The small ticket was stuck at the bottom of the envelope and it took a few seconds to fish it out. I placed it on the table in front of Jon and watched his reaction. He bent over and studied the ticket for a moment, looked up at me then back at the ticket and finally asked, "Holy shit, is this what I think it is?"

"If you think it's stinkin fortune then yes, it is." I was grinning from ear to ear.

Jon leaned back in his chair, staring at the ticket and shaking his head. He ran his hand through his wavy white hair and said, "Holy shit, holy shit, holy shit." He looked at me and before he could ask what I knew would be his next question, I said "After taxes two hundred and eighteen million, give or take."

Jon looked up from the ticket, with an expression more serious than I had ever seen him use before. He let out a long, slow breath. "I hope you haven't told anyone about this."

"Well, just Delilah and Ozzie, and now, you." I waited for his reaction and it was what I expected.

"Shit, Linc, this is the kind of thing you have to keep under wraps until you get a plan worked out."

"I realize that, Jon. I did some looking around online and all the legal advice said, "Keep it to yourself and trust no one.""

"Okay, online legal advice is a start and, as your real-life lawyer I agree." he said, still looking serious.

I knew I had to tell him the things that were going through my head on Sunday morning but I gave him the abridged version. "Delilah is going to be my wife and Ozzie is my closest friend and confidant. They are part of everything I do."

Jon picked up the ticket by its edge and waved it in my direction. "Okay, I guess I understand that. I think if I were in your shoes I'd have told Kim about it too. She's my wife and an equal part of my life so I would definitely have to bring her in on it." He paused then said, "I suggest we get Oz and Delilah to sign confidentiality agreements to tighten things up, if you're okay with that."

"Jon," I said, trying to carefully choose my words, "Delilah and Ozzie, and you, will be the only ones who know about this. Believe me, man, I understand what could happen if word got out. My employees would expect big raises, every salesman in Arizona would be hounding my ass along with every charity, and Chloe would suddenly re-appear in my life to try and claim a piece of it."

"Don't worry about Chloe," Jon replied, "the divorce settlement I helped you arrange was ironclad and forever. She can't lay claim to a damned thing."

Jon stopped toying with the ticket long enough to notice that I hadn't signed my name to the back of it. "Geez, man, this isn't signed yet, it's like you're carrying around millions in cash if you were to lose it." He slipped a pen from his notebook and slid it over to me, along with the ticket. "Here, sign this thing right now, your full legal name, and I'll make you a copy of it."

I followed his instructions, handed the ticket back to him and said, "Alright, so to get back to what we were talking about, there would still be a hell of a lot of trouble if anyone found out and it will be trouble I don't need, so let's talk about what needs to get done here. I assume we want to set up a blind trust." As soon as the words left my mouth I hoped that Jon didn't think I was trying to circumvent his expertise.

He looked at me and nodded. "A blind trust is usually the course of action in these situations. You get identity protection which is okay under Arizona law, so as long as you keep a low profile you should be safe. The down side is that a blind trust is expensive to set up and expensive to manage, and there's no guarantee any investments will perform any better than investment vehicles you're already into."

"Well at this point it's the privacy I'm looking for more than the investment value" I explained. "If it doesn't make one damned penny it's still two hundred and eighteen million dollars that I didn't have last week."

Jon smiled and nodded. "Linc, it sounds like you're taking the right view of all this. Let me put a few ideas together and we can review them before you claim the cash. I think you have six months to claim it, right?"

"Yep, six months to let the curiosity die down while we plan what we're going to do, but to be honest, I don't want to wait that long to at least make the claim. I'm thinking more like a few weeks or so, do whatever legal shit we have to do to make me invisible and by then people will have already moved on to thinking about the next big winner."

Jon leaned toward me. "You know, the timing here is good because there's a bill in front of the state legislature to force the Lottery Commission to reveal the names of winners ninety days after a claim. But those people never do anything quickly so I think we'll be grandfathered on the existing rules which should keep you safe."

I leaned back in my chair, crossed my legs and exhaled loud enough for Jon to notice and comment, "Yeah, let out that big sigh of relief, but just be ready for what we have to do. As your attorney but mostly as your friend, I can tell you this isn't going to be easy for you."

"I know that, nodding as I responded. "I confess I've been worried about all kinds of things since all this happened, like my security and my privacy and how this is going to change my life. It's like nothing will ever be the same again and I'm not exactly sure how to feel about it."

Jon leaned forward, one hand on the table and the other rubbing his chin., He looked me square in the eye, and said in a very matter-of-fact tone, "Linc, you come first in this whole thing but it's not just how you feel about it that you have to be concerned about. Like it or not, and whether or not they've said anything specific, your future wife and your best friend already have their own feelings about this. Their lives are going to change too and that will affect you in lots of ways, large or small that you haven't even thought of yet. And it's still too soon to tell if you or either of them will be able to handle this new wealth."

I knew Jon was right. I had to do everything possible to make sure I kept myself in check. I couldn't let myself become the squirrel that Delilah feared or the asshole that Ozzie worried about. It was going to be a huge challenge and as I sat there in Jon's office I couldn't honestly predict if I would be successful. And on top of all that I had to worry about the fact that Delilah and Ozzie, each in their individual ways, would be part of that same struggle.

3

Man, I Love This Job

It had been nearly two weeks since the big day. Jon Aiken had put together confidentiality agreements for Delilah and Ozzie to sign and, on Jon's advice I didn't bring Jeff Norris in on things. Jon had built the framework of a trust to protect my identity before I claimed the money. Once I made the claim through a representative from Jon's office, who would be someone who I wouldn't even know, the trust would contact Jeff to discuss an investment strategy for my money but it would be in the name of the trust. I felt strange about not working with Jeff on a personal level but Jon had convinced me that the fewer people who knew about the money the better my life would be. Without knowing exactly who he was working for, Jeff would develop an investment strategy for an unknown business owner in his mid-forty's, a strategy that was diverse and conservative enough to grow my winnings over time. And when the time was right the trust would contact a different investment firm to help Delilah and Ozzie with plans for the twenty million dollar bequests they would each be receiving. Jon felt that course was safer so Jeff wouldn't make any kind of link between my trust and Ozzie and Delilah.

As each day passed immersing myself in my routine became easier and easier but the money still tugged at my mind. Not in a regular or constant way but more like an out of left field interruption when I was thinking of something else. Money had always been a motivator for me which just made me pretty much like everyone else in America. Now I had more money than I could ever need and possibly more money than I could handle as well. I thought back to that rainy afternoon at my house, when Delilah, Ozzie and I had celebrated the wonderful news, and how that news totally eliminated money as a motivator for me. I wanted Carr Creative to maintain its momentum and profitability for all of the wonderful people who worked for me but in the back of my mind was a fear that, without the need of personal income, I might lose my drive to be the best. I had to force myself to stay focused on the day to day needs of the business, my health and my relationships. I couldn't let myself become a squirrel or an asshole.

Wayne and his team had made a lot of headway on the ProInsure ads and I was starting to feel more comfortable with the bear in the pick-up truck. I spent an entire morning in "The Garage" with Wayne and his team going over the preliminary online ads. The Garage was the nickname we had given to Wayne's little piece of the office. It was at the rear of the building and was separated from the rest of our office space by two large, glass-paneled garage doors. It was an appropriate and friendly way to separate Wayne's odd but gifted group of artists and internet geeks from the other departments. Though the garage doors were almost always rolled up, when they were pulled down it was a signal that Wayne's team was in its own little zone and privacy was requested.

Our marketing staff had done some follow up focus group sessions with what we felt was a good cross section of consumers. Surprisingly, the bear was a hit with almost the entire group and it was even thought to be much more appealing than the poodle in the minivan. It still had a redneck flavor that bothered me but if it passed muster with the focus group I figured I should just stop worrying about it. As Wayne said to me at our update meeting, "Boss man, we're gonna be the face of Jethro."

Things were going well enough at the office that Ozzie and I found some time to break away from our duties and get some work done on *Operation New Daddy*. Delilah had just finished her design for the landscaping of a big resort project and took a few days away from her office to relax and join in on the planning. With some ideas from Ozzie I had written the outline of a script and we did a run-through of it to see how it sounded. Delilah had already coached Ozzie on the right words to use when he approached Lisa Martinez, the wronged woman, about getting involved in our little con. Her advice worked well because Ozzie said that after he talked with Lisa any hint of embarrassment she might have felt was masked by an eagerness to get back at Mike Perino, his philandering neighbor and her date-gone-wrong.

We sat at our favorite table at Las Mesas in a corner where it was reasonably private, a bottle of Chardonnay at the ready. Ozzie had ordered it and said that he had actually developed a taste for it. It was obvious that his budding relationship with Michelle, the woman he had met on an online dating site, was having a positive effect on him. He poured us each a glass and said, "Okay, let's see what we have here,"

The script called for Lisa, her attorney and her best friend, who was also a nurse, to confront Perino, first via a registered letter sent to his office and then with a face-to-face meeting at a location to be determined. The letter would state that Lisa was examined by her doctor and determined to be pregnant, that it was her belief that Perino was the father and that she demanded financial restitution sufficient to cover the costs of her doctor's fees during pregnancy and delivery and an additional sum to help with the cost of child care so Lisa could continue working. We all agreed that, if we wrote it with the right amount of thinly disguised malice, the letter would put enough guilt and fear into Perino to make sure that he wouldn't do anything that would point a finger in his direction.

Ozzie had just one concern. "Okay," he started, "Perino gets this registered letter out of the blue. It's on a law firm's letterhead and it's a no nonsense message with a not so veiled threat of legal action that will be taken if Lisa's terms are not met." I nodded and he continued. "So we're hoping he'll be too ashamed or too afraid to get an attorney to fight it because if he did Lisa would spread the word about their little tryst. Is that the idea? Is that really going to work?"

"Well, that's how I see it playing out," I answered. I looked over at Delilah. "What do you think, honey, is that how you see it going?"

She nodded and looked at Oz. "I never met this Perino guy but from what you've said about him he's a real sleaze, a sleaze with a wife and five kids and he wants them to think he's Mr. Perfect. So I have to believe he'll want to keep a lid on anything that might upset his perfect little family." She paused a moment and then looked at me. Her expression telegraphed an obvious feeling of apprehension. "But even though he's a sleaze, who in the hell are we to get involved in his personal life?"

"I get your point," Ozzie answered, "and I have thought the same thing a hundred times. But this guy is a deacon in his church and president of the Rotary Club. He even has aspirations to run for City Council. It tells you a lot about the guy's ego that he smirks and brags about his conquests and somehow thinks it will never come back around on him. It's almost scary that a guy could be so arrogant but I agree with your original point. I doubt that he would even want to tell the story to an attorney let alone drag it all out in public."

"So, Oz," I asked, "given all of that, do you feel better about it? It sounds like you do."

"Yeah, I guess so, but there's one other thing and it might be harder to pull off. When Perino gets the lawyer's letter I'm betting the first thing he does is go online to check them out and he'll find out they don't exist."

I was waiting for that little detail to come up and I was ready for it. I looked at both of them and said, "You probably remember back when we pulled off *Operation Budweiser* and we invented a couple of lawyers for the meeting with Jason." They both smiled and nodded. "Well I got to thinking that this probably won't be the last little con I want to pull and more than likely some of them will need a lawyer somewhere in the mix."

Delilah's eyes widened. "Please don't tell me you're going to hire lawyers for these things."

"Nope, even better," I said, grinning, "I'm going to invent them. I already have Stacey on Wayne's internet team putting together a basic website for a fake law firm; Yale and Roth, Attorneys at Law. I told her it's part of an ad campaign concept and that it's confidential."

"Linc, that sounds very close to something illegal or fraudulent to me," Oz replied. "Setting up a fake business must violate some kind of law." He looked at me, his nervousness written all over his face. "Man, I think you need to slow down and get a grip, it sounds like you're pushing the risk boundaries here and that's not like you, Mister Cool and Controlled.'

On the one hand I felt bad that Ozzie saw me as a guy who wouldn't take risks or push boundaries but on the other, his comment was something I was ready for. "Not to worry," I said. "First of all, no one will know this firm exists because they won't be advertising or doing anything whatsoever to make themselves known, other than having a website that is in no way interactive. If someone does an alphabetical or a Google search for a lawyer our little firm begins with the next-to-last- letter of the alphabet so no one would ever have the patience to get to our name. Beyond that, no services will ever be provided and no money will ever change hands."

Delilah added, "So you're saying it's a "no harm, no foul" kind of thing."

"Exactly," I answered, "no harm, no foul and no problem." As the words left my lips I hoped I'd eventually get to a point where I really believed them.

Even though his expression told me he was still nervous and more than a little skeptical, Ozzie chimed in "Okay, I guess that makes sense, but there's a lot more to this. You'll have to have faces on the website, not just names. It's got to look real"

"I have that covered. I asked Apex Casting to get me ten people, male and female, who can pass for trial lawyer types, you know, stiff, pompous and full of themselves, with snarky smiles.

We'll have them made up and dressed to look like the kind of people you don't want to go up against in court. They'll pose for the headshots and before long it will look like a real law firm. And simply because I can't resist being part of things, I intend to be one of the faces, in heavy make-up of course so no one recognizes me."

Delilah's response wasn't exactly a surprise. "Whoa, big fella, are you sure you want to get that involved in things?"

"Absolutely sure, these little schemes of mine are like my children. I give them birth and help them grow and I need to be in the middle of it all."

Ozzie and Delilah exchanged the same skeptical look and she tuned back to me and said, "Honey, slow down a little, we might be in squirrel territory here."

My smile was a quick attempt to lighten the mood but I don't think it worked very well.

After an uncomfortable lull in the conversation Oz sighed and said, "So, moving on, how about names for all of these fake lawyers? I liked the name you had for the lawyer when we played the joke on Jason. What was it again, Greesi or something like that?"

"Yeah, it was Greesi, and I want to have some fun with the names on the website too so if either of you has any ideas, by all means chime in." The conversation seemed to be finding a more comfortable level.

We spent a few minutes laughing and throwing out suggestions. Ozzie came up with George Cheetum and William Paumpus while Delilah offered Margaret Fauxni and Adrienne Tokker. I favored Warren Feeman and James Trustnaught, and we all agreed that we needed to mix in a Smith and a Johnson here and there just to make the firm look like something close to being real.

When the fun died down a little Delilah looked at me and said, "Honey, it sounds like this is going to be really expensive. I know you're probably planning to pay for it yourself but how do you keep your money separate from the company's when it comes to paying *Apex* and anyone else?"

"Good point," Ozzie added. "Finance is my department and we can't have Carr Creative tied to any of this silliness.

"Relax," I said, looking at both of them, "I already have Jon Aiken working on the groundwork for a new venture, a little company that will help us do these things. It will even cover the cost for Stacey's work on the website. It's going to be called CONjunction." I emphasized the word con and they both started to laugh again. "You know, CONjunction, where the cons come together."

"What the hell man," Ozzie said, "you're actually starting a company to do your cons. Amazing. I expect to be on your team."

Delilah was still laughing. "Me too," she said, trying to regain some level of seriousness.

"Way ahead of you," I answered "I wouldn't think of doing this without you two. You're both listed as executives in the company. I'm listed as the President so in case there's ever any trouble and something comes back to bite us in the ass it will only be me in the crosshairs and not you."

Delilah's expression suddenly turned more serious. "Honey," she asked, are you sure you're not taking on too much? You know what your doctor said about keeping a sensible pace to things."

I knew she was right and I appreciated her regular reminders to take better care of myself. "I know what you're saying," I answered, "and believe me, I'll be careful."

After a few more drinks and then a few more and some more review of the script *Operation New Daddy* was almost ready to implement. We agreed previously that Ozzie would be the point of contact for working with Lisa Martinez, and he said that once he had told her about the plan to wipe the smile from Perino's face he knew she would be eager to get it all started. Delilah would play the role of Lisa's nurse and friend and I would play the attorney, wearing the same make-up as in my website photograph. The plan was to suggest a meeting with Perino at a neutral place and not the offices of Yale and Harris because Lisa, the plaintiff, had requested it that way. Obviously, the fact there were no offices for a fake law firm was the real reason for the decision. Our fake lawyer would allow Perino to suggest the meeting place so the man wouldn't feel like he was being squeezed or pressured. We didn't want to risk scaring him off.

I would finish the work on the fake lawyer website and the writing of the letter to Perino. Delilah came up with a brilliant idea that we all agreed would really help sink the hook into Perino. Her younger sister, Ramona, had asked Delilah to be closely involved with Ramona's recent pregnancy. Delilah went with her to her doctor's appointments and stayed with her right up to the moment of delivery. During the process Delilah acquired several copies of the baby's sonograms. With a little touch-up on the labels to change the mother's last name to Martinez, our little team of con artists would present Mike Perino with a black and white image of his soon-to-be-born son. Just talking about it made me eager for the day I'd be there to see the look on that self-absorbed guy's face.

I was strangely excited about this particular con even though I sensed that Delilah and Ozzie didn't feel quite the same way. This was the first one we'd ever concocted that wasn't just a simple prank meant to get a few laughs. This one had an edge to it, a feeling like we were slapping someone across the face. It had been Ozzie's idea, born from his disgust for a disgusting man but I found myself enjoying the darkness of it all. I could tell that Delilah and Oz heard the glee in my voice and they noticed the twisted little smile that only came out when I was plotting a new scheme. Ozzie looked at me and asked, "Is it my imagination or are you getting into this con a lot more than the earlier ones?"

I couldn't help but smile. "Okay, I admit it, this one feels different. It feels kind of like, I don't know, like revenge on a guy I don't even know."

"I'm in the same place," Ozzie replied, "but let's just keep a tight rein on things, okay? Let's not get too mean or vicious. This thing has a chance of turning back on us if we overplay it."

Delilah added, "I'm with Oz on this one. We have to be very careful to not get carried away with things and I confess I'm more than a little uneasy with this one. Let's keep our egos and our anger under control."

Whatever enthusiasm the two of them felt I knew their nervousness was just as real. But we all agreed that Mike Perino deserved a little wake-up call and if we just followed the script we'd be okay.

We finished our business and our wine and left the restaurant. Delilah rode with me back to my house. She had been spending nights with me more frequently and we had decided to make our cohabitation official within the week She had already contacted a moving company, filled out change of address forms online and at the post office and was in the process of boxing up more of her personal belongings to move into my house. It felt to me like things were happening fast but we had been talking about her move for so long, the fact it was finally happening just seemed to hit me in an odd way. I had been living alone for so long I knew I would have to make a hundred adjustments after she moved in.

For about a week we had been discussing the idea of eventually buying a new house and Delilah had gotten into a daily routine of touring realtor websites to see what was on the market. I enjoyed hearing her comments when she'd find a listing that was ridiculously over the top. Comments like, "Oh here's a nice little eleven thousand square foot charmer with its own guest house and a six-car garage. I don't know, honey, would that be enough house for us?" We could afford any house we wanted but we still acknowledged that we had both come from humble roots. Finding a bigger new home that would still be true to who we were as people would be a challenge.

We knew that because of the need to keep the lottery winnings under the radar we'd have to wait for a while before we made any major purchases. We couldn't lose sight of the importance of that fact. Besides, I loved the 50s-era bungalow I bought right after my divorce. It was in the Willo Historic District near the downtown business area and it had been the perfect place for me. But with the new money and pending marriage it seemed that, like it or not, a newer, larger house would be the logical step to take eventually.

When I thought about all of the other adjustments I was already facing from my lottery money and the adjustments that

Delilah would face with her twenty million dollar gift, I knew the months and years ahead would be very interesting to say the least. They would be interesting, wild and, in a very real way, scary.

At Delilah's request we stopped for our usual orders at Pei Wei, our favorite Chinese take-out place. The rest of the evening was conversation that mixed business, the con and, of course, the omnipresent lottery money. A firm called Sonoran Wealth Management had contacted both Delilah and Ozzie earlier in the day to schedule meetings to discuss the details of the bequests they had received from an unnamed trust. Very soon my new roommate and future wife, along with my best friend and business partner would officially be millionaires. I was still trying to figure out if I could keep my own head on straight with all of my new wealth and now the two people I loved the most would be dealing with the same problem. All three of us could end up being normal or even squirrels. Or assholes.

4

Operation New Daddy

The internet is its own strange and fascinating little universe. In it you can find answers and entertainment as well as trouble. The term *Big Data* was a regular part of the dialogue at the office and was an essential part of the fact-finding that we did every day. It had become a whole new way of researching, buying, selling and doing business and was a very big part of the content we created for our clients. Now I was trying to make it a part of my cons.

It had taken a little longer than expected but I finally managed to finish the website for Yale and Harris, The fake law firm was essential to pulling off the con and, I had a gut feeling it would be brought into any other schemes I came up with. Apex Casting had helped us pull together an interesting mix of actors for the headshots on the website. Every one of them was successful in taking on the look of someone who offers a handshake with the right hand while the left hand is reaching for your wallet. I honestly wanted the website to look genuine but it was hard for me to ignore my desire to have fun at the expense of egotistical trial lawyers and the litigious world they lived in. I scrolled through every page of the site and decided that, even though my snarky sense of humor was evident in the names of the lawyers and their exaggerated resumes, the average person looking at it would only see a bunch of lawyers and a lot of text about how the firm fights hard to get its clients the money they deserve. The money they deserve. Anyone who goes online to search for a lawyer looks for those four words. They were the four words we hoped would send a chill down Mike Perino's spine.

Finally on Tuesday morning our website was live, with a contact e-mail address, a fake street address and even a phone number that rang to a recording that promised a reply call. That number was connected to a phone in my office, and I would be playing the role of Ira Steele, the attorney for Lisa Martinez. The registered letter had been sent to Perino at his office and by now I figured the son of a bitch was close to wetting his pants in fear that his sexual indiscretion would somehow become public. If he was even half as slimy as Ozzie described him, he would already be busy working on a scheme to hide his deeds and escape the consequences.

The letter informed Perino of Lisa's pregnancy and instructed him to contact Attorney Ira Steele via e-mail or phone to arrange a meeting to discuss the situation and explore a path to a resolution. It also stated that no formal lawsuit would be filed if terms of a settlement could be agreed to outside of court. I hoped that would discourage Perino from contacting his own attorney and make our little charade even riskier. The letter also said that, at the plaintiff's request, Perino was to select an appropriate public venue for the meeting. We wanted to plant the seed in his mind that this meeting was only to present the facts of the situation, figuring that alone would be enough to scare the living shit out of him.

At about eleven-thirty Ira Steele's phone rang from a small table in the corner of my office. I let it ring three times, took a deep breath and then answered it. "Ira Steele," I said in a very stiff, all business kind of tone.

There was a moment of silence then a nervous sounding man stammered, "Uh, yes, uh, this is Michael Perino calling, about the letter you sent me."

I purposely delayed my response for a few seconds, hoping the silence would add to Perino's discomfort. "Oh, yes Mr. Perino, thank you for getting back to me." I tried hard to sound as rigid and unemotional as possible. "Can I assume you have taken the time to read the entire letter and that you fully understand what we are dealing with in this situation?"

Perino's nervousness was evident in his halting, almost soft voice. "Yes, Mr. Steele, I've read your letter several times. I was totally shocked by it and, to be honest, I'm not sure what to say."

"To be honest." I thought to myself, "interesting choice of words from the mouth of a serial philanderer." I paused again and then said, "Well, Mr. Perino, your shock notwithstanding, I have a client who is very upset and very frightened by the circumstances she is faced with and it's my job to help her get through this. And getting through this will involve a financial burden that she is not prepared to deal with on her own." I stopped at that point, figuring the words "financial burden" should have a few seconds to sink into Perino's head without any interference.

Perino's reply was harsh but not totally unexpected. "Come on, this girl is young and pretty, she's probably very popular. What makes her, what makes you think it's my baby?"

The comment made me hate the guy and I hadn't even met him yet. "Ms. Martinez explained things to me in great detail, including the fact she has not dated anyone in the past six months and that she was quite intoxicated from the Mojitos you kept buying for her when she never requested them."

Again, I got a reply that wasn't unexpected. "That still doesn't prove her baby is mine."

I didn't want the entire con to play out on the telephone. It was important to all of us to see this slime ball sweat and squirm in front of Lisa Martinez. "Mr. Perino, there is much more to discuss regarding this matter and my client has made it clear that she wants to be a part of the discussion. I feel that by virtue of the fact we are offering you a chance to meet privately we are protecting your privacy as much as Ms. Martinez's. If you would like to argue the facts of the case in court we are fully prepared to do so."

I was certain the mention of a courtroom drama would make Perino squirm and his response proved me right. "Uh, okay, we'll do it your way."

"And do you have a place where you would like to meet with us?"

There was a long silence on the other end of the phone, then Perino said, "How about Maria's, it's a little lunch place on Thirty-second Street just south of Baseline?

The first thing that popped into my head was that the area south of Baseline was largely Hispanic and Indian in population, and probably far from anyone that would know or recognize a slick businessman like Perino. Knowing that his office was located quite a distance away in the heart of the downtown Phoenix business district I could only wonder how he knew about a little place called Maria's. "Okay," I answered, "we will find it and meet you there. Let's make it Thursday at one o'clock. I'll arrange for a table. Since you seem to know the place is there a quiet part of the restaurant, say a patio where we can talk openly and in private?"

His response took a while to leave his mouth. "Uh, yes, ask for the patio table, the one with the green umbrella, and say it's for Mr. Mike."

It was pretty clear that Perino wanted to have the meeting in a place where he felt safe, even to the point of selecting a specific table. "That's fine," I answered, "we will see you at one o'clock on Thursday." I paused then added, "We look forward to it."

Delilah and I had a couple of days to make sure we had our story laid out clearly and on Wednesday evening Ozzie and Lisa Martinez joined us at my house. I told them about my conversation with Perino and was surprised that any feelings of embarrassment from Lisa were either gone or masked by an obvious desire to get some small measure of revenge. Delilah and Lisa went through their lines regarding the medical examinations, Lisa's ongoing discomfort and worry about her condition and of course, the best way to present the fake sonograms to get the maximum impact.

Everything seemed to be in order and there was a general feeling among us that the con was going to be interesting to say the least. Despite our intention that no money would change hands and no threats would be made to Perino, I couldn't shake the feeling that this con was somehow different from our previous pranks. This one had a dark and crispy edge to it and I had to admit that I shared Ozzie and Delilah's nervousness but I also felt a rush of adrenaline that my previous pranks and cons had never produced. I wondered if I would have concocted this kind of a con before the lottery happened. Since that day there must have been a hundred times when some little conversation or circumstance had prompted a strange feeling of invincibility in me. I was ridiculously wealthy and could afford to take control of any situation. Each time that kind of thing popped into my head I had to stop myself and try to remember to stay grounded in my regular life. It was getting harder and harder to do that.

On Thursday at about twelve-thirty, Delilah, wearing a drab, gray dress and almost no make-up, came to my office. I was wearing a dark blue suit and business-like red tie. After double checking that we had the materials we needed and a quick run-through of our script we left to pick up Lisa. Delilah drove while I put on the same fake mustache and hairpiece I had worn for the website headshot. At five minutes to one a hostess at *Maria's* seated us at a patio table with the green umbrella that was unusually separated from the rest of the tables. She told us that Mr. Mike called and said he was on his way and for us to please order a drink on him. Delilah and I had never met Perino but a few minutes later we could tell by the look on Lisa's face that the overly-tanned man with the dyed black hair and gray suit heading toward us was the man we were waiting for.

Perino stopped when he reached the table. "You must be Mr. Steele," he said as he extended his hand. In mid handshake he turned to Delilah and said, "And you are?"

"I'm Nicole Blakely," she answered, "I'm Lisa's nurse and friend." Perino offered his hand to Delilah but her cold, confident expression, with eyes riveted on his, made her handshake something less than cordial.

Finally, when he knew he could stall no longer, he turned to Lisa and said, "Hello again."

I studied her expression and thought, "Man, if looks could kill." Lisa said nothing.

We had made sure that the only empty chair at the table was directly opposite Lisa's so she wouldn't be any closer to him than necessary and so he would have to keep turning his head back and forth to talk to Delilah and me. It was a little tactic I had learned from my boss in my first job out of college. By taking turns talking and asking him questions we could keep him off guard and in the process, each time he turned his head he risked making eye contact with the one person who made him the most uncomfortable.

Before any of us could speak a smiling young woman with a thick Hispanic accent stopped at the table and asked if any of us would like a drink with our lunch. Delilah, Lisa and I all declined but Perino ordered a gin and tonic. I couldn't help but wonder if he was a regular lunch hour drinker or if his nervousness over our meeting had dried his throat a little.

"Okay," I began, knowing I had to be the one to control the conversation, "my letter to you, Mr. Perino, stated the purpose of this meeting. Let me say up front that it is not our wish to take a punitive posture with this discussion and that we are here primarily to state the facts of the situation and to present our position on finding an equitable solution." Before he could respond I turned to Delilah and said, "Ms. Blakely, would you please tell Mr. Perino the facts of Ms. Martinez situation from a medical stand-point?"

Delilah gave Perino an icy glare as she opened a blue file folder, thumbed through several pages of documents, and then began. "Lisa, Lisa Anne Martinez is near the end of her first trimester of pregnancy." She paused, hoping Perino was mentally ticking back the days of the calendar to the night he and Lisa went to the hotel room together. She gave him a few more seconds and then said, "That timeline is in keeping with the date that Ms. Martinez told us that the two of you met." She was playing the part flawlessly and I was so proud of her.

Perino's face was expressionless as he stared at Delilah. She continued. "Her pregnancy seems to be going well and a few days ago we took these sonogram images." She spread three black and white images on the table in front of Perino, all of which bore the name Martinez, Lisa A. and the altered date of three days ago.

For the first time, Lisa spoke, saying simply, "That's my son."

Perino's previous lack of expression had suddenly become a face of obvious distress. I waited a moment to see if he would comment but he just stared at the sonograms so I said, "Okay, let me explain how things work from a legal perspective."

I watched carefully, studying Perino's face as he turned toward me and nodded, and then I said, "The State of Arizona allows Ms. Martinez to start the paperwork to establish paternity now while she is pregnant. If you wish to deny paternity of the baby we can and will order a genetic test after the child is born." I paused again and Perino was still nodding, almost as if he was in a daze. "However, an *Acknowledgement of Paternity* is a legal document that establishes the child's father without the need to go to court. While this form will become a matter of public record we have no wish to reveal your name. If no one makes a formal inquiry your name will not be known." I was really enjoying myself.

Perino leaned back and I could hear an audible sigh of relief. I pulled a small stack of papers from my folio and laid them in front of him. "I have printed out for you a copy of the *Maricopa County guidelines for Proof of Paternity* and I'd like you to review them in detail. You may contest paternity but if you do we will ask the Court to order genetic testing. That testing has an accuracy rate of over 95 percent. You must submit to the testing if we request it in court."

His face now fixed in a tense scowl, Perino loosened his tie and said, "I'll, I'll read through this carefully, and today."

"Good," I replied, "and let me finish by saying that if we have to request a test and it establishes the fact that you are the father, we will obtain a court order naming you as such with all that entails."

By this time Perino looked like a beaten man. I was surprised when he looked straight at Lisa and calmly said, "I'm very sorry this happened."

Lisa was more surprised than anyone and replied, "Thank you." I was glad she stopped with those two words. The less she said the more likely Perino would be left up in the air to wonder about her feelings.

Delilah scooped up the sonogram images when she saw the waitress heading toward the table. Before the young woman could say anything Perino looked at her and said, "We need just a few more minutes please." She didn't do much to hide her impatience as she sighed and muttered, "Okay, I'll be back in a few minutes."

Perino turned directly toward me, leaned forward and asked, "What needs to happen for this to go away?"

It was the response we had all hoped for. "Well," I answered, "we are preparing a detailed list of the fees and costs that Lisa has already incurred and can expect to face up to her delivery. There will also be costs attached to child care and follow-up doctor's visits. I can have my office send you a complete accounting." I gave that a few seconds to sink in and then added, "It is our hope that you will make a reasonable contribution toward those costs."

Perino gathered up the papers from the table, folded them in half and slipped them inside the lapel pocket of his suit coat. "Mr. Steele," he said, his nervousness now looking like borderline panic, "I would appreciate it if this goes no farther than the four of us. I guess I don't have to tell you how something like this needs to be kept as low-key as possible." His face glistened with perspiration and he tugged at his tie as if it were choking him.

"I absolutely agree," I replied, "and you can rest assured this can be resolved as quietly as you would like." I hoped those words would convince him that his predicament didn't require him to contact his own attorney. I was still nervous about that so I added, "It will be up to you to control the number of people who know about this."

With that he slowly stood up, looked at Lisa for an awkward moment then turned to me and said, "I'll get back to you as soon as you send me that information, and send it to me at my office, please." He politely nodded to each of us, turned and then quickly walked back through the restaurant. We watched intently from our patio vantage point as he hurried through the parking lot to his car and drove away.

There was a palpable sense of relief. We looked around at each other and Delilah was the first to speak. "Oh my God, honey," she exclaimed as she reached across the table and grabbed my hand, "that was so amazing. I think we actually pulled it off."

I offered a sheepish grin as Lisa, shaking her head, chimed in. "I was so scared about doing this but Delilah is right, you were amazing. Have you guys done this stuff before?"

Before I could answer Delilah said, "Oh, believe me, Lisa, he has done it before, many times. He should do this stuff for a living." She turned back to me and said almost proudly, "Like it or not, I'm in love with a damned chameleon!"

The returning waitress was a welcome interruption and we all ordered white wine and salads. Even though I cautioned them to not forget that the con wasn't quite over yet, we couldn't help but feel we were celebrating the success of our plan. There would be no further communication with Perino, no hospital costs shared, no phone calls or e-mails and no request for money. I was convinced by the look on his face and a gut feeling that we had accomplished our mission: to give an immoral creep his comeuppance. I was afraid to admit to myself that the whole con gave me a feeling of power that I couldn't quite understand and that I probably shouldn't enjoy. But I did enjoy it. I enjoyed it a lot.

Our success was confirmed on Monday morning when Ozzie came into my office. "Well, it looks like we did it. My neighborhood is shy one asshole."

"You mean Perino, what happened?"

"Well, on Saturday morning I watched him putting luggage and two cardboard boxes into his car along with what looked like enough hanging clothes to fill a closet. The rumor in the neighborhood was that he was moving out although nobody seemed to know the details of why."

I leaned back in my chair feeling smug and relieved. From where we stood it looked like Perino had finally had an attack of conscience and it led to a "come to Jesus moment" with his wife. We sat in my office drinking coffee as Oz continued to tell the story and when he was finished he leaned forward, his elbows on my desk. I could tell he didn't share my satisfied feeling. He sat silently for a moment and then said, "You know, Linc, I have to confess that I'm not sure how to feel about this con."

I sort of knew what he meant but I asked anyway, "Why is that?"

"Well, Perino is garbage, we all agree on that. He has bragged about so many women and so many times he has gotten away with things, and for all we know he might have really impregnated some poor woman. But here we are with a man who has left his family. He never did anything bad to me or you or Delilah and now his life is turned upside down and we're the ones who did it. I never expected it to turn out like this."

Nothing Ozzie said was untrue, even though I was surprised and more than a little pissed off by his sudden sense of regret for an idea that originated with him. But what we didn't know was if any of Perino's past transgressions had hurt another family or disrupted some other woman's life. I looked at him, nodded, and said, "You're right, man, he never did anything to us. It wasn't our business but come on, admit it. Don't you think we accomplished something here? Didn't we maybe stop him from using another woman and throwing her aside like he did to Lisa?"

Ozzie nodded and sighed. "Yeah, I suppose you're right but I guess I just don't feel as triumphant as I thought I would." He looked at me with an expression I hadn't seen from him before, like he was feeling guilty, and then he added, "I called Lisa this morning and she told me, when you were all sitting there under that umbrella you really looked like you were into the role, like you were in some kind of a zone and really in control of things."

"Yeah, I guess I kind of got into it, so what?"

Oz just kept going. "Sorry, but I gotta ask. Would you have acted that same way, would you have done things the same way if the lottery hadn't happened?"

I was surprised at the tone of his question and what he was implying. "What is that supposed to mean?" I was trying not to sound offended even though I was.

"I don't exactly know what I mean," he answered slowly. "It's just that there was a lot of risk involved with this one, the risk of

Perino finding out you made up a fake law firm or the risk of Lisa losing her cool. Hell, your fake hairpiece or mustache could have blown away in the wind. Anything like that and Perino could have figured out it was a con and made a lot of trouble for us." He paused, then added, "It just seems like you were different this time around, like you were utterly fearless or something."

I sat back in my chair and crossed my legs, tapping my hand on my knee and trying to find the right words. Then finally I said, "Okay, man, I know what you're trying to say and I can't say I blame you for feeling a little bad about screwing over Perino. I admit I was kind of worried about the risks myself but I think I handled it the same way I handled all the other cons. My money never entered into it."

Ozzie looked at me, nodded, but didn't say anything. I looked him right in the eye, trying not to let my anger show and said, "Oz, just remember, you started this one. Even though you weren't there when it all played out you were as big a part of this one as I was so don't ask me to apologize for what I did."

"I'm not asking you to apologize," Ozzie answered, "I was just thinking out loud that's all. There was a long, uncomfortable pause and I figured he was as aware as I was that we hadn't had a disagreement like this in years. Then finally he added, "I just hope this thing wraps up and the guy fixes things with his wife and with his kids."

Not having children of my own probably made it easier for me to pull off the con but my friend was a father and his big heart was showing loud and clear. "Okay Oz," I said, "what's done is done. We sent Perino a message and we can only hope that now he'll work as hard at fixing things with his family as he did with counting the notches on his belt. Let's move on."

I sat there for a moment, savoring the feeling of power I had felt with the con and at the same time thinking of the heart rhythm episode I had endured while sitting at my desk just a half an hour before Ozzie had walked in. It was one that lasted longer than most previous ones and it definitely had me rattled. It scared me enough to call my doctor and make me think of my father's untimely death related to his heart. And it made me think of three things people seem to crave; money, power and time. Two out of three would not be enough for me.

5

Another Visit to the Trailer Park

With the blind trust in full operation and Delilah and Ozzie's bequests final and legal I thought it would be easy to get back to normal and put the lottery in my rear view mirror once and for all. I had done a quick accounting of the costs related to *Operation New Daddy* and even with the expenses related to CONjunction, the fake lawyer website, the printing of business cards and everything else, my lottery winnings had already earned a hundred times more in interest than the entire con had cost. It was as though I couldn't spend enough money to offset the interest income and, try as I might, I couldn't get my head around that. My new income situation wasn't what I expected it to be, namely, that it would be something I could put into the background and not think about. That was a naïve notion that I was embarrassed to admit was beyond my control. But I had to admit that the potential for raising hell and having fun was intoxicating. It was a feeling of power that I enjoyed and I was working on a whole bunch of ideas to help me do it again.

So many things in my life just felt different. I couldn't pinpoint exactly how but nothing, nothing at all, felt the same as it had just a couple of months ago. Not the way I looked at people, not the way I viewed the world around me and not even little things like how I slept at night. I knew I shouldn't have been surprised by that but that didn't make it any easier to deal with. I knew the money and everything that came with it were right smack in the middle of things. That much was certain. I knew I was changing but I still couldn't figure out exactly how. It was an interesting problem to have.

Things were running smoothly at Carr Creative. Through my new trust Jon Aiken, the person he appointed as the trust representative and I had come up with a way to award substantial bonuses to every one of my employees. They all knew that the business was doing extremely well and no one seemed to question how I could afford that kind of generosity. Within the office only Ozzie and I knew the truth. I felt good about finally being able to reward my staff's hard work and creativity. I arranged to have the bonuses paid out over a six-month period so it wouldn't look like the company suddenly spent a big wad of cash. It was impossible to be too careful.

The ProInsure campaign was underway in print, on television and on the internet. The early feedback from customer polling and the client was way beyond anything we expected. My earlier concerns about the campaign's potential to look condescending and insulting to a large segment of the population seemed to be unnecessary. On the contrary, ProInsure's in-house marketing team told us they had never seen such an overwhelming and positive response to a national campaign. Their customer service staff conducted a survey among existing customers and the comments ranged from, "I loved the new commercials, the bear is adorable" to "You sure seem to know what matters to average people." Either our condescension wasn't obvious or the audience wasn't sharp enough to see it. I suspected the latter.

Our successful read on what the trailer park was all about seemed to be seeping into the work we were doing for other clients as well. The boundaries and definition of "trailer park" were broader than any of us expected, much broader. A new campaign for a chain of dental clinics featured a heavy-set, middle-aged man in a plaid shirt with a mouthful of nasty, crooked yellow teeth at the beginning of the spot but with a perfect Hollywood smile after he visited one of our client's offices. His closing line was "I may be a redneck but that don't mean my teeth can't be pretty." I actually winced the first time I saw it but a few moments of reflection led me to the conclusion that, unfortunately, there were a lot of people out there who could relate to it.

Another campaign for one of the largest car and truck dealership groups in the Southwest featured the on-going activities of a very sexy, blue jeaned and tattooed young woman who strutted around the car lot talking about the great deals on Dodge trucks. At the end of each commercial she stood at the back of a pick-up, opened the tailgate and hopped up on to it, then leaned back in a very provocative pose and said, "Real men, Dodge men, know what to do in this bed." It felt tacky and embarrassing but it had already sold a hell of a lot of Dodge pick-ups.

Wayne and his team of odd but brilliant geeks had really honed in on the things that moved, mattered to and motivated this ever-growing audience. Our clients might have had some reservations about the way we seemed to be talking down to their customers but their improving bottom lines and sales figures kept them from ever asking us to change or stop what we were doing. Whatever the message was, good, bad or pointless, it was reaching an audience that received it, barely gave it a thought and then moved on to the next good, bad or pointless message. No one seemed to take the time to think about the content or process it. They simply acted on it. I couldn't help but feel complicit in the dumbing down process and felt more than a little guilt for having gotten so good at it.

Because of that we weren't totally surprised when two other clients, the Smokehouse Barbeque chain and HomeGrown food stores told us they liked what we did for ProInsure and wanted us to do similar campaigns for them. As Wayne said when we wrapped up our weekly creative review with his team, "Boss man, I'm actually starting to like Jethro."

One of the unexpected benefits from our trailer park work was that it had provided us with an enormous database of information about the things the average person cared about and didn't care about. Wayne's team and our marketing staff worked with a variety of consultants to lay the groundwork and use that information for understanding exactly whom it was we were talking to and what made them tick. The information included a wide variety of demographic information like median age and income broken down by zip code, racial and ethnic populations, education levels, voter registration data and even people's shopping and dining preferences. I was particularly interested in the information that was strictly from Arizona. The state was my adopted home and I loved so many things about it but I never got used to and could never accept the political climate. It was dominated by politicians who were hell bent on promoting guns, hating gays, starving public education and keeping the public in the dark about what they were doing. And somehow the folks in the trailer park went right along with things and didn't seem to question it. Either that or they simply weren't paying attention.

For my own peace of mind I probably should have left all of that information buried in a file cabinet or computer folder. The more I dug into the data the angrier I became and, given my heart issues, that wasn't a healthy situation for me. I knew from being a long-time news junkie and reading every bit of internet, print and TV news that came my way that Arizona schools were falling farther and farther behind the rest of the country. I knew that public libraries and universities were scrambling to maintain programs and keep their doors open. Like the rest of the country, our highways and infrastructure were badly in need of repairs and our public employees were facing pay cuts and lay-offs. But what surprised me most was the almost non-existent amount of outrage from the public. It seemed as though a small percentage of the people agreed with the policy makers, an equally small percentage disagreed but the majority simply didn't care enough to form an opinion. At every election cycle voter turnout was abysmally low. Could it really be that so many people bought the line of bullshit their representatives were spewing? Could it really be that so many people weren't paying attention? Could so many people have set the bar so low? Our team had come to the conclusion that the answer to all of those questions was yes. It turned out that the data we had gathered to create an ad campaign also shed a lot of light on the reasons for all kinds of problems within the state and it led me to the conclusion that the negative aspects of the trailer park seemed to be a self-fulfilling prophecy.

I had just finished a half hour of reading the reams of information and finding myself getting more and more churned up inside when Ozzie walked into my office. "Hey, man, gotta minute?" he asked as he sat down in front of my desk. I couldn't help but notice that the previously gray hair around Ozzie's temples had turned dark brown like the rest of his hair. I assumed it had something to do with his new romance but I didn't make any kind of comment.

I leaned back and let out a huge sigh. "Yeah, sure, I could use a break from this shit."

Oz glanced at the piles of papers and binders strewn across my desk. "What's all this stuff?"

"Well, my friend, to me it's absolute proof that the trailer park is much bigger than we thought." Oz had a confused expression on his face but before he could say anything I continued. "This is the mountain of demographic and customer information we got out of the ProInsure campaign. Some of it is polling, there are some egghead studies and some of it's just plain focus group opinion. But I gotta say that as useful as it was in putting the concept together it's not exactly stuff that gives you a warm, fuzzy feeling about the future."

"What do you mean?" Ozzie asked as he leaned forward and picked up a blue three-ring binder from the desk.

"Well, you just picked up a good example," I answered. "That binder is a study of how much people spend on food every month including what they spend on groceries as well as fast food and junk food. We have an obesity epidemic in this country and people are lined up at the drive-through windows at Burger King and Taco Bell."

I picked up a red folder off the top of the stack and laid it in front of Oz. "This one shows the results of a survey on people's attitudes on buying American versus foreign made products and guess what, the bottom line is they simply don't give a shit as long as they can save a fucking nickel."

Ozzie seemed to be studying my face and he paused before he asked, "Forgive my ignorance. I'm a finance and numbers guy but what the hell does this shit have to do with buying insurance?"

It was a valid question and it reminded me of how often advertisers get lost in the minutiae of statistics. "It has to do with the way we view the client's customer. We're expected to know him or her from top to bottom, inside and out, know what makes him tick, what turns him on and what pisses him off." I picked up a thin, black folder labeled *Controlling the Customer: The Relationship Between Consumerism and Perceived Cultural Stratification* and held it up in front of Oz. "This little tome with the big pretentious title basically says that people define their self-worth through the things they buy and that it's our job to steer that process. According to the authors it's our responsibility to make people think they can be the equal of or better than anyone as long as they buy the right car or wear the right clothes."

Ozzie nodded and said, "That's nothing new, that's been a core belief of advertising from day one."

"Yeah, you're right, but this study is different. I've read all kinds of things like this before but this one has some really scary science behind it, things like IQ studies. Shit, there's even a section called, here let me find it." I flipped through the pages then stopped and read aloud the title of the chapter, "Here it is, *How Advertisers Can Help Negate Socioeconomic Realities.*"

I looked at Ozzie and said, "This is what we do here, we change people's reality. We fool them into thinking they're something that they're not. I guess I've been so buried in the details of running this place that I lost sight of the sad fact that we sometimes work over on the dark side."

"Just take it easy, man." Oz answered, "We do exactly what our client's pay us to do; help them sell their shit to people who might not realize they want it or need it. That's the way it's been for years. That's advertising."

When it came to the business Oz had always been my sounding board and I knew there was a very large grain of truth in what he said. But for some reason, over the past few days I couldn't shake the feeling that what I was doing, what I had been doing ever since I founded the company was somehow sleazy at least some of the time. I put the black folder back on top of the pile and leaned back in my chair. "Sorry man, I guess I'm just in a funk. I'm trying to decide if there's a victim here or if people are just their own worst enemies." The more I thought about it I leaned toward the latter. It was like the United States had become a three thousand mile wide trailer park full of people who didn't care, who didn't think and who didn't pay attention. I knew I had to try to stop feeling as though it was my fault.

Ozzie looked at me for a moment, like he was trying to read my mood and then he finally said, "Look, I can come back later if you want. It's nothing that can't wait."

"No, sit tight, I'm just venting. It's been a crazy week and I guess you just walked into the line of fire." And then before Oz could get started with his part of the conversation I said, "Hey, man, it's after five and I'm thirsty. How about you tell me what you wanted to tell me while we're sitting at the bar at Las Mesas, and I'll buy."

"Sounds good," Oz said as he stood up. "Just gotta call and check on the boys. They're still not used to the new house and the new neighborhood, you know how that goes. Let me do that and then I'll meet you there." He hurried down the hallway while I packed up my computer bag.

The traffic was heavier than usual and an accident on Camelback Road made the drive even longer, but it gave me time to think again about all of the studies and statistics that had put me into such a bad mood earlier. It was hard for me to not dwell on it. The reports, the surveys and the focus groups all seemed to say that it was getting easier and more profitable to manipulate the consumer and that the consumer himself was making it easy for us do it. What we referred to at the office as the trailer park was real and it was growing. Sad but true.

I was sitting at a red light when for some strange reason a phrase popped into my head, the words that form the foundation of the medical profession's code of ethics: Do no harm. I couldn't help but wonder if advertising and media should follow that same philosophy and that included me.

The crowd at the bar had already settled into every available stool but I managed to find a tall bar-side table. The faces around me were the usual mix of young professional types and blue collar folks stopping for a drink on their way home. Las Mesas was a wonderful, friendly melting pot of a place and I always felt right at home in its low-key embrace.

I was doing my usual scan of the bar, looking for familiar faces when Ozzie came up behind me. "Man, that "Camelback Crawl" was worse than usual," It was more of a sigh than a statement.

"Yeah," I answered, "I wish there was another route to get here but all things considered, it's the shortest way."

"You order yet?" he asked as he settled on to his stool

"Nope, but here comes Sarah so get your mind set on what you want because it looks like she's really slammed and it could be awhile before she gets back to us."

The words were no sooner out of my mouth when a very cute, very haggard and very pregnant young woman reached our table. "Hey, Linc, hey Oz, how y'all doin'?"

"Hey, Sarah, we're fine but more importantly, how are YOU doing?" I looked down at her stomach as she grinned and rubbed her left hand over her swollen midsection.

"Oh, I'm doin' okay I guess. She started kickin' this mornin' and hasn't stopped much all day. I think she's almost ready for her big debut."

Always acting like a father, Ozzie asked, "Sounds like she's knockin' on the door, what's your due date again?"

"The fifteenth, but I don't think I'm gonna make it that far, this little girl is ready to say hello!"

I couldn't help but feel bad for Sarah, a nice young woman who needed to wait tables to pay her bills and on top of that bring a new child into the world. "Well, don't push yourself too hard."

"Thanks, Linc, I appreciate that, now what are you drinkin' this evening, your IPA or your bourbon?"

I knew I was going to miss a server who knew my tastes in advance. "I'm going to go with a Maker's Mark with just two cubes." I turned to Oz and said, "Your turn, and it's on me, remember."

Ozzie held up his index finger as he scanned the beer menu. "Just one moment, almost there." Then he looked up at Sarah. "I'm gonna have the Stone Arrogant Bastard Ale."

She looked at him and smiled. "What, the premium stuff? Looks like Linc is rubbing off on you."

Oz grinned and said in a voice dripping with sarcasm, "Rubbing off on me, come on, Sarah, you know it's more than that. "I idolize this guy."

We watched her shake her head and walk away and when she was out of ear-shot I said, "Hey Oz, I just wanted to finish up where we left off in my office. Again, I'm sorry for laying all my pissed-offness on you but that market research shit really got to me. It's like all I can think about lately."

Oh, don't worry about it but I have to say that's the kind of thing that makes me glad I'm on the numbers end of things. I'd probably become an alcoholic or serial killer if I had to deal with the kind of shit you and Wayne deal with every day."

"You know it's funny you say that because Wayne and his team are trying hard to keep all of the trailer park stuff in balance and it's a struggle."

"What do you mean? I thought Wayne was sort of having fun with it all."

"Yeah, that's true or at least it was at first. He said Carr Creative was the face of Jethro but somewhere along the line Jethro went from being an inside joke to being the real face of real people and that changed the whole equation. Have you seen what they have hanging over the entry door of the Garage? It's a poster size portrait of Jethro Bodine, you know from the *Beverly Hillbillies*. And under Jethro's face are the words, In Jethro We Trust. Now Wayne's people are trying to find ideas that are simple enough for

Jethro to grasp but not so simple that the clients will think we're just phoning it in. I tell you, it's not easy."

I knew Ozzie was sympathetic even if he couldn't totally relate to the situation but then I remembered our reason for coming to Las Mesas in the first place was to talk about something he tried to bring up in my office. "Hey man, that's about enough of Jethro. What was it you wanted to talk about in my office before I went on my little tirade?"

My question seemed to have an odd effect on Oz because he looked at me for a second then looked down at the napkin he had nervously been folding and unfolding. "Well," he started, but before he could continue Sarah showed up with our drinks. She set each one in front of us and asked me, "You all gonna order an appetizer or anything else?"

I looked at Oz who was shaking his head. "No, I don't think so, Sarah," I answered, just a quick drink this time around." She smiled and walked away and I turned back to Oz.

He was still playing with his napkin and seemed nervous and after a moment of silence he said, "You know, for some reason I just had a flashback to a moment we shared at the *Upper Deck* back in our Oregon State days.'

It was a comment that I wasn't expecting. "When? What moment?"

"Remember the night you and I were there sitting way back in the dark corner by the restrooms, hoping that Chloe and Kim wouldn't see us if they came in, and you called it "TAB," our God-given right to Take A Break?"

"Yeah, of course I remember, it was something a twenty-one year old guy comes up with when he's terrified of a relationship with someone who wanted things to go in a totally different direction than he did." I looked at Oz for a moment and then joked, "Hey man, does this mean you want to break up?"

Ozzie broke into a grin. Memories of our wild and crazy days always did that to him. But the grin quickly faded and he said, "Man, talk about an ironic choice of words." He paused and took an unusually long sip of his beer, set the mug down on his mangled napkin and said, "Given all that's been happening lately and how everything seems to be moving along in the right direction, I was thinking it might be a good time for me to sort of slow down and catch my breath, maybe cut back my hours at the office and spend more time with the boys."

All things considered Ozzie's words didn't exactly come as a surprise. He had been my friend for a very long time and I knew him as well or better than anyone did. He was only a marginal student in college and throughout his working career, including his time as my partner, he did good, solid work but only as much as was needed at the moment. I used to tease him that he would have made a great hippy if it wasn't for his small tinge of ambition. Sooner or later I figured he would want to take advantage of his new-found wealth but I didn't think it would happen so soon. I leaned forward, my elbows on the table and my eyes trying to read my old friend's mood. "Oz, we all knew that the money was going to change things for us and I guess you're the first one to feel it." I could tell he was earnestly trying to be open and honest with me and I suddenly had a strange feeling that my best friend might be slipping away from me. "What do you mean by cutting back? I need you, buddy."

"I know, and don't worry I'm not quitting or anything like that. I just want to free up some time for me and also for the boys. You know I've never really taken them on a vacation of any kind? We had some weekend visits to San Diego and I took them to the Canyon once but that's it, just our usual "three guys in a car" kind of stuff." He paused for a moment looking like he had suddenly entered a daydream. "It sure would be nice to have a female companion to join us."

I wasn't sure how to respond so I said, "Hang in there, man, just give the internet dating thing a little time and maybe it'll lead to something good." It sounded easy and hollow, like the kind of thing someone says just to fulfill a conversational duty but I honestly didn't know what else to say.

"Yeah, well, whatever," he replied, fulfilling his own conversational duty. "I just want to get away and clear my head a little. So much shit has happened lately and I need a little time in a place that isn't here."

"I know what you mean, Oz. Delilah and I have been talking about a nice, long getaway someplace too, maybe even make it an elopement and honeymoon adventure."

"Then that's exactly what you should do, as long as I still get to kiss the bride when you get back."

I smiled and tried to turn the conversation back to its original purpose. "So what do you mean by cutting back, like part-time, twenty or thirty hours a week or what?"

"Yeah, something like that eventually. I'm meeting next week with Karen to see if we have everything we need to wrap up the fiscal year and then you and I can go over it with Jeff. After that we could be on autopilot for a while and I was gonna take the boys and hit the road for a couple of weeks. School doesn't start again for almost a month."

I waited a few seconds before I said anything, wanting to make sure my message was clear. Finally I said, "Oz, the three of us are in a very weird place right now with all of the money and the secrecy and the walking on eggshells. If you told me that you *didn't* need a little getaway I'd think you were crazy. Believe me, I know how you feel and I feel the same way, I just want to make sure we all keep our shit together and not do anything, or fail to do anything that causes problems."

"You mean problems with the money?"

"Yeah, of course the money but the company too." Suddenly, I felt a little bit sheepish because I'd been wanting to talk with Oz about my getting away for a while and asking him to cover for me. "You know, besides getting married I've been working on a couple of ideas for CONjunction and I was thinking of taking time to really work on them but I need back up at the office."

Oz nodded and said, "And that back up would be me."

"Well, that was my thinking but with what you just told me I guess I should come up with a Plan B." The words were no sooner out of my mouth when I realized that I probably laid some real pressure on my best friend, but then again he had also laid some on me. "Wait, man, that didn't come out the way I wanted." I looked at Oz and his expression seemed to be leaning toward the irritated side so I said, "You go ahead with your plans, you sure as hell deserve a break and the boys deserve an adventure with their dad. I can get Wayne to take charge for a while. He's done it before."

Always accommodating, Ozzie shrugged, seemed to shift gears and said. "Are you sure? I mean, I can put things off for a little while if you want me to." It was a nice offer even though his tone sounded a bit insincere.

Suddenly, when I heard the words "put things off" I felt like I'd had some kind of an epiphany and it took Ozzie to make me see it. I hesitated then answered, "No way, I'm being very unrealistic here and I guess it's time I face the facts" I leaned forward so I could lower my voice, looked around to make sure no one could hear me and said, "Oz, you just made me realize we've been very careful with this whole thing and we've been looking over our shoulders too much. It's been a few months of putting things off and I think it's fucking time we started letting ourselves be exactly what we are."

"And exactly what are we?"

I had noticed that while we'd been talking much of my lovely double shot of premium bourbon had been badly injured from the melting of the ice so I took a nice, slow sip. "Well, old friend, we are two very rich men with lots of other things that trip our triggers besides our jobs." That comment caused a little flashback to a quote I had heard many years ago by a a political cartoonist, and I repeated it to Ozzie. "I want to achieve a lifestyle that doesn't require my presence."

I took another quick look around the bar room and said, "Listen, promise me you'll give me a few days and help me figure out some way to reassign some of the work in the office, kind of an unofficial transition plan, for you, for me, for the firm. I mean a way to keep things moving that keeps the firm strong and allows us a chance to do what we want to do. We can worry about the legal shit later. What do you think?"

Ozzie seemed surprised, almost shocked by what I said. For a moment he just looked at me with a quizzical expression but it soon turned into the devilish grin that was his trademark, and he said, "Holy shit, I was wondering how long it would take you to get to this point, and I'm glad I was here to witness it first-hand."

I laughed out loud, reached over and clinked my glass with his. "Here's to us, two old friends with love in our hearts, mischief on our minds and money in our pockets."

Oz smiled and said, "Watch out world, here we come." We sat there for a while and just looked around, commenting on the usual collection of drinkers and diners around us. Then, out of the blue Oz asked in what sounded like a very cautious tone, "So what are the CONjunction plans about? I hope there's something I can help you with."

I wasn't sure if I was ready to share my ideas with Oz or anyone. The jokes and cons I'd pulled off in the past were fun. With the exception of *Operation New Daddy* the schemes played out, usually people laughed and then everyone went home afterward. But what I had come to label as "the trailer park data" had really messed with my thinking. I was pissed off and frustrated by it all to a point where it sometimes got my heart pounding and I had to take a break from it to calm down. I was still trying to figure out why. I felt like I had to do something with the information, to take some kind of stand and make things change somehow. It was both the "something" and the "somehow" that I couldn't quite pin down. I owed Oz an answer so I just said, "Oh, I have a couple of things churning in my head and you and Delilah will be the first to know." Fortunately, Oz didn't probe any deeper.

While we were finishing our drinks Sarah came back to the table. "Anything else guys?"

I looked over at Oz. "Nope," he said, "for once I'm going to leave this place with just one drink in my belly."

"Me too," I said to her. She handed me the check folder and I said, "Hey you, in case your beautiful little girl gets here before I see you again, good luck."

Sarah smiled. "Aw, thanks Linc. I'm gonna miss you guys while I'm on family leave."

She walked away and I slipped my credit card into the slot of the folder and then wrote her a tip for a thousand dollars. Oz waited at the table while I hand delivered it to the manager so I could explain and he could verify the amount. I also asked him to keep it low key. When Oz and I walked out the door it really felt like our talk had helped me clear a big hurdle. I wasn't sure about the how and why of it all but I couldn't escape the feeling that the chance for adventure the Powerball winnings offered me was getting closer and would soon be ready to launch.

6

Moving Right Along

When you live in the desert, summer is strangely like the way people in the east live in the winter. You stay indoors as much as possible and things seem to slow down. The oppressive heat and monsoon rains alter your lifestyle in the same way the bitter cold and blizzards do to people elsewhere in the country. All you can do is tough it out and wait for the calendar to change. It's a good time to bear down and get things done.

Things around the office of Carr Creative were humming along at a pace that none of us could remember experiencing. It seemed like a strange time to be thinking about getting away from things. Two new employees came on board with us and almost everyone was working late or going into the office on weekends, everyone except Ozzie. It was a grind but somehow we all managed to meet our deadlines and maintain our collective sanity. Ozzie and I had created what we thought would be a workable, near-term and decidedly informal restructuring plan while all around us the activity of an increasingly successful business seemed to demand more of our involvement not less. But what should have been heady times for me were blunted by the feelings I had ever since I started reading the research from the trailer park campaigns. I just couldn't seem to shake my continuing fixation on the downside of the work we were doing in the office.

The mountain of information we had gathered to pull the ad campaigns together was hard to handle. It helped us understand the customers and meet our client's goals so, in effect, we did our job, but it also was very upsetting to me on a personal level. As I took more time to dig into the research I noticed my own attitudes on many topics starting to change. We had known for a long time that our target audience on the campaigns wasn't exactly the cream of the American crop but seeing the actual science behind that feeling made me start to see them in a different light. And along with that my earlier concerns about being insulting or condescending to them had started to melt away. That feeling was both liberating and bothersome.

There was evidence in the studies and particularly in the focus group results that indicated the people who appeared in the research weren't necessarily stupid or lazy, although there was also some evidence of that as well. They just weren't motivated by any obvious or familiar measure and they just didn't seem to care very much about anything outside their own little worlds. Sure, through our work we were manipulating their spending habits but they made it easy for us because the people in the focus groups were very vocal and very blunt about what was important and unimportant to them.

By a wide margin they appeared to be apolitical, especially when it came to issues that required more than minimal thought and reflection. In one case, members of a group were asked if they identified themselves as *politically active* or *non-active* and eighty-eight percent responded with *non-active*. The same group was asked the reasons for their political inactivity and the list of answers included, "Why should I vote because my wife never agrees with me so her vote just cancels out mine." Another respondent said, "It's too hard to register" and another respondent said, "I don't understand the issues, they're too confusing." The one that really sent chills down my spine was, "It don't matter who gets elected cause' they're all crooks." I was starting to wonder where the boundaries of the trailer park began and ended.

Just to keep my sanity I decided to channel some of my frustration and bewilderment into one of the cons that had been churning in my head. Dan Franks, an old friend of mine from my early days in Phoenix was working on the election campaign of a political newcomer. Raul Mendia, a self-made man born and raised in the barrio of South Phoenix was running for City Council in a district that had slowly shifted from a mostly White population to a slight Hispanic majority. Raul was the clear underdog to the incumbent, Bob Gradwell, a smarmy, self-absorbed businessman and the golden boy of the Republican machine in Maricopa County. He was a polarizing presence in his district and, with funding help from a PAC with unidentified membership, had rolled over his opposition in two previous elections. When Dan approached me about helping with Raul's campaign the part of me that always rooted for the underdog took over. Of course I'd make a substantial contribution to the campaign fund but I could also smell an opportunity for a con, a little scheme that would help Raul in his uphill fight.

I spent a good part of the next two days turning my raw idea into a finished script. I went over the concept with Oz and he started to put together a short list of the actors we'd need to pull it off. It would all play out at a town hall style candidate's forum that had been scheduled for less than two weeks down the road. Because the con involved a legally organized political campaign I knew I'd have to be very careful with what I did and how it would be viewed from the outside. Delilah had worked on a friend's school board campaign a few years back and she guided me on how to set boundaries on our activities to stay within the campaign laws.

Over the next weekend I fine-tuned the details with Delilah, and Ozzie managed to find a little time to join us to do a quick run through. Finally, when I was comfortable that it all felt realistic and workable I called Dan Franks and I put it on the speaker so Delilah and Oz could hear what Dan had to say. The hard part of the call would be making the con sound reasonable, useful and, most importantly, legal. In my line of work I knew the importance of semantics so instead of using the word "actors" I used the word "volunteers." Instead of saying that we should "follow the script"

I said we should "control the tone of the questions." The overall message to Dan, and by extension to Raul, was that we were marketing and media experts, our product was Raul Mendia, and our plan would help to blunt the momentum that Bob Gradwell was shown to have in the polls.

Dan listened to my plan and he was very quiet, just letting me talk but saying nothing in response. It had me puzzled because I couldn't tell if he simply didn't understand the plan or if he understood it and didn't like it. Or even worse, that he understood it and thought I was suggesting that we do something illegal. When I finished explaining it I paused to hear his reaction. All I could hear was dead air broken by an occasional "uh" or "hmm." Finally I just came right out and asked, "So, Dan, what do you think?"

There were another few seconds of dead air at the other end and then he replied, "Linc, I have to say I'm new to all of this so I'm not sure how to answer." There was another pause and then he asked, "Is this stuff legal?"

That was pretty much what I was expecting him to say but Oz and Delilah's expressions seemed to indicate that they were surprised. "Dan, relax, this is simply a plan to make sure Gradwell doesn't rig the event in his favor. He sort of has that reputation."

"How, by rigging it in Raul's favor? That doesn't seem right."

"No, not really. We aren't rigging anything. Political campaigns are rough and tumble sometimes. I've been hearing and reading the shit that Gradwell has been saying about Raul and his supposed favoring of the Hispanic voters over everyone else. To me that just reduces the election to a referendum on race and that's awful on so many levels."

There was more silence on the other end, and then Dan finally said, "Okay, let's do it. What do you need from me?"

I knew from what Delilah had told me that town hall style events were organized by both candidates' committees, with each side selecting and bartering on the details. Dan had told me earlier that he was worried about who would get to select the moderator who would control the questions. It was a legitimate concern but

I saw things from a totally different angle. "Dan, I think I have an idea that will really lock us in tight on this little event."

"What's that?" he asked.

"Well, remember the other day on the phone you told me you were worried about what would happen if Gradwell gets to choose the moderator. I know that's a big concern but I think there's a way to get around that or at least blunt that advantage. From what I understand the venue has already been picked, right?"

"Yep, it's going to be held at the lecture hall at Rio Salado College, both Gradwell and Raul agreed to it. It can only accommodate about four hundred and fifty people but the location is great because it's smack in the middle of the district."

"Okay, that's good. Now who is going be fielding the phone calls for access to the event, it's going to be a call-ahead reservation deal, right?"

"Yeah, because the seating is limited the candidates agreed that they didn't want any pushing and shoving at the doors the night of the event. A woman we know, she's not officially on the committee but she's sort of a friend of ours, works in the office at the college and she volunteered to handle the phone calls."

"What did the Gradwell people say?"

"They seemed overjoyed that we would be willing to do that kind of mundane chore for them."

I thought about the situation for a moment, long enough that Dan asked, "Linc, you still there?"

"Yeah, I'm here. This thing sounds like it's going to work out just fine. Can you give me the name and number of the woman who'll be fielding the reservation calls? I'd like to go over a couple of helpful tips with her."

I wasn't sure how Dan would react to that comment so I was relieved when he said, "Sure, got something to write with? It's Anna Gomez and her number is 602 555-2820. That's her number at the school."

"Great," I said, glad that Dan couldn't see the grin on my face. "I'll get in touch with her in the morning. Thanks, Dan, and I'll get back to you in a few days."

After I hung up the phone I sat there for a moment with a couple of little tweaks to the plan churning in my head. I looked over at Delilah. "How do you think that went, babe?" I asked her.

"It sounds like he bought into the whole thing." She paused and I noticed her raised left eyebrow. "But I'm really curious about those helpful tips you mentioned." Another pause and then, "Something tells me that once again you're going to be working out on the edge of legality here. Am I right?"

Despite my efforts to look completely serious I knew that I had a slight grin on my face and Ozzie picked up on it. "There," he blurted out, "there's that little smirk. I've seen that smirk a thousand times and it always precedes something a little, shall we say, risky."

Delilah was looking at me with a skeptical expression and Oz was waiting for a response to his comment. "Okay, I know this one probably sounds a little, let's use your word, Oz, risky. We usually have a lot more control of the situation and who is going to be involved. This one isn't going to be quite so neat and tidy. We'll be pulling this off in a building owned by the County with candidates for a City office talking to four hundred and fifty citizens. There will probably be off-duty City cops there for security and the local TV stations will be covering it."

After an uncomfortable pause, Delilah said, "And I can tell none of that seems to bother you. It's almost like it turns you on. Honey, it seems like we're getting even closer to squirrel territory here."

I smiled, hoping to reassure her as well as myself. "No, we're not, at least I don't think so. We won't be running the show here, just kind of steering a few things just a little bit."

"Okay, man," Oz said, "maybe you better let us in on what you mean by steering."

"Well, let's just say, if we do our jobs right and follow the script, the vibe in that auditorium will be music to Raul's ears. Music with a distinct Mexican flavor"

Ozzie grinned and said, "Man, you've got brass balls, very, very big brass balls."

I nodded in agreement. "Yeah, and I hope that'll be enough."

7

The Big Mexican Switcheroo

Las Mesas was more crowded than usual and the noise level was uncharacteristic of the normally mellow and low key ambience of the place. It had been the favorite hang-out for Delilah, Ozzie and me since it had opened over a year ago but word of mouth was slowly turning it into another urban hipster hang-out and that was the last thing we wanted to see.

"Man, I gotta tell ya' Linc, you really outdid yourself this time," Ozzie shouted above the din as he lifted his glass in my direction.

Delilah took her glass in hand and followed suit, "Absolutely, honey, what you pulled off was amazing."

It felt good hearing accolades from the two people I most cared about and knowing that I had put a self-important idiot politician in his place only added to my good mood. I held my glass high, looked at Ozzie and Delilah and said, "Thanks, but it was a team effort and as usual I couldn't do this shit without you two as my partners in crime."

The clinking of our glasses was the perfect punctuation to the successful completion of *The Big Mexican Switcheroo*. In less than two weeks we had managed to meet with Raul Mendia's election team, help them organize the details of the town hall debate and carefully arrange the reservation-only access. We made sure that

81

Councilman Bob Gradwell's usual list of hand-picked lily-white friends would not dominate the attendance with the intention of asking him pre-arranged, softball questions. Since his election six years earlier Gradwell had all but ignored the voices and problems of the large Hispanic neighborhoods within his district and I had carefully crafted our little charade to get his attention.

Delilah put her hand on mine, gently squeezed it and said, "It's like you always say, honey, it feels good to do good and that's exactly what you did with this little con"

"You know, I confess I'm finally starting to get comfortable with the word con," I said, smiling into her beautiful blue eyes. "In fact, I like it."

"Hey man, she's right," Ozzie chimed in. "and I'm glad you're finally coming around because this one wasn't a practical joke or a charade, it was a flat-out con job, a beautifully designed and executed one and you should be proud of it. I know I am."

I leaned back in my chair and took a quick look around the restaurant to make sure no one was close enough to hear our rather unusual conversation. "Okay, I admit we did a pretty good job of pulling it off. Like I've said before, these cons are my children and when I give them birth it's fun to sit back and watch what they do."

Ozzie smiled and said, "Yeah, but you gotta make sure one of your children doesn't wind up going to juvenile detention or prison in the process."

I laughed almost as hard as Delilah did, even though hers seemed tinged with more than a little nervousness. Then I continued, "I was glad to be sitting there in the crowd. And I have to say it was worth all of that work just to see Gradwell practically shit his pants when that sweet, elderly Mexican woman asked him why the crumbling streets and sidewalks in her neighborhood hadn't been patched or repaved in over five years while the street he lives on was repaved and the entire boulevard replanted in the same period."

Ozzie almost choked on his wine when I said that. "I know, did you see the sweat running down that shiny, bald head of his? And when he answered her with his usual, "Please let me look into that for you, ma'am," I expected someone in the crowd to throw a folding chair at the fat son of a bitch."

Delilah laughed and added, "And, Oz, that guy you hired from the casting agency was the sweetest, most perfect looking, little, down-on-his-luck old man I ever saw. When he stood behind that microphone in his tattered jeans and quietly asked Gradwell why the neighborhood recreation center was shut down for lack of funds but a big, new indoor recreation building was approved for the Councilman's neighborhood, Gradwell's silence was deafening."

"Yeah," I replied, "That was a very satisfying moment. I hope Raul was taping it or taking notes because if he manages to beat Gradwell and take over the district he's going to have his hands full. Gradwell has totally ignored those people for six years and their neighborhood has gone to hell. Those folks are about ready to bust loose."

Ozzie leaned forward, elbows on the table and a smug grin on his face "I wonder if Raul noticed that there weren't as many white faces in that audience. How many ringers did we end up hiring to fill the extra chairs?"

"Oh, about fifty or so. Meta Rosenberg at the casting office did a great job of finding people who really looked like what you asked for; average, every day Mexican folks. Not a movie star or model or wanna-be in the bunch, just real folks. She asked me if we were doing a TV commercial so I made up a story and told her we were just going to do a dry run for a future ad campaign."

"Fifty!" Oz said, obviously surprised. "I never told her to hire that many."

"No, I told he, and relax, it's coming out of CONjunction's pocket."

Our server set another shot of bourbon in front of me and I noticed Delilah's raised eyebrows as I took a sip. Then I continued. "You know, what really made the whole thing work was Anna Gomez taking all of the reservation calls. Anyone who called to reserve a spot had to get past her. When I talked to her about things to say when the calls came in I flat out asked her if she could tell the difference between a White person's voice and a Mexican's She told me she has a good ear for people's voices and accents, and if she had any trouble she'd talk to them for a minute to find out a little about them. She said she'd have no trouble being able to tell if it was one of Gradwell's buddies on the other end of the phone or someone from the neighborhood.

"Delilah leaned forward, eyes wide and asked, "So that's what you meant by steering things?"

"Well, yeah, I guess that's what you could call it. I gently suggested to Anna that if the voice didn't sound like someone from down the street she should tell that person there were no more seats available. Without her ever saying so I knew she understood what the goal was and she soldiered on all the way to the deadline. She was the gatekeeper on this thing and it worked out beautifully. I just hope she never talks about it to anyone." While I refilled their wine glasses I added, "Gradwell's people pushed really hard to be the ones selecting the moderator. I told Dan Franks to argue a little and then back off. He did that and Gradwell's guys thought by getting that they won the battle and had things all tied up in a neat little package. But what we managed to do was take away that advantage because their moderator had to field questions from a room full of our people, meaning Raul's people.

"You know," Ozzie said, "I don't pay that much attention to politics and I can't prove it but I gotta believe that slime ball Gradwell has done this kind of thing before too, and, I gotta tell you, if we'd ever found out about it at the time we would have been screaming to the media the next day."

"But there's a difference here," Delilah interrupted, "and maybe it's splitting hairs, but what we did was merely level the playing field for a change and give the little guy a fair shot at winning." She looked over at me and said, "At least that's why I think we did it."

"It is, and sometimes you just have to play by the other guy's rules if you want to beat him," I said. "When the whole thing was over and people were heading for the exits, Dan Franks came over to me with this strange little smile on his face. He said, "I don't know what it was you did and maybe I don't want to know but all I can say is thank you."

Oz looked around the room and then leaned forward to make sure I could hear him over the crowd noise and said, "You know Linc, I gotta say this con felt totally different from the other ones, almost dangerous or something. It was even better than *New Daddy*. This was way beyond being a practical joke, this one seemed like it was a slap upside somebody's head, or actually a lot of people's heads."

I didn't even try to hide my proud little smile. "Yeah, and I hope it hurt the bastards."

The surprised look on Delilah's face got my attention. "Be careful, honey," she said, "it's okay to enjoy the moment but keep this stuff in perspective and do it for the right reasons, okay?" She obviously didn't share my taste for battle.

I smiled and nodded but didn't say anything more. Oz was right. This one felt different and I had to admit I liked the feeling. I had taken a big step in the effort to bring down a very insensitive and very divisive politician. It was a very different kind of con than I had ever pulled off before. I knew that it skirted the edges of legality but, in my own way, I rationalized my little tinge of guilt with very little trouble. I had created a lot of cons in the past. I was damned good at it and I had never done it for money or to profit from it in any way. This one felt good and I was happy about what the results might be. And I had the desire and the money to do even more. Much more.

We continued our little celebration over crab cakes and wine and, in my case, bourbon. Delilah leaned over several times during dinner to suggest that I slow down on my drinking but it was Friday evening. It was a good note to end the week on and also served as a send-off for the three of us. In a few days Ozzie and his sons were going to leave on a trip to Hawaii so they could try their hands at surfing, gorging on seafood and watching girls. And Delilah and I had finally decided to take the plunge. We had reservations at a resort in British Columbia and had arranged to fly our parents there as well. We'd be married on a patio overlooking a gorgeous mountain lake. For the first time since that rainy Sunday when my whole world changed I felt like things were settling into some kind of a new normal, if constant change can be called normal.

We were having a great time and we could have stayed longer if it wasn't for an early Saturday morning meeting with Jon Aiken that I reluctantly put on my schedule. Jon's team was very meticulous when it came to money and he was really staying on top of the investment plan that Jeff Norris' team had created for the trust. I had to admit to myself that I was eager to see what my money was doing.

Ozzie offered to pick up the tab, insisting that it was his turn. Before I could protest he grabbed the vinyl folder the waitress had set on the middle of the table, looked over the tally and said, "Shit man, maybe I spoke too soon. You be drinking some expensive bourbon and we be drinking domestic wine."

Delilah rolled her eyes and said, "Then I'll get it" She leaned forward and reached for the check but Ozzie smirked and waved her off. "I'm just messing with you guys. Thanks to Linc's generosity I can finally afford to pick up the tab, but just don't get too used to it."

On Monday I got into the office early. The day was a combination of my usual work plus organizing things with a variety of people. With Wayne for his handling of the reins while I was gone, with Oz to make sure the necessary financials were sent to Jeff Norris' office and with Delilah on finalizing the details of our wedding trip. Somehow in the midst of it all I managed to find a little time to savor the feeling of success that came from *The Great Mexican Switcheroo*. My daily reading of the op-ed pages in the *Arizona Republic* seemed particularly satisfying. For the first time in his tenure on City Council Bob Gradwell was sweating bullets. The general feeling from the newspaper's editorial staff, and the way I interpreted it was that Gradwell had really stepped in some shit and he was having no luck cleaning his shoes. Between comments from the editorial writers and a number of letters to the editor, Raul Mendia had shown he was a man of the people he wanted to represent and Gradwell clearly wasn't. I was happy about what we pulled off and hoped that very soon the election results would let me put that con in the win column.

8

Turning a Corner

There is an upside and a downside to travel and the best you can hope for is that the two sides will balance out. It was the first time since I'd started my own business that I had taken two consecutive weeks away from the office. I thought it would be hard and for the first few days I admit I had trouble cutting the electronic umbilical to Carr Creative, but it eventually got easier. The first day of the trip was settling into the resort and the second day was filled with errands and some local sight-seeing. When we got to day three I finally felt relaxed and prepared for the big event. Even though I didn't want to admit it to myself the money made it a whole lot easier to relax.

We spent the evening before the wedding relaxing on the deck of the restaurant sipping some great local wine and waiting for our dinner order. I was feeling very mellow which made Delilah's comment all the more surprising. "Honey, it's not like I'm counting or anything but you've had a whole lot to drink today. Mimosas at brunch, a beer this afternoon and now we're on our second bottle of wine. Don't you think you should give it a little break?"

It wasn't the first time she had commented on my consumption levels but I didn't expect one at a time like that. "Babe," I said, "tomorrow is our wedding and I decided to start celebrating the moment I woke up this morning." I expected a smile in return but I didn't get one.

She looked at me more seriously than the moment would suggest and said, "Wouldn't it have been nice if your father could have been here to be part of things?"

Her point was clear. My father had lived with the same heart rhythm issue as mine and had passed away when he was just fifty-three. His doctor told him to quit smoking and cut back on his daily drinking but Dad wasn't a very good listener. I sighed and answered, "Okay, I get your point but remember Dad was a heavy-duty smoker and I'm not."

Delilah's serious expression didn't waver. "You said nobody ever knew if it was the cigarettes or the drinking or both but, either way he died way too young and damn it, I want to grow old with you."

Every word she said sounded just like things I had said to myself a thousand times. I didn't tell her every time I had a rhythm episode because it would worry her too much but whenever my heart rhythm problem would flare up I'd cut back on my drinking, watch my diet more closely and even walk or run in the morning before I went to the office. But after a few weeks I'd slip back into my bad habits again. Delilah's expression on the night before the biggest day of her life bothered me and I knew it was my fault. I reached across the table, took her hands into mine and said, "Babe, you're right and I'm sorry." I squeezed her hands and added, "It feels so good to have someone care so much."

Finally she smiled. "Honey, I'm not asking you to give up drinking. I know you enjoy it and hell, so do I. I just want you to take better care of yourself, that's all."

I smiled, nodded and said, "Okay, message received."

The wedding ceremony, on the stone terrace of the hundred year old hotel overlooking Otter Bay, was more emotional than I had expected. Having been through a wedding before, I was surprised that my second one could actually bring tears to my eyes. Delilah was stunning in a very simple white dress and her last minute decision to pick some small, blue wildflowers from the resort's garden and put a sprig of them in her hair seemed like the perfect enhancement to her blue eyes. I wore a dark gray suit and a blue tie and even though I felt that I looked pretty sharp I was no match for my beautiful bride. The resort had found us a retired judge from a nearby town to perform the ceremony and his calm, relaxed personality helped me keep my nerves under control. It was a short but moving ceremony, and it led to pretty much the happiest day of my life.

After a few days of sight-seeing and consuming more food and wine than was sensible I was finally able to distance myself from my work, at least the official work of the company. The ideas for a couple of cons that had been simmering on the back burner of my mind for weeks just wouldn't stay away. Even though they were a constant distraction I knew I had to focus all of my energies on Delilah and nothing else, if that was possible.

In anyone's life a wedding is many things. Of course it's all of the romantic things that couples get caught up in and both Delilah and I felt like a couple of happy kids on a magical vacation. Even with my odd sense of humor I had always considered myself to be somewhat of a tight-ass but Delilah had a way of loosening me up and helping me get in touch with the parts of me that I didn't indulge very often. It was an amazing honeymoon to say the least.

It was about day seven or so that I found myself starting to reconnect with the ideas for my new cons. One of them involved a charity golf tournament that I had played in in previous years and was a sponsor of for this year's event. The other one was still a work in progress, something rolling around in my head and not yet focused. It was also something that seemed almost overwhelming in its scope, and the risks involved were real but strangely appealing. I tried hard to keep it pushed to the back of my mind but it kept popping into my consciousness on a regular basis. If it played out the way I imagined it would dwarf any of the schemes I had ever tried before. And until I got the concept, the details and, most importantly the possible consequences clear in my head I didn't want to say a word about it to anyone.

Because of my fixation on the two cons, much of my plan to relax and focus on Delilah was compromised and I could tell she wasn't happy about it. I was lying on a chaise lounge pretending to be reading the morning newspaper, when she walked out on to the patio and sat down on the chaise beside mine. For a moment she just looked at me and I turned to her and asked, "Hey, babe, what's up?"

"That was supposed to be my question," she answered in a flat tone. Her usual upbeat demeanor was missing.

I wasn't sure what to say next but she saved me the trouble. "You seem pre-occupied like you're in some kind of a daze, is everything okay?"

"Yeah, everything's fine, I guess I'm still not used to being away from the office routine"

"Oh, come on, it's not the office that has you sitting around in a fog." She waited to see a reaction from me and when she didn't get one she added. "I know I've only been your wife for a few days but I've known you long enough to tell when your mind is off on its own somewhere, and right now it's definitely not in the here and now."

She was right and I had to admit that it felt good to have someone like her be able to read me. It had been over six years since a woman had been around me on a regular basis, and even longer since a woman actually cared about what I was thinking. I put down my newspaper and sat up, facing her. "Okay, you got me, it's not office stuff I'm thinking of, it's a con, actually it's two cons."

Her slight smile was my first clue that she was interested. Her hand on my knee was the second. "I remember a comment Oz made that Sunday at your house," she said, "that you couldn't go three straight days without pulling a joke or a con. So, what has it been so far, about two weeks?"

"Yeah, at least." I turned to sit on the edge of the chaise, facing her. I took both of her hands in mine. "Babe, I'm not sure what these two little schemes will turn out to be. One is pretty straightforward and kind of feels like our last one."

"You mean, *The Great Mexican Switcheroo*?"

"Yeah, they both have politics at the center of them."

She waited almost nervously and then said, "So I take it there will be winners and losers involved again."

One of my ideas was pretty straight forward but the other one, the big one, the one that actually scared me, was still a work in progress. Until I had it totally fleshed out I wouldn't even know how to describe it to someone. "Well, I answered, "I guess you could say that. The first one is pretty well set but the other one is still just a vague idea and I'm not even close to putting it all together. I'd rather concentrate on the first one because I have the script worked out in my head and it's kind of time sensitive."

"What do mean, time sensitive, you mean like you need to do it soon?"

"Yeah, like in a couple of weeks, and I'm gonna need some help with it until Ozzie gets back."

"And I take it you mean me." I couldn't tell if she was asking or offering.

"Well, if you have some time after we get home I could use some help, mainly coordination, phone calls and e-mails, that kind of thing, and of course looking over the script and offering any ideas you might have on how to make it better. The rest I'll have to handle by myself."

"Well, okay, I guess I can help," she said slowly, "I know I have a couple of meetings and a presentation to work on so before I commit it would help if I knew what the con was all about."

Putting together a really good con usually took me a while so I could walk it through my head a few times to see how it felt. This one was only about eighty percent there but I knew that Delilah deserved to know why my head was in the clouds so I decided to lay it out for her. "Okay, here it is. It's still kind of rough around the edges but hopefully you can help me smooth them out when we get home. I took a breath and then began to describe *The Bentley Caper.*

For three consecutive years I had played in the Greater Phoenix Charity Golf Classic. It was a pretty big event in the Valley, with a list of players made up of the movers and shakers of local politics and business, and sometimes a professional athlete or two. Over the years it had grown from a small event to one that generated several million dollars to the coffers of local food banks, women's shelters and child-care facilities. It had also become an essential place to be seen if you had a reason to get in front of the television cameras and the Valley media. I enjoyed being part of it to help the community and this year I was not only going to be a player, I was also on the line for a sizable sponsorship.

Along with the usual sponsor forms and information packet I received regular e-mail updates on the people who had signed on to be part of the event. One morning a few weeks back, while I was sitting at my computer, an update popped up and I took a minute to look down the list of players. One name in particular jumped out at me, Representative David Pierce. I wasn't at all surprised to see Pierce's name on the list because he was a shameless publicity hound who seemed to spend more time in front of a camera than he did in his legislative office. Pierce was from an influential conservative family and was the quintessential political hack who curried favor from a small handful of East Valley business owners and a few incumbent and entrenched Republican politicians. His political reputation was built on intolerance for minorities, gays and pretty much anyone who wasn't an old, white male. He was also a preening, self-absorbed jerk who had an overpowering need to be the center of attention. To me he was the poster boy for what was wrong with Arizona politics, and to me that meant there was a target painted on his back.

Since I had played in three previous tournaments I knew how things worked with the television cameras and photo-opportunities with sponsors and celebrities. It took me all of ten seconds to realize the tournament was an opportunity for a con. The success of *The Great Mexican Switcheroo* was still fresh in my mind and so was the way it had made me feel good to smack down a bad-guy politician. So while I had been juggling my work, the wedding and the honeymoon a very mean and snarky scheme had been brewing.

Delilah seemed totally attentive so I continued my explanation. I knew how the tournament events worked and I knew that Pierce would be looking for a photo-op, some way to get his grinning face in front of the cameras. I had to come up with a way to create and control that opportunity and with a little bit of head scratching and lying awake at night I came up with the concept. The con would be based on Pierce's ego and his need for attention, and the catalyst for his undoing would be a shiny, brand new Bentley convertible. I had met Rolf Lange, the owner of the Scottsdale Bentley dealership about six months before at a business leadership luncheon and he seemed like a very nice guy. We talked around the edges of having Carr Creative do some advertising for the dealership but nothing ever came of it. I figured this little con might give me the perfect excuse to contact him again.

The plan was to have a shiny and gorgeous new Bentley parked near the eighteenth hole. It would be a chance for Rolf to get one of his cars out in the midst of several thousand people, many of whom could actually afford to buy one of them. I would hire several auto show models to stand around the car and help with questions and referrals to the dealer. That was just Part One of the caper. Part Two was where the fun would happen. Since I had ponied up a fairly sizable sponsorship check I knew that I could ask for and get a favor or two from the committee.

I continued my description of the con, explaining the kinds of actors I'd be hiring, the basic script they would follow and how it would build to the final outcome I was hoping for. I stopped talking for a moment to see if Delilah had any questions. She didn't ask one but she leaned forward, looked at me intently and said, "So far I'm not hearing anything that's going to make me laugh at this one. It sounds kind of edgy again and I'm not hearing what possible good can come out of it."

She was absolutely right but that's what I was hoping for. When we wrapped up *Operation New Daddy* and *The Great Mexican Switcheroo* I had felt a kind of dark satisfaction that surprised me. Delilah had cautioned me to keep things in perspective but I couldn't help feeling a sense of empowerment. And it felt good.

"Well, babe," I explained, "this one is going to play out on local TV so it's going to have a whole new kind of feel to it and yes, an edge."

Delilah looked at me, shaking her head. "So whatever happens, good, bad or ugly, there's going to be an audience watching you." The frown on her face made me a little uncomfortable. After a pause she sighed and said, "Okay, tell me the rest."

I could tell she wasn't exactly enthusiastic about my idea so I tried to choose my words carefully as I continued describing the con. "In a nutshell, the idea is built on the lure of a gorgeous, expensive car and making an egomaniac believe it can be his." Delilah's expression didn't change as I continued. "I'm still working on the final details but my two golfing partners and our fake course marshal will help me get Pierce so focused on the car that he won't be able to think of anything else. The tournament won't matter to him, the charity, the crowd, nothing will register in his mind except the shiny Bentley, the Bentley that he can't really have. We'll be with him every step of the way, setting the hook, playing along with things and watching him set himself up for a fall. And if we do it right it will be a fall to remember and one that happens in front of the crowd and the cameras.

That was the end of my thumbnail description of the con and I leaned back in my chair, waiting for Delilah's response. Through my entire monologue her expression hadn't changed. All I could interpret was a strong sense of disapproval. I figured the next words had to come from her so I didn't say anything else.

Finally, she let out a long sigh, looked down at the ground and then at me and said, "Honey, this is going to sound like I'm joking but I'm not, not even close. I think you've finally reached serious squirrel level here. I don't see any purpose for doing this other than to be mean. I know how you feel about Pierce and, to be honest, I think he's an asshole too. But I don't see any good coming from this and the entire thing doesn't seem to have a point."

Although I was hoping for her to love the concept and ask to be in on it I wasn't totally surprised at her reaction. Delilah had a great sense of humor but a very strong aversion to anything that was mean or unkind. This little caper, if I went through with it, had one purpose and one purpose only; to make an arrogant politician make a fool of himself in public. To me it would be a worthwhile and noble effort but I could tell that Delilah didn't share that feeling.

She was silent, looking down at the ground for an uncomfortably long time then she looked at me with a face devoid of expression and said, "I've never seen this side of you before."

I probably should have waited for a few seconds, taken a breath and thought about my choice of words but instead I just blurted out, "Maybe it's because I never had the luxury of having this side before."

Her eyes widened, her surprise obvious. "And by luxury you mean the money."

"Yeah, I guess that's what I mean." I had no sooner said the words when I realized I probably sounded very cocky and smug. I paused thinking about what I really wanted to say and then began what I hoped was an explanation she'd understand. "Honey, what are the things that keep people from taking chances in life?"

"There are all kinds of things I guess, probably fear mostly."

"Yeah, I agree, but fear of what?"

"Oh, fear of failure, that's probably the big one, and fear of getting into some kind of trouble."

I nodded, trying to go more slowly and carefully than when I started this odd little conversation. "I believe people are afraid to take chances because of the repercussions, real or imagined. That might mean some kind of social consequence like offending or angering someone. It might be a professional consequence like getting in trouble with the boss or a financial one like losing money."

Still looking at me with a frown on her face, she answered, "And you obviously can't get in trouble with the boss and don't have to worry about money, but how about offending someone? Doesn't that bother you? She paused for a moment and then said, "Linc, you have a great name in the community and you shouldn't risk messing it up."

"Babe," I said, "there is no way the public will know this is a con or that I'm involved in any way. I know you don't exactly feel the same way about politics as I do. You've told me before that

I shouldn't let those elected idiots get under my skin but they do. I've even tried to avoid watching and listening to news talk stations just to keep my frustration under control, but then some guy at City Hall or the legislature makes some inane comment and I'm sucked back into being angry and outraged." I paused and then added, "It's just the way I'm wired."

Delilah had listened to me patiently and now she was just staring at me. I knew that nothing I had said changed her mind. Her gentle spirit was one of the things I most loved about her and, all things considered, I was sort of glad that she stayed true to that gentle spirit and didn't feel compelled to agree with me. She reached over and held both of my hands, looked me straight in the eyes and said, "Honey, I know you take your politics seriously and I admire you for that but this con seems to go way beyond that. I don't like the way this thing smells. It smells like trouble and it smells mean. I'm afraid you'll be on your own on this one."

All things considered her response didn't come as a surprise and fortunately for both of us the tension of our conversation didn't last long. We put aside any further talk about the con and spent the rest of the day, our last day at the resort, going for a long walk in the foothills and then relaxing by the pool. The warm, mountain air and beautiful lake vistas created their own kind of intoxication that we enhanced with ridiculously expensive wine, albeit in smaller quantities than usual. It was a decadent feeling that I'd never had before but I decided not to worry about it and just enjoy it.

There was no rush getting back to Phoenix. We rented a car and drove down to Portland for a few days of shopping and a microbrewery tour and then moved on to San Francisco. A slow, meandering route along the coast took us through scenery and towns straight out of a romantic old movie. We finally got back to Phoenix on a Friday morning and used the weekend to get back into our routine, or more accurately, to continue to create our routine.

Being away from the office for two straight weeks had made me certain that I'd return to find things in disarray, with fires to put out all over the place but that wasn't the case at all. When I walked in on Monday morning I saw that Wayne had done a great job of keeping our bunch of geeks and artists focused and productive. It was clear that Jethro and the trailer park were still very real parts of much of our work and I was glad that Wayne had managed to bring everyone on board with the idea. What used to be a snarky joke about a part of our culture populated by unmotivated underachievers was now just business as usual for Carr Creative. I also learned that Karen had squared away the fiscal year-end information and Jeff Norris was well underway with his review of things. Ozzie was due back on Wednesday. Things seemed to be totally under control

I made the rounds through the office and took a few minutes to chat with every one of my twenty-three employees. The secrecy surrounding my Powerball money had made me so cautious about what I said and how I acted that it had created a strange kind of self-imposed exile for me. I had come to feel defensive and distant from the people who had become my family over the past few years and I didn't like the way it felt. Stopping by each person's desk and shooting the breeze for a few minutes was almost therapeutic. It also made me aware of how disconnected I had become.

After a quick lunch of delivery-pizza at my desk I sat in front of my laptop and opened up my notes for *The Bentley Caper*. Despite Delilah's comments and lack of support for the con I was still very motivated to follow through on it. A story in the previous day's *Arizona Republic* only added to my enthusiasm. It described David Pierce's latest fight to restrict the voting rights of people that he referred to as "questionable" but which meant no more than *non-White*. It was something he had tried several times before, each time wrapping it up in high-handed terms like *voter fraud protection* and *enhanced accountability*. His conservative base bought his line but most other people, at least the ones who took the time to pay attention, could see right through it for the voter suppression it was.

Without Ozzie's help rounding up the other players I had to call Apex Casting myself. It didn't take them long to find me two young men who I was told were both fairly experienced at playing small parts in commercials and also were scratch golfers. It took a little longer but they also found me a middle-aged man to play the role of the course marshal. The next day Apex emailed me the resumes and headshots of all three actors and as I looked over everything I couldn't help but feel this was going to be a good, solid con.

It took me a good part of the afternoon to finish up the rest of the plan. I called Rolf Lange to make sure things were set to have the car on display. After being put on hold for an awkwardly long time Rolf finally answered. "Hey, Linc, sorry for the long wait, I was on another call."

"Oh, no problem, I just wanted to make sure the car is set and your people know what needs to happen."

"Well, my team is ready at this end and we're excited about getting our brand in front of such a great crowd. All we need is for you or someone to stop by and choose the car you want."

"Rolf, you know your cars better than I do, they all look gorgeous to me. Just pick one that'll make people's heads turn and draw a lot of attention."

"Then I'm going to go with the new GT Speed convertible. We just got one in yesterday and it's absolutely sex on four wheels."

"Sounds perfect, let me know if you need anything else from me and let's have a drink in the clubhouse afterward." After I hung up I sat there for a moment, feeling that everything was coming together like I had planned it.

The last detail was the hiring of three female models with auto show experience to handle the showing of the car, chatting with the visitors and providing referrals back to the dealer. I also had to call the organizer of the tournament to confirm the placement of my foursome as the last group of the day. I knew from my involvement in previous years what the course marshals wore so I was ready to pass that along to our actor. When it seemed like everything was in place I leaned back in my chair, closed my eyes and tried to picture what it would be like standing on the eighteenth green while the con played out, as I set the hook and reeled in Pierce. CONjunction was ready to add another con to its resume and it already felt good.

9

The Bentley Caper

Golf is probably the most frustrating game a person can ever take up. The mechanics of the perfect swing elude even someone who has played the game for a lifetime, and even mastering the form and rhythm of the swing can be undone by the wind or a bad club selection. During my teenage years I had spent many weekends caddying for the members of Spruce Hollow Country Club. It was a way to make a few dollars in tips, learn the game by watching people play it and on many an occasions, observe the best and worst in people. From seeing subtle attempts at cheating on the course to not so subtle bragging at the bar in the grill room, I learned a lot about golf and the people who played it.

I was an average high school kid, the off-spring of good, solid middle class folks who knew that money, even in very small amounts, could only come from working for it, from doing tasks that weren't necessarily easy or enjoyable, and that sometimes involved working for people that regarded you as someone of lesser value or importance. I remember wondering what it must be like to be rich, to have a life where everything, and I mean everything was within reach. The people I caddied for were those people. I admired them and hated them at the same time. Rich people were different and yet now I was one of them.

I tried hard not to dwell on that kind of thing. To me the best part of golf was spending three or four hours at a stretch amid some of the most beautiful and pastoral settings one could imagine, acres and acres of pampered green lawn bordered by hundreds of trees and flowering shrubs. Small ponds and streams and gently rolling hills bordering perfectly maintained stretches of impossibly perfect grass. A golf course was a piece of heaven on earth.

On that day the Phoenix Country Club was one of those settings. For many years it had been a part of the history of professional golf but today there are many local residents who couldn't tell you where it is even though it's located right in the heart of the city. With its high, masonry walls, fences draped in red bougainvillea vines and its scores of soaring palm trees, a person could drive right past it without knowing it was there. The Phoenix Open had moved to Scottsdale many years ago and these days the club had become the domain of local golf fanatics, business executives and their families. The course still had a lush maturity to it that made it the perfect setting for the charity event.

For a variety of reasons the build-up to the tournament felt different than the prelude to the earlier cons. Delilah was still staying miles away from any involvement and Ozzie's late return from his vacation had made him a non-player in the event as well as the con. Even though I was excited and eager to get it started it just didn't feel the same without my two regular accomplices. My ideas were always hatched when I was alone and could turn the concepts into some kind of coherent, methodical plan but the execution was the part that made my pulse race. It was scary, risky, exhilarating and satisfying in a way that was hard to describe. But with no one to share in the action and the satisfaction that came with it I wondered if I would feel the same way when this one was finished.

Standing at the first tee was another reminder of why I loved living in Arizona. The late summer heat would arrive around mid-day but for now the morning air was clear and reasonably cool and dry. I had just met Scott Kerry and Trevor Dunnigan, the two young actors who would be my partners in golf and in crime for the next few hours. I explained the con to them and their reaction was a mix of enthusiastic laughter and visible nervousness. We had just finished going over the script and talking about their respective roles when our other actor walked toward us.

"Sorry I'm late, gentlemen," the grinning, middle-aged man said. "I'm Jack Lewis, or should I say, I'm Course Marshal Lewis." His wild, gray hair stuck out of his khaki visor and, along with his thick, black rimmed glasses, made him look like some kind of mad scientist. His voice was tinged with the hoarseness only years of cigarettes could cause and his slightly crooked grin only added to his colorful look. I couldn't wait to see him in action.

I went over the script with him and we confirmed that his khaki pants and dark green polo shirt matched the outfit worn by the course marshals. He also showed me the official USGA Rule Book that course marshals used throughout the country. Jack had done his homework. We all talked some more about the con and when he felt comfortable with the script Jack tipped his visor to the three of us and then walked off toward the eighteenth green. The plan was for him to hide out there, keeping a low profile until he saw our foursome on the tee. He would then position himself near the fringe of the green, slip the lanyard with his fake Course Marshal ID around his neck and begin his little part of the act.

The foursome in front of us had just finished teeing off and had begun their walk down the fairway. I looked back toward the parking lot and saw David Pierce walking toward us. "Here he comes, guys," I said to Scott and Trevor. "Isn't it nice of him to finally grace us with his presence?" I hadn't discussed politics with my two partners but I knew they could tell from my script that I didn't have much more than contempt for Representative David Pierce.

When Pierce was within speaking distance I turned toward him, extended my hand and said, "Good morning David, may I call you David? I'm Lincoln Carr."

Pierce finally reached me, leaned forward and shook my hand. "Good morning, David Pierce, nice to meet you." Then he turned and exchanged introductions with Scott and Trevor. I watched Pierce's practiced demeanor and how he seemed to walk a fine line between smooth and slippery.

I interrupted the handshaking. "Hey guys, we better get our butts in gear, the foursome in front of us already hit their second shots."

We all set about being golfers and exchanged small talk, bullshit and all of the things guys do to get to know each other. It was on the second tee when Trevor pulled out his cellphone and pretended to read a text message. He looked over at Scott and said, "Well, that was a message from my friend, Mark. So far nobody has gotten within forty or fifty feet on eighteen."

Scott nodded. "Let's hope it stays that way, man, I want a shot at that car."

Pierce looked at both of them and asked, "What car, what's going on, is there a giveaway of some kind?"

I made it a point to play it safe and stay out of the conversation and I let Trevor respond. "Yeah, didn't you see it sitting there near the eighteenth green? It's a Bentley Sport convertible."

"So what's the deal, is it a closest to the pin thing?" I could hear the excitement in Pierce's voice.

"Yeah," Trevor answered, "whoever is closest to the pin in regulation. It's a par five so it's your third shot that counts."

Scott chimed in, "You know that thing has a twelve-cylinder engine with almost six hundred horsepower."

"And it has that new Platinum Metallic paint finish. It looks amazing." The two actors were playing off each other like they had done it many times before.

Pierce was staring at them and hanging on every word and I couldn't help but wonder if he had an erection from thinking the car could possibly be his. "I was running late," he said," so I had to take a shortcut by the cart shed and come right to the first tee," he blurted, "so I guess I missed seeing it."

"Well keep your eyes open, Trevor replied. "Once we get over that knoll and up on to the next tee box you should be able to get a look at it. It's kind of far away, but you'll know it's a Bentley." I liked the way Trevor was working the mark. He and Scott seemed to be enjoying the con as much as I was.

While we played the second hole and walked toward the third tee Pierce seemed to be distracted. He practically ran up the steep slope to the tee box and when he looked across the fairway and saw the Bentley in the distance he just stared in silence. Trevor, Scott and I all exchanged careful smiles. I continued my silence regarding the car so that Pierce couldn't later accuse me of setting him up.

We were lucky that the foursome playing ahead of us seemed to be fairly talented because, little by little, they pulled away until we lost sight of them altogether. I was having a decent round, with a score of forty-one at the turn. I tried to keep my conversations with my teammates focused on golf but the three of them continued their chatter about the Bentley. Scott talked about the eight-speed automatic transmission and Trevor told Pierce that the car went from zero to sixty in four point one seconds and had a top speed of two hundred and three. Pierce had a strange, almost glazed look in his eyes. Staying true to the script, both Trevor and Scott kept up their sham text-messaging in an attempt to keep Pierce hopeful of winning the car. By the time we reached the eighteenth tee it was obvious that his mind was on nothing but the gleaming convertible that now sat so invitingly close to us.

Even though Scott would be teeing off first I walked out to the center of the tee box and stared toward the crowd gathered at the back and sides of the green. After a few seconds I saw a man in khakis and a dark green polo shirt slowly walking toward the edge of the crowd. Then I saw him take off his visor, wave it twice and put it back on. It was Jack's signal to me that he was ready.

Scott hit a nice drive of about two hundred and twenty-five yards down the left side of the fairway, Trevor matched it and was also along the left. I managed to hit my best drive of the day, a graceful arc of a shot that landed right in the middle of the fairway and almost equal in distance to Scott and Trevor's shots. It was Pierce's turn and I knew if he hit his drive the way he had been hitting them all day he might have a bit of trouble to overcome.

He hit a shot that faded to the right and landed just a few feet into the shag and about two hundred yards out. He let out a growl and then yelled, "Fuck!"

We all knew the importance of our second shots. We had to get our balls close enough to the green where a nice easy wedge or nine-iron could loft the ball up on to the green. Pierce's ball was away so he would hit first. After an appropriate amount of time to study the wind and his lie he stood over his ball, looked up toward the green and back down to his ball. Looked up, looked down, looked up, looked down. "Come on, you idiot," I thought to myself, "Just hit the fucking thing."

Finally, he took a slow, smooth backswing, swung through and then lofted the ball high and to the right. It landed softly in the fringe about fifteen yards from the green. It would be a very makeable third shot for him and even from a distance I could hear him exhale with relief. He stood in the spot where he had taken his shot, looked longingly at the Bentley and smiled.

Our script called for Scott, Trevor and me to make sure that our second shots would be short enough to ensure we would all be away in relation to Pierce's ball so we would take our third shots ahead of him. From what I could see the plan was executed perfectly and by doing that we put a little extra pressure on him. He would see where our balls were lying on the green if we played it right, and where he would have to hit to get his inside of them. The Bentley was in full view just about a hundred feet from the green. To add to the tension I noticed the media setting up along the cart path between the green and the clubhouse, like a gauntlet of microphones, cameras and voyeurs. It was the kind of scene that Pierce usually welcomed but I hoped today he would feel differently.

As we all walked toward the green I saw Jack positioning himself near Pierce's ball. It was off to the right of the green, my ball was dead center just short of the slope up to the green and Scott and Trevor were both eyeing their shots from the left. I grabbed my pitching wedge and stood over my ball. Trevor looked over at me with a noticeable smirk and I saw Scott look my way, smile and tip his visor. Then I looked over at Pierce who was so busy staring at the Bentley he seemed oblivious to the fact that Jack was standing less than ten feet behind him.

I hit my ball first and watched it land just over the fringe on the front edge of the green. I have made many better approach shots than that one but given the circumstances it was right where I wanted it to be. Scott hit next and ended up in about the same place as I had. Trevor's shot was a little too strong and he ended up on the back of the green a long way from the pin. The three of us made eye contact and exchanged nods and smiles and then we all turned to watch Pierce. He was standing about forty feet from me but it was close enough to see the tension on his face. From what Scott and Trevor had been telling him about the shots that players ahead of us supposedly had hit, and from him seeing where our three balls were lying, he probably believed that a good shot to the center of the green was the only thing standing between him and the Bentley. The lack of a ball marker on the green that would confirm the earlier and potentially winning shot seemed to escape his notice.

He stood over his ball holding his wedge in his right hand while he looked at the car one more time. Then he hovered over the ball and positioned himself for the shot, choking up slightly on the grip of his club. His club head rested in the grass behind the ball as he looked up at the pin and then down at the ball. Up at the pin and down at the ball. Over at the Bentley, up at the pin and down at his ball. When he looked up at the pin and the Bentley one more time Jack called out, "Time, gentlemen. I'm afraid we have a penalty situation here." Pierce turned and looked at Jack in shock, shook his head and sputtered, "What, what the fuck are you talking about?"

Jack played his role perfectly, maintaining a straight face and a crisp, professional tone as he replied, "Sir, while you were addressing the ball and then looked away, your club head made contact with the ball. That is a violation of USGA Rule 18-2b which assesses a one stroke penalty for club contact that moves the ball after address." Pierce's face was frozen with rage and before he could say anything else, Jack said, "With the one stroke penalty, sir, you are hitting four instead of three and, therefore, not hitting in regulation."

Pierce turned and looked at me, then Scott and Trevor and finally back at Jack. "Look, asshole, you can shove your USGA up your ass. I didn't touch the ball."

Jack was a pro and it showed. "Please, sir, there's no need for vulgarity here. Please abide by the rules of the game and the course, and finish your round."

Pierce had all but convinced himself that he had won the car and now here he was, standing on the edge of the green thinking that some unnamed course marshal had taken it away from him. He was obviously not going to let it go. Jack took a few steps back and I found myself worrying that Pierce would go after him and maybe even take a swing at him.

Scott, Trevor and I had counted on there being some amount of a ruckus at this point so we all took advantage of the situation, walked up on to the green and made our putts, leaving Pierce the only player not yet finished with his round. Because Pierce was still throwing a tantrum and making no move toward completing his shot, and because we had to follow the plan, after they made their putts Scott and Trevor walked away and disappeared into the crowd. I walked toward Pierce who was shaking his finger in Jack's face and swearing a blue streak. "Okay, David, let's calm down here," I called to him," it's just a round of golf."

While I tried to keep Pierce's attention Jack also melted into the crowd. "Come on, let's head for the grill room and I'll buy you a drink." I offered. Pierce was actually shaking with anger as he walked toward me and nearer to the flag.

"Fuck your drink, fuck you, fuck this course and fuck that marshal," he said as he turned around, searching the crowd for Jack. "That car over there was mine. You guys hit lousy shots and just set the table for me to win it until that asshole marshal fucked me up."

I noticed that the remote camera man from Channel 12 had moved on to the fringe near the green and was close enough to us that I knew his microphone could pick up the conversation. So far the con had moved along flawlessly and I couldn't resist the temptation to set the hook into Pierce. "Wait, what are you talking about, win what car?" I asked loudly enough for everyone to hear?

"You know god-damned well what car! That Bentley was mine for the taking and that fucking little shit of a marshal screwed me over!"

"David," I said, trying to appear calm and compassionate, "there must be some kind of mistake here."

"Yeah, there's a mistake here, a big fucking one and I want it fixed now!" His face was red, he was sweating profusely and his breath was uneven.

The shocked look on most of the faces in the crowd told me that my con had worked. There was no car giveaway and everyone knew it, everyone but Pierce. Finally, through the confusion and noise a reporter from Channel 12, with her cameraman at her side, cautiously extended her hand-held microphone toward Pierce. She was an attractive young blonde who looked nervous and was probably there just to get a few comments from the sponsors and participants in what had always been an enjoyable charity event. Unfortunately for her David Pierce's was the only recognizable face still left on the course. She smiled awkwardly and asked, "Mr. Pierce, did you have a good round today?"

Pierce glared at her, his face still full of rage. He made a growling sound, muttered, "Fuck this place," and then pushed the microphone away, but not before it picked up another distinct sound. Pierce's anger and huffing and puffing caused him to let loose with a very loud fart. My mission was accomplished. David Pierce had thrown a crude, childish tantrum in front of the local media and shown himself to be the arrogant, boorish jerk that I knew he was. My con was a success and the public fart was a bonus.

10

The Times they are a Changing

It had been a month since the honeymoon, since Ozzie got back from his vacation and since I had watched *The Bentley Caper* play out. It had been the first month of my new life and my new routine. Adjusting to being married and having someone else in my house didn't turn out to be the problem I had anticipated except for adapting to the new choreography of two people using the same bathroom in the morning. Delilah had already made some minor changes to the décor of the house and had drawn up plans for some changes to the landscaping. Otto and Bowser needed only a few days to get acquainted and that surprised both of us. As Delilah liked to remind me her moving in with me was simply a matter of geography, a new location for her but everything else was still the same. I didn't agree totally but I figured I'd get to that same point eventually.

The local buzz and the political fallout that resulted from David Pierce's eighteenth-hole meltdown had died down as far as everyone else was concerned but I still felt the satisfaction, the absolute elation of helping undo the political aspirations of a total asshole. His fall from grace, witnessed by the local media and a thousand bystanders was jaw dropping and complete. The political cartoonist and writers of the newspaper's op-ed pages had been handed a gift from editorial heaven; the public self- destruction of a self-important blowhard. And the thing that I couldn't shake, the thing that was stuck in my head and wouldn't let go was that I had made it happen. I created it. I pulled together the players and set them in motion. I shepherded the action and I paid for it. It was like a very satisfying little performance played out on a statewide scale and all I could think of was, what will I do in the next act? I felt a tangible kind of power and it felt great. It seemed that the possibilities were endless.

It had also been a good month for Ozzie. The stubble that he had let grow on vacation had thickened into a very substantial beard and he looked like an older version of the scraggly, fun-loving guy I had met in college. He had also picked up his guitar again and was playing it regularly just like in his younger days when he played in a band, smoked pot and looked like the most unlikely accounting major in the entire school. All in all he seemed more relaxed and stress free than he'd been in a long time, also due in part I guessed to the developing relationship with Michelle, his new internet romance. He wasn't totally forthcoming with the details but he said that he had lost his skepticism about internet dating. Michelle, he said, was warm and funny with an extremely engaging personality, and knowing that, sooner or later I would ask him for other information, he told me she was a very pretty redhead and was six years younger than he was. I decided not to probe for more. I could see from his face and hear in his voice that he was happier than he had been in a very long time and I couldn't wait to meet the woman who had captured my friend's heart.

With three quarters of the year behind me, I took some time to meet with Jon Aiken at his office for an update on the trust. As a guy who had always just worked hard, saved and invested carefully, albeit in a small way, I figured that my money must have earned some interest or maybe even increased from a safe, little investment somewhere. Jon handed me a sort of executive summary of my earnings-to-date and I flipped through the thin, black, spiral-bound folder. Jon must have sensed that I was having trouble making sense of all the spreadsheets and column after column of numbers. "Linc," he said, just turn to page eight, bottom right corner, the figure in bold, black type.

I found the page and ran my finger down it to touch the number he had referenced. I ran my fingertip back and forth over the number and felt the same, hard to grasp feeling I had felt on that rainy Sunday morning. The heading for the number read *Earnings to Date* and the number below it, in bold, black type read, *$3,147,016.42.* The same feeling of disbelief came over me. The report said that, in six months, for doing absolutely nothing but putting my money in play here and there, in investments handled by people I didn't even know, I had earned over three million dollars. I thought back to a comment that Delilah had made on that rainy Sunday, when she said she was having trouble getting her head around the idea of so much money. I had made three million dollars by doing nothing and that was something *I* was having trouble getting *my* head around.

My surprise must have been evident on my face because Jon chuckled and said, "Come on, man. If you're going to wet your pants please don't do it while you're sitting in my leather chair."

I grinned, shook my head and answered, "Relax, your chair is in no danger but this is just too much to grasp."

"Get used to it, Linc. Your kind of money makes even more money and it can make it faster than you can spend it." He paused then added, "But please don't try."

"Don't worry about that. Except for CONjunction I've been keeping my spending small and under the radar."

"Good to hear. You've come this far and you don't want something to trip you up. How are Delilah and Ozzie handling their parts of all this?"

"Oh, pretty well I'd say, at least they're not doing anything to call attention to their situations. Becoming overnight millionaires doesn't seem to have hit them any harder than it has me."

"Yeah, as far as you know." Jon's comment seemed somewhat cautionary.

I looked at him, paused and then asked, "What do you mean by that?"

"Linc, you've been my friend and my client for a long time and I've given you advice on a whole lot of different things, but I confess this is something that's totally new to me and I don't feel I have anything to say except take it slow, keep your eyes and ears open and be prepared to be surprised."

I wasn't exactly sure what he meant but it gave me a slightly uneasy feeling. I nodded and answered, "Thanks, I will."

Less than a week later, with Jon's words still sticking in my head something else happened that I knew would bring about more change in my life. Delilah made the decision to leave LDP Partners, the landscape architecture firm for whom she'd been working, and to set out on her own. She was a very creative woman but her bosses had her working on mundane commercial and streetscape projects. When she started working with the firm she had been asked to sign a contract with a one-year no-compete clause but two of their biggest clients told Delilah they wanted her to do their future work. We had Jon Aiken's office working on a strategy to get around the contractual problem. Then after a week-long search she found a small stucco and tile-roofed office building for sale just down the street from Carr Creative that she bought for the business and as an income property for the future. We agreed that she needed to keep the purchase very quiet so no one close to us would ask questions. When her office space was ready she immediately hired three people to help her launch her new venture which she had named Terra Nueva. I was proud of her and knew she would do well. I also knew she was going through the same adjustments that I was with being newly married and sharing a house and two pets, and now she was also trying to handle and new business and her own sudden wealth. Again I recalled Jon's advice to be prepared to be surprised. Instinct told me to walk and talk carefully for a while.

For the first time since I had started my business I was having trouble staying focused on running it. So much had happened. So many things had changed. For years I had made Carr Creative the center of my world but now, with my marriage, with CONjunction and mostly with my money, going into the office every day just didn't seem to be the same. I still couldn't seem to shake the anger and pessimism that came with all of the data we gathered for the trailer park commercials, and that same anger and pessimism had become the fuel for my next con. It was the one I wasn't ready to reveal to anyone and the one that kind of scared me. But it also gave me a rush that was intoxicating.

Things at the office were humming right along. We had landed three large, new accounts including one with Devich Capital, a consumer lending firm with a nationwide customer base. Despite the easiness with which I could be distracted lately I had spent a solid two hours studying Devich's advertising history to learn what they did, what worked, what didn't work and why. I was nearing the end of the review when I heard Wayne's booming voice.

"Hey, boss man, got a minute?"

I looked up over the top of my glasses and saw Wayne filling the doorway. "Sure, come on in," I answered. I settled back in my chair knowing that the conversation would probably be the usual meandering mix of business, profanity and humor. "Have a seat. I was going to be knocking on your door later anyway to talk about Devich so maybe we can kill two birds with one stone."

Wayne dropped into one of the chairs in front of my desk, and I wondered how many more times the chair's frame could survive. "So, man, I just wanted to see how you're doin', how things are goin' in your world."

It seemed like an odd comment and I couldn't help but think Wayne was on some kind of fishing expedition with me. "Uh, I'm doing okay." I waited to see what came next.

He shifted his weight in the chair and said, "That's good, that's really good." He seemed a bit uneasy. "I was just wonderin' because you seem kind of distracted lately, like maybe you've got too much on your plate." He looked at me as if he was waiting for something but then said, "Actually, boss, pretty much everyone in the office seems to think you're in like this kind of fog or somethin'."

Wayne had always been a strong manager and the guy I could go to for anything I needed to make the firm a better one, so I knew for him to come to me like this there had to be something to it. I leaned forward, pulling my glasses down and rubbing my eyes. "Oh, it's not a fog, it's just trying to keep all the balls in the air and adjust to all the changes in my life." I hoped that would be a sufficient answer.

Wayne grinned and said, "Yeah, a beautiful young wife and a new dog. I should have such problems."

I returned his grin. "Well, actually, that's the fun part of the adjusting. I guess it's probably the extra workload and Oz cutting back and a hundred other little things." Suddenly it dawned on me that my constant thinking about my cons and the new one that was starting to take shape in my head were probably what was making me look like I was a little out of touch. People notice when your mind wanders and mine had been wandering all over the place ever since I got back.

Wayne leaned back. There was a cry of pain from the chair and he said, "Well, okay, but just let me know if I can do anythin', somethin' to lift the fog."

"Thanks, man, I appreciate it."

Wayne got quiet for a moment and looked down at the floor then back at me. Then he said, "Linc, I don't know if I should say this, if it's any big deal, but while you were gone I got a call from Meta over at Apex Casting. She wanted to know something about the invoice for the group of Mexican actors you needed for something and I didn't have a clue what she was talking about. I asked around my team and nobody knew a thing about it"

Sooner or later it had to happen. There was more than a little overlap between what we did at Carr Creative and what I had been doing with CONjunction. I had made sure to have Ozzie run two completely separate sets of books to keep the finances clean but there was still the need to work with Apex and a few other companies with which Carr Creative had a long time relationship. I tried to read Wayne's face for any sign of suspicion or anything negative but didn't see one. "Well, Wayne, that's one of the things I wanted to talk to you about, along with the new stuff for Devich, so I guess we can start killing the first bird."

I paused for a moment so I could choose my words carefully. Nothing I had done with CONjunction was illegal, but that didn't mean I wanted a lot of people looking at it too closely. The cons were mine and they were personal. So far there had been no need to involve anyone outside of my little circle. But as my newest con had been taking shape in my head it was becoming clear that to pull it off I was going to need resources and people way beyond what I was used to. I tried to keep a light tone when I answered Wayne. "Geez, I told Meta to make sure that invoice didn't get mixed in with the other ones for Carr Creative."

"Well, don't worry about that," Wayne said, "when I told Meta I didn't know what she was talkin' about she checked into it and called me back. She said somebody in their billin' office screwed up and that the invoice was for a company called Conjunction or somethin' like that, but she said she still needed to talk to you about it."

"Okay, I'll call her, it's no big deal, just a little consulting gig I worked on before I left." I watched for Wayne's reaction and he seemed a bit puzzled. I knew I owed him some kind of an explanation. "Let me fill you in on a few things. I started doing some extra consulting work and I decided to do it on the side because it had nothing to do with the things we're doing at the office."

"And that's this Conjunction Company?"

"Yeah, and it's just called CON-junction, the "con" means consulting and the junction means where it comes together." I didn't feel ready to tell him the real story just yet.

Wayne nodded and seemed to be satisfied with my answer, but after a pause he asked, "So if you don't mind my askin', what kinds of things are you workin' on with this?"

Given Wayne's position with the firm it was a reasonable question and so was his curiosity. The cons I'd pulled so far were proof that I wasn't going to be able to keep Carr Creative and CONjunction totally separate for much longer. When I answered him I tried to choose my words carefully. "So, remember a few months ago when I asked Stacey to help me set up a website for a law firm called Yale and Roth?"

"Yeah, I was up to my eyeballs with ProInsure and Jethro so I didn't pay much attention to it. To tell you the truth I never even went online to check it out."

"Well, that little website is, how can I say this, just one piece of a much larger operation."

"Operation?"

"Well, that's as good a word as any to describe CONjunction."

"You seem to emphasize the first syllable, the CON part, what's that all about?"

It was obvious that to some degree, like it or not, I had to bring Wayne in on what was going on. "Wayne, I'm gonna tell you exactly what's been happening and why people think I've been in a fog lately. And I'm gonna ask you to keep this totally to yourself. Besides Ozzie, Delilah and me you will be the only person who knows what CONjunction really is."

Wayne's expression was a priceless combination of glee and curiosity. He leaned forward. "Well, this sounds interestin', even a little mysterious. Go ahead, lay it on me, man."

I took a deep breath and said, "Okay, you know how I like to play practical jokes on people and have a little fun with them." Wayne nodded. "Well, those practical jokes have somehow grown into much more elaborate, shall we say con games."

"So that's the CON in CONjunction," Wayne offered.

"Yep, and it was Ozzie who always insisted on calling them cons when I just saw them as jokes. But little by little the jokes got bigger, they got more complex and they required more people to pull them off. I had to write scripts for them like they were little plays or movies. The law firm website came about to make one of them work and be more believable. It worked so well we decided to keep the website just in case we ever needed it again."

Wayne was hanging on every word so I continued what, in a way, seemed like a confession. "A while back Ozzie had an idea for a con that wasn't really a joke or anything close to being funny but it seemed like something that needed to be done."

That one piqued Wayne's curiosity. "Whoa, wait a minute, a joke that wasn't funny but needed to be done. That sounds kinda weird."

"Well, I wouldn't say it was weird but I will say it had an edge to it that turned out to be very satisfying. A bad guy got his comeuppance."

"So who was the client?" Wayne's interest seemed to be growing.

"That's an interesting question," I answered, suddenly feeling very sheepish. "Actually, CONjunction doesn't exactly have clients. What we have are targets or, as they call them in the crime dramas, marks."

"So no clients, that's interesting. How do you pay the bills?"

'Let's just say that CONjunction exists for purposes other than making money." The words sounded kind of strange and even ominous and Wayne's face indicated he felt the same way. "I know that probably sounds unusual, but it's the best way I know to describe it. When I filed the paperwork to form CONjunction, LLC, the function of the firm was listed as "Media Consulting" but its real purpose, the real reason I created it is to simply pull off some small things that might make a difference in the world."

It was hard to tell if Wayne was picking up what I was putting down and after a brief pause he said, "Geez, boss man, it almost sounds noble."

I couldn't help but let out a laugh and I said, "Before you give me credit for doing noble things you should know that some of the work that CONjunction has completed isn't anything even close to being noble. It's more like a package of practical jokes wrapped up in good intentions and tied with a big, snarky bow."

It was obvious now that Wayne was totally caught up in my explanation. His wide eyes and smile made it clear that I had struck a chord in him and he proved it when he said, "Okay, boss, whatever it is you're doin' I want in on it."

Up to this moment my jokes and cons had been the sole property of myself, Ozzie and Delilah and that made me feel very protective of them as far as involving anyone else was concerned. But those cons were also relatively simple and small in scale. The idea that was percolating in my head would require far more effort than the three of us could provide. It would mean hiring people and asking them to work full time on nothing but the con. And given what was involved and the risks, I would probably have to devote myself to it full time as well. I looked at Wayne and, as usual, his humor and energy were infectious. "Well, I think we should talk about that," I said. "We'll get together eventually and at the very least I could use your critical eye looking at what we create." I hesitated for a moment, not sure if I should say much more but then I shrugged and said, "And I confess, the fact that you know the trailer park like nobody else does will make you invaluable."

Wayne's face beamed and he bellowed, "Wow, does that mean I can bring Jethro in on this with me?"

I laughed and said, "Absolutely, we'll even give him his own fucking office."

Wayne was obviously pleased. "So when do we get started?"

"I'm not sure but it's gonna' be awhile, like a month or two at least. I have quite a bit of research to do and I have to run my ideas by Delilah and Ozzie."

"Yeah, that reminds me," Wayne replied, as the same curious expression he wore when he came into the room returned to his face, "what about Oz? He told me he was cuttin' back his hours on a permanent basis. Is he okay? He's not sick or somethin' is he?"

Suddenly I felt uncomfortable. I had managed to keep my lottery wealth totally secret for over six months but things were happening fast and I had a sinking feeling that the word was close to getting out or was at least to a point where someone could put things together and reach a conclusion about what was going on. Ozzie had bought a new house, vacationed in Hawaii and was cutting back his hours. Delilah left her job and started her own business and a simple check of public realty transfers would tell someone that she also bought a three million dollar office building. On top of all that, I had started a second business that had no clients and didn't make money. When you put it all together it painted a very strange picture.

I shook my head and answered, "No, nothing like that, Oz is healthier than all of us. He just told me he needed a little break and wants to spend more time on family matters."

"Yeah, I heard he has a new lady friend and it's gettin' serious."

"Yeah, it sure looks like it. He's been a bachelor and single dad for a long time and I'm keeping my fingers crossed that this new romance is going to last."

It was only half an answer but it seemed to satisfy Wayne. At the very least I hoped it would buy me some time and a chance to figure out how to make sure nobody else got too close to what was going on. The people in the office were a tightly knit bunch and if Wayne was getting curious then I was certain everyone else was too.

"I feel the same way." Wayne answered, "He's a great guy and it's about time he found someone."

It seemed like the perfect time to shift gears and change the subject. "So, big guy, if I've convinced you that I'm not losing my mind and Oz isn't dying, how about we talk Devich. Where do we stand with the new look and the campaign rollout?"

Wayne's bushy, gray beard didn't begin to hide his smirk. "Boss, this thing with Devich is tailor-made for us. Did you get a chance to look over the pile of stuff I left on your desk?"

"I haven't quite finished it but I think I have the general idea. They want to go after a chunk of the lending business that Walmart has, right?"

Wayne let out a laugh that sounded like it started at his ankles. "Yeah, can you believe it? All of the research and crap we got out of the ProInsure campaign that made us the experts on Walmarters, and now we're gonna' use it and go and compete with them. It's a very sweet and tasty irony."

"Walmart is a tough competitor, it has pockets deep enough to last a long time," I said. "And they charge something like thirty-six percent interest on their loans so this is a high stakes situation."

Wayne nodded. "Yeah, and most of the money they lend is in the form of a purchase card so the borrower's money goes right back into the Walmart cash register. But Devich has worked out deals with five major retailers with more to come. I think they've positioned themselves really well."

"Part of what I read in the report was that Devich goes after pretty much the same demographic as Walmart and that means we're working on familiar ground."

"Yeah, it does, low income folks, minorities, people in rural areas, not terribly well educated and always a day late and a dollar short."

"So then, we're back to the trailer park." I said, trying hard not to smile.

Wayne made no such effort. His ear to ear grin made it obvious that he was enjoying the new challenge. "Linc, this client's middle name is Jethro. You should hear some of the ideas the nerds in the Garage have already come up with."

"Any bears in pick-up trucks?"

Wayne looked like he was ready to burst out laughing but he managed to maintain what, for him, passed for a businesslike demeanor. "Nope, and no hot babes in pick-up trucks either. We're lookin' at everythin' from a talkin' debit card to a NASCAR tie-in to the on-goin' adventures of a blue collar couple named Joe and Maria who always seem to be in some kind of jam and in need of cash. The guys are havin' a ball and the slang is bouncin' off the walls. There's even a duel goin' on between the fake Southern accent and the fake Hispanic accent."

Wayne's enthusiasm always rubbed off on the people around him and this conversation was no different. I leaned back in my chair, paused a moment and then asked, "Hey, do you remember when we first got started on ProInsure and I said I was worried about our stuff being condescending or insulting to the target group?"

"Oh yeah, I remember it well. You were so afraid we'd be seen as talkin' down to folks and makin' the message too simple."

"So how do you think we're doing now?" I asked.

Now, since he first sat down Wayne became quiet, and a thoughtful, serious look came over his face. "Boss." he said, "I gotta' tell ya', we're walkin' a fuckin' tightrope these days. It's like I said when we first started on ProInsure, we're tryin' to create advertisin' artistry for people who probably won't get it. I try to keep a tight rein on the craziness around the Garage because my folks tend to get carried away sometimes. That big picture of Jethro Bodine hangin' on the wall started out as a little in-house joke but it turned out to be fuckin' inspirational." Wayne was known for his light-hearted approach to life and his serious demeanor was beginning to crumble right before my eyes. The tone of his voice was changing as he continued. "Every time we've laid our ideas and our pitches in front of the focus groups I've held my breath just waitin' for somebody to object and say we've gone too far with the simple shit, and then say we're bein' insultin' or, even worse, that the campaign is dumb or crude or somethin', but that doesn't happen and then, like some fuckin' bolt of lightning came down, some guy calls out, "Wow, this is great, I really like it," and it's all I can do to keep a straight face."

Wayne was back to being on the edge of bursting with laughter. "So," I interrupted, "it sounds like you and your team have figured out how to speak 'trailer park'."

Wayne finally broke out in his trademark roar of a laugh that I was sure could be heard throughout the entire office. "Speak it, man we're fuckin' channelin' Jethro. It's like he's part of our DNA. Hell, we've even got banjo music playin' in the Garage!"

Whatever reservations about talking down to the trailer park that still might still have lingered inside me disappeared with Wayne's words. I had started Carr Creative with a handful of small retail accounts and eventually landed some corporate and institutional clients and, until recently, hadn't ventured very far from that type of account. Now, thanks to Wayne and his group of oddballs, we had turned a hundred and eighty degrees and tapped into the psyche of a part of America that I had always ignored, or at least tried to ignore. The success of that effort was making the firm a lot of money and that fact, all by itself, struck me in an odd and profound way. I was making money based on my knowledge of people that I didn't associate with, that I didn't know in any personal way or even particularly care for and I knew more than ever it was time to do something more with that knowledge. Something very different.

I waited for Wayne to come down from his trailer park euphoria and when I was sure he was calm I said, "Hey man, it sounds like you have things under control as usual. I have to run and take care of a few things but I'm gonna' want to continue this conversation."

Wayne looked at me with a slightly confused expression. "Uh, okay, man, just say when." He stood up and his chair squeaked its gratitude.

As he opened the door he looked back and asked, "So everythin's cool with you and Oz and the whole fuckin' planet, right?"

I grinned, nodded and said, "Yeah, more than you know."

11

Pillow Talk

The late summer heat had finally started to show signs of giving way to fall and the danger of monsoon storms was fading. The days were warm, not hot, the nights were cool, not warm and the Arizona skies had returned to the crystal clear blue that tourists paid a lot of money to sit under. Football season was underway and the city and county election season, with the August primaries finished, was grinding toward the November spectacle that usually disgusted me but that I couldn't tear myself away from either. It was an interesting part of the calendar and this year I had been anticipating it for a variety of reasons. Summer had been filled with changes both personal and professional and I knew that more change was coming. I hoped I was ready for it.

I was sitting on my patio flipping through an unusually large pile of Saturday mail when Delilah called to me. "Hey honey, what happened to my gardening partner?" She was standing over our herb and vegetable garden, surrounded by a dozen potted plants, an array of digging tools and several large bags of soil from the garden supply store. Bowser was at her side, sniffing the bags and everything else within range of his constantly active nose.

"Oh, sorry babe, I got lost in this stack of mail." I stood up and walked over to help her on what in past years had been my project, and mine alone. Now that I was married to a landscape architect backyard gardening had taken on a whole new dimension that I knew would no longer be limited to simple projects. "So what do you think?" I asked, "Did we figure the plant selection right for the space?"

"I don't know, I guess so, I just wish we could have a more ambitious approach to this, like planting everything we have here plus room for corn and some root vegetables." I could hear the frustration in her voice. It was the same tone I had heard every time we talked about buying a bigger house, and I knew that decision would be coming sooner rather than later. We didn't really need more house we just wanted more house. Knowing how much money was sitting in the trust really seemed to blur the line between need and want.

"Well, let's get this stuff in the ground and see how it looks," I said, "then we can talk about a bigger garden."

We went about the process of spotting, digging, planting and feeding and in about an hour and a half our garden was ready for the growing season. Delilah stood back and looked things over while I went in the house to get us a couple of beers. When I got back to the yard she was standing in the far corner, scanning left and right. "I have a feeling you've got another project in your head," I said as I handed her bottle to her.

"Gee, it's kind of early for beer, don't you think?" she asked. The look on her face told me she was back in worry-mode about my health.

Well, maybe just a little but hell, it's Saturday and the sun's shining." My attempt at being glib was a failure because her expression never changed. "Okay, babe, I got the message and I'll keep it to just this one. So do you have some other project in mind?"

She sighed and said, "Well, I've got lots of ideas but not enough yard.

We had kept things under wraps for nearly seven months but, given what had been said during my conversation with Wayne and the changes Ozzie had made in his life it was obvious that the three of us were at a crossroads with our secret. I knew that Delilah shared my reluctance to reveal our situation and that her reluctance was mixed with a very strong desire to start enjoying our money and living our lives accordingly. I was sure that Oz felt the same way. I looked at Delilah, noticing again how she could be sweaty and windblown but still look drop-dead beautiful. "Darlin'," I said, "let's sit down on the patio and have a conversation."

She looked at me with a curious expression and said, "Uh, okay."

We sat down and I wasn't sure where to start so I just blurted out, "I think it's finally time to come out of the closet and reveal that we're stinking rich." They were words I'd been wanting to say for months and I hoped they were as light-hearted and funny to her as they seemed when they came out of my mouth.

Delilah always had trouble hiding her excitement over things that she felt strongly about, whether good or bad. When she was unhappy or angry her face took on a stoic appearance and fortunately I had only seen that a few times. I teased her that she would make a lousy poker player because she was blessed, or cursed, with having a very expressive face. I looked at her for a moment and could tell that she was more than a little excited by my suggestion, even though she didn't say anything. I waited a few seconds to see what might be coming back my way but when she maintained her silence I said, "I had a conversation with Wayne the other day and it sounds like our secret is getting closer and closer to getting out."

"Uh-oh," she said, her nervousness clear, "what happened?"

"Well, it's just that shit is building up. Little by little stuff that the three of us have done is starting to come together and forming into a very odd scenario that seems to be drawing some attention."

"Such as?"

"It's kind of a combination of things and I guess it's our fault, all three of us, for not paying attention to what the others were doing. Wayne accidentally got an invoice that was meant for CONjunction and he brought it to me. That led to a conversation about how everyone thinks I've been in a fog lately, about Ozzie suddenly cutting back his hours and involvement with the firm and even to you starting your own business."

"So do you think he put everything together or was he just being Wayne?"

"He didn't come right out and ask what was going on but he's a bright, insightful guy and you, Ozzie and I have left a pretty big trail of bread crumbs for him to follow if he wanted to. There's Ozzie's big, new house, his two week Hawaiian vacation and his desire to only work part-time when he's still in his forties. Then there's your new firm and hiring a staff all at once. That obviously involves some serious start-up costs and would make someone wonder who's fronting you the money. And, on top of all that, I had to tell Wayne that I started CONjunction, a consulting company with no clients and no billable hours. Put it all together and it looks like someone robbed a bank."

"Yeah, or won the lottery." The look on Delilah's face had become more serious. "What do you think we should do?"

"Well, for one thing I think we should get Oz in on the discussion because whatever we do we have to have a unified plan, we're all in this together."

"Agreed, but let's talk just between us first because we stand to take the brunt of the problems if this thing isn't handled right." She took a small sip of beer, reached down to pet Bowser who had just sat down beside her chair, and said, "You know, I've been thinking about this decision ever since the day you won the money. I knew that we all had to lie low for a while and act normal, and I think we've done a pretty good job of that although I have to say, just between you and me, that Ozzie's buying that big house must have set some tongues to wagging."

"Yeah, I agree. He just went out and did it and never even told me he was thinking along those lines. To be honest, I was kind of pissed off but I bit my tongue and didn't say anything. He and his boys had been bumping into each other in that little house for years and teenagers need a lot more room than little kids do so I wasn't totally surprised that he wanted to find a bigger place."

"But, still, it puts us in the position of being afraid to buy our own bigger house for fear of raising more eyebrows." Delilah's tone showed that she shared at least a part of my frustration with Ozzie. She hesitated for a few seconds and I could tell she wanted to say something else.

"What's the matter, babe? I can tell something is really bugging you."

"Well, since you asked, there's something that has bothered me ever since this all got started, but I know Oz is your best friend and I was kind of afraid to say anything."

"Okay, let's hear it," I said

"Well, for all this time we've been thinking that the big secret of the money was a three-way deal, that as long as you and Ozzie and I kept our mouths shut everything would be okay. But how do we know how much his two sons know? Daddy buys a big new house, takes them on a Hawaiian vacation and then decides he wants to hang around the new house and spend time with them and we're left to think everything is cool. In your entire life did you ever know a teenager who could keep a secret? And now that Oz and Michelle are getting serious we have someone else to worry about." She looked down, paused and said, "To be totally frank, Ozzie makes me very, very nervous."

Everything Delilah said made perfect sense and I suddenly realized that my closeness to Ozzie had created a blind spot when it came to believing he could and would control the situation. Delilah reminded me that two impressionable teenage boys whose father had suddenly become wealthy could screw up everything, and so could a new girlfriend. And as uncomfortable as it made me feel I had to admit so could Ozzie.

"You know, you're right. I guess I've been pretty naïve about the whole secrecy issue. Oz understands the consequences of the whole thing, of what will happen if the word gets out, at least I think he does, but his kids don't. I'm betting he didn't tell them the whole story, just what he needed to say to make the new house and vacation sound normal."

Delilah's stone-like expression was not typical of her but, given the conversation, it was understandable. "We can only hope that's the case," she said, "but I can't help but think that somewhere down the road Oz is going to say or do something with the money that will be too obvious for his boys or somebody else to ignore. From what he says they're both smart kids and you gotta' believe they'll put two and two together and get twenty million."

For the first time I was starting to feel the same uneasiness that Delilah felt, maybe more, but I also knew there was more than Ozzie to consider. "Okay, let's put that aside, forget Ozzie's situation for a minute here, there's a lot more to think about "I said, trying to keep things on a positive note, "It's been seven months or so since we set up the trust and built the big wall around our secret. In that seven months there have been four Powerball winners, I know that because I've been watching very closely, so I gotta believe that nobody is still wondering about who won the money the week that I did."

"Yeah, you're probably right. People are too caught up in their own stuff to think about what happened to somebody else months ago. At least I hope that's the case."

"And here's something else to remember." I added, "Even when you add up Ozzie's house and your new business and CONjunction, it still doesn't necessarily look like a fortune. The donations we made to the animal shelters and the *Wildlife Fund* were made by the trust so. we wouldn't be connected and it was the same with the money we gave to the art museum. It's not connected to us as far as any paper trail is concerned." I leaned back and sucked down the rest of my beer, stifled a burp and said, "Here's an idea, tell me what you think. We don't say a word unless someone asks and then, if that happens, our story is that the three of us split twenty bucks worth of lottery tickets, the Arizona lottery not Powerball so they won't be thinking it was a kajillion dollars. We won a nice piece of change but not a fortune and then shared the winnings equally. We'll make it sound like there was enough money to have a little fun with but no more than that."

Delilah nodded. "I like it, very simple and clean and it should sound like we don't have much left over. Remember, your biggest fear was that everyone and his brother would be pounding on your door asking for something."

"Yeah, and it still is but as long as the three of us are careful and we just take our time with any more big life changes we should be able to keep things relatively low key. Of course Oz had damn well better be careful how he presents himself too."

Delilah nodded, her skeptical expression still obvious. "Yeah, he got his new house and his tropical vacation, so as long as he doesn't buy a Maserati or a Ferrari or buy Michelle a million dollar engagement ring he should be able to stay under the radar. And I'm sorry to say it, but as I sit here listening to my own words I find myself starting to think something like that might actually happen."

"You know," I replied, "as long as we're talking about this let's get Oz on the phone and set up a meeting to lay this out once and for all." I picked up my cell phone and punched in his number on speed dial. Ozzie picked up on the first ring. "Hey buddy, got a second to talk?" I asked. Fortunately he was home alone. "Hey, man, Delilah and I have been talking here and we decided it's time for the three of us to get together, sort of a "come to Jesus" talk about the money and maybe coming out from under our self-imposed veil of secrecy."

There was a moment of silence at Ozzie's end, then he said, "Uh, sure, I take it you guys think it's finally safe."

"Yep, we do, sort of, and we want to get on with our lives just like you do but we all three have to be on the same page of the same story or this thing could blow up in our faces."

"Yeah, and we've come too far to screw it up now. When do you want to meet?"

I looked over at Delilah. "He wants to know when to meet."

"How about for happy hour today, here, say five-ish?"

Oz heard her suggestion and said, "Casa de Carr at five it is." He paused and added, "Is it okay to bring Michelle with me?"

I waited for a few seconds, wanting to make sure I didn't sound insensitive. "Uh, I think we should keep it to just the three of us, at least this time. This thing started with the three of us and I want to be really careful before we bring anyone else in on it." Oz didn't respond right away and thinking that I might have offended him I added, "But once we get this all squared away I want to include her, and, if it's okay with you I'd also like to see if she might be CONjunction material in the future."

Ozzie's laugh told me he was okay with my request. "You know," he said, "I have a feeling she just might make a first class player in our little group."

Oz got to my house a few minutes after five and the three of us sat on the patio, enjoying Delilah's array of appetizers and just for the occasion a bottle of what I used to consider a pricey Pinot Noir. After my phone conversation with Oz, Delilah and I had spent about an hour putting together a short priority list of things we wanted to do with my share of the money. At the top of the list was a new house, followed by smaller, miscellaneous things like furniture and a new car to replace my old Explorer. At the bottom of the list was just the word CONjunction.

Knowing that Oz wanted to get on with his Saturday evening with Michelle, I made sure everyone's glass was full and then started the conversation. "Okay, the October meeting of the Three Crazy Rich People Club is hereby called to order."

Delilah smiled and answered, "Rich, yes, but as far as crazy, speak for yourself."

"I agree," Oz chimed in, "crazy is a relative term."

For the next half hour we talked about our individual needs for expenditures and we agreed that keeping them to the staples of life like a house, a car and maybe a vacation here and there would help tamp down any curiosity. We also agreed to stick to the story that the three of us had split a lottery ticket and also split the relatively modest winnings. That story would only be told as a last resort to anyone who pressed hard for information. We all hoped that no one would have the balls to be so intrusive and actually ask.

I watched Delilah's face and body language while the three of us talked. Her concern about Michelle and Ozzie's sons was still evident. It was a topic that we all needed to address but I knew it had to come from me so I said, "Hey, Oz, I'm just curious. What have you told Alec and Josh about the money? Did they ask any questions about the big, new house or the vacation?"

I expected a totally different reaction from him, maybe even a defensive one, but he answered, "Nope, I haven't told them about the money and I guess, so far at least, they think that Uncle Linc and I are making big, fat salaries at the office."

"How about your cutting back your time at the office," Delilah interjected, "did they ask any questions about that?"

One question about his kids didn't seem to register with him but a second question did, and he let us know that he was a little irritated. "Whoa, time out here, what's with the concern about my boys all of a sudden?"

I knew I needed to say something to keep things from getting out of hand. "Relax, man, we're not singling out the boys or anyone else. We've been talking about a new house and that got us to thinking about our agreement to keep things under wraps and when we could all eventually start spending some money."

Oz still seemed to be on the defensive. "So it comes back to me and my new house is that it? Did I break the rules or something?"

"No dammit," I said, "stop with the defensive shit already. Delilah and I started this whole conversation because Wayne and some people at the office seem to be sniffing around the edges of your situation and Delilah's too. I had to field a whole bunch of questions about my being in a fog lately, Delilah's sudden opening of her new firm and your cutting back your hours. Put it all together and it makes a problem, or at least the potential for a problem that we have to deal with."

When Oz didn't say anything right away I added, "And the best way to head off any trouble is to find out who knows what, how it could be a potential problem and how to fix it."

It was an honest response to Ozzie's concern and it seemed to sink in with him. "Okay, sorry, now I get it." he said somewhat sheepishly. "So first of all you don't have to worry about my boys. Someday when the time is right and the need for secrecy is behind us I'll tell them about the trust funds I've set up for them and about all of the cloak and dagger shit that Uncle Linc, Aunt Delilah and I had to go through. But until that day comes you can rest assured they won't be a problem."

In her characteristic loving fashion, Delilah got up from her chair, bent down and wrapped her arms around Oz and said, "I'm sorry if we gave you the wrong idea, but we just don't want any of this to cause trouble between us."

Oz reached out and hugged her in return. "No problem at this end," he said.

Seeing the need for a break in the action I walked into the kitchen and opened another bottle of wine even though we weren't quite ready for it. For the next hour the main topic of conversation was the fact that our need for secrecy, anonymity and fudging the facts would be a fact of life for a very long time. We also went over our respective lists of things we wanted to do with our money, the personal lifestyle things, the charitable work and the sharing with friends and family. When it seemed like we had our plan all worked out and were in agreement on the basics I poured us all more wine even though Delilah tried to stop me. After a moment and a sip, Oz asked, "Okay, Linc, it's on your list, not mine. It's your gig and your money but I gotta find out about CONjunction, about what you have in mind. Do you mind filling me in?"

I fully expected him to ask the question and I knew that Delilah must also be wondering about that particular line item on my part of the list. All things considered I would have preferred to wait until I had my next con, the big one, fully formed and worked out in my head but since all three of us were involved with the cons then all three of us had to decide where things would go in the future. And because of my history, I also considered myself the majority stockholder and the one in charge of our fun little venture. One way or another I would make sure that it would continue operating. "Well, I want both of you to know that CONjunction is going to be with me, with us, going forward and

I wanted to get it on my list of expenses, you know, just for the record."

Neither of them said anything so I continued. "I don't want to get into any detail about the cons I have in mind for the near future and there's no doubt that more ideas will pop up along the way, but just let me say that CONjunction is going to grow and by that I mean beyond the three of us."

"You mean Michelle?" Oz asked.

"Well, yeah, if she wants to join the fun but I meant actually hiring a few people and making it a real business, well sort of a business. It'll let us try more ambitious stuff, stuff that'll get people's attention and maybe, hopefully make a difference."

Delilah leaned forward, wine glass in hand and said, "Okay, let's talk about this for a minute. Remember when we started on this journey and we joked about you becoming a squirrel?"

"Nope," Ozzie interrupted, "it was about him becoming an asshole."

"Hey wait a minute," I said, "you guys are part of CONjunction too and, except for *The Bentley Caper* you've been up to your eyeballs in the fun. I admit that I tend to lose myself in the cons sometimes but I assure you both that my head is on straight and I have everything under control."

I looked for Delilah's reaction to my comment and she looked down at the floor, back up at me and said, "Honey, I admit the Bentley con bothered me. It just seemed to be mean and almost vengeful and I started to wonder if there was some part of you coming out that I didn't know about. But after it played out and I read the things in the newspaper I started to understand why you did it. I remembered something you said to me shortly after we met. You said that a person has to live his politics and I guess that's what that con was about, you living your politics, even if it was stretching the point"

"Relax, man," Oz said, "as far as I'm concerned CONjunction is a gold mine of possibilities and I want to be part of it no matter what. I just wish like hell I could have been here for *The Bentley Caper* because it ended with a public fart and you know how much I love fart jokes."

That comment ended whatever tension might have still been in the air and I replied, "Okay then, let's all agree that CONjunction will live long and prosper and we'll all have a blast along the way." I raised my nearly empty glass toward their nearly full ones and offered a toast. "To CONjunction, may it lead to fun, fun with a purpose and fun that makes a difference." The words were no sooner out of my mouth when I felt a twinge of doubt that the results would always match the goal.

Our glasses clinked in unison and Delilah asked, "So, honey you gotta tell us, what's the next con stirring around in that crazy head of yours?"

I looked at her and then at Oz and said very calmly, "Be patient, give me a few more weeks and then I'll fill you in."

Give us a hint," Oz pleaded.

I paused to carefully choose my words. "Let's just say that it's going to be big and maybe even a little scary. It's going to be political and I think it's time for Jethro to join in the fun."

12

Laying the Groundwork

A person would be hard-pressed to drive through any town in America without eventually seeing a mobile home. It might be a lone trailer nestled on a small lot along a narrow road or a sprawling trailer park covering acres and acres in a rural area. They could range from a quaint, little one person size box to a huge, modular double-wide with skylights and an outdoor deck. But no matter how humble or grand it might be, it was still a trailer.

The manager's office at the Sunset Estates mobile home park consisted of a small, gray 1970s-era single wide trailer set up on concrete blocks painted white, with a row of barely-alive sage bushes running around the entire perimeter. Based upon its position it appeared to belong to the resident of the large beige and white double-wide that shared the driveway near the entrance to the park. Beyond it were rows and rows of all manner of mobile homes, mostly doublewides which seemed to be well maintained, driveways filled with pick-up trucks and older model compacts and an unusual number of barking dogs roaming the streets and yards.

I pulled up along the right side of the driveway by the office to make sure I didn't block any traffic. A red and white sign in the trailer's front window read, Manager and Rental Office. I got out and walked toward the small wooden porch at the front door, and my foot was no sooner on the first step when a chubby, middle-aged woman with curly, platinum blonde hair and bright pink lipstick opened the door.

"Mornin' sugar, how can I help you?" she called out in a raspy, gasping voice that sounded like it belonged to a much older woman.

"Good morning," I answered. I was glad that my sunglasses were hiding my eyes because I couldn't help but notice how her loose fitting tank top did little to hide her enormous cleavage and ample midsection. "I was wondering if you had any rentals available, you know, a by the month kind of deal."

She looked at me, then over at my Explorer and back at me. "Yeah, I think I can fix you up. How much room do you need, you got a family?"

"Nope, it's just me and my girlfriend. We travel a lot so we won't need much room." I wasn't sure how my next comment would sound but I let it out anyway. "And once in a while, if we're on the road, a friend or two might want to stop by and relax."

"Well, wait here for a minute and let me get the keys to a nice little two bedroom beauty I have near the back corner. I think you'll like it." As she walked back through the door she turned around and said, "I'm Dolly, by the way."

"And I'm Alan." I waited at the bottom of the steps and fidgeted with my fake mustache. It itched and I was afraid to scratch it for fear of making it come loose. I scanned the neighborhood and noticed a few of the neighbors peering in my direction.

Dolly reappeared, walked down the steps and asked, "You mind walkin'? It'll give you a chance to see the place'

"No, it's a nice morning, lead the way."

As we walked, Dolly's chatter never stopped. "We have a real nice bunch of folks here, mostly workin' people, some with kids. Got lots of divorcees, you know how that goes, you split up and you gotta have a cheap place to live for a while so you come here. Don't have a lot of renters, most of the folks own their own place but don't let that bother you cause' everyone's welcome. Watch out there, don't step in the dog poop. Man, that just burns me when they don't clean up after their pets, it's a real problem on this street."

As we walked past the dumpster corral the stench of a hundred people's garbage wafted over me and I instinctively held my breath. We turned the corner and I dropped back to walk behind her when a car passed us coming the other way. Dolly looked as big from behind as she did from the front. Finally, she said, "It's this nice tan and white one up here on the right, nice yard in back and an extra wide driveway. The owner just had the inside professionally cleaned."

I looked at the aging aluminum box and wondered how many people had lived under its corrugated roof. Dolly unlocked the front door and I followed her inside. Her comment on the trailer being professionally cleaned hit home when the strong smell of disinfectant reached my nostrils. The cleaning people probably did their best but the smell of cigarette smoke was still obvious. Dolly stood in the kitchen and said, "Go ahead, sugar, look around and see why this is one of our most popular rentals."

It felt odd in some unexplainable way to admit to myself that in my entire life I'd never set foot inside a mobile home. I had seen them in photos and on TV shows so I had preconceived notions of what they looked like but I had never known anybody who actually lived in one and as I stood there and scanned the place it was exactly what I had always envisioned. I walked slowly down the narrow hallway, peeking left and right into the rooms, each one small and dark. The flooring and wall covering had seen better days, the ceiling panels sagged and the window blinds looked to be original. I walked into the bedroom at the end of the hall and looked out the side window. It was at most twenty feet from the side window of the trailer next door and it made me wonder how many romantic scenes and private arguments in both trailers had played out in front of the neighbors.

When I got back to the kitchen Dolly asked, "So what do you think, pretty sweet isn't it?" I couldn't tell if she was just working her sales pitch on me or if she actually thought the trailer was nice, but either way I had to fight to keep a straight face. "And if you want your girlfriend to see it first I can hold it for a few days. Just give me a hundred dollar deposit and I'll make sure nobody comes and takes it out from under yah'."

"No, I like the place and I'm sure my girlfriend will too. Let's go back to the office and write it all up."

We retraced our steps through the mine field of dog poop and when we got back to the office trailer I sat in a metal and vinyl kitchen chair that served as visitor seating in front of a big wooden desk. The desktop was covered with piles of paper, framed photographs of little dogs and a large pink glass ashtray filled with cigarette butts. Dolly sat down at her computer and I gave her the information she needed for the rental agreement. She printed out the four page document and showed me where to sign. When that was finished she said, "Now I'm gonna need a security deposit and first and last month's rent." She hesitated a moment and then said, "And I'm kinda surprised that you never asked me how much the rent is. You must have some deep pockets, huh?" She let out a hoarse laugh that brought on a hacking cough.

I grinned and said, "Oh, I just figured you'd give me a fair rate and you seem like a real nice person."

To keep as low a profile as possible I used my middle name on the agreement. To Dolly and my new neighbors I was L. Alan Carr. She looked over the papers, then looked at me and said, Mr. Carr, Alan, I'm gonna need a check from you right now to make this all nice and legal."

Since I only had checks with my real and complete name and address on them, I asked, "How about I pay you in cash?" Dolly seemed to be impressed as I opened my wallet and pulled out a wad of bills that I had brought for the occasion.

The rent was four-hundred and fifty dollars a month with a security deposit of the same amount, so for the princely sum of one thousand three hundred and fifty dollars I was the new tenant at 20831 Valley Vista Road. I was an official resident of a trailer park and I wasn't sure how I felt about it. It wasn't like I actually owned the place. I was only renting it so that made me feel less connected to the surroundings. Holy shit, I was actually renting a mobile home! I said goodbye to Dolly, got into my car and drove away slowly, taking in the sights, sounds and smells of my new neighborhood. I stopped at the entrance to the highway, looked into the rearview mirror and peeled off my fake mustache then carefully slipped it into a Ziploc bag and put it into the glove compartment. I was Lincoln Carr again.

The next few weeks were a juggling act for me. Things at Carr Creative were going so well it was like the office was on autopilot. Even with Ozzie's transition underway there didn't seem to be a problem or a hiccup in sight. Wayne and I had some time to put together a framework for his taking over more control and he had already started filling some of the voids I was creating with my regular absences from the office. The juggling came from trying to grow CONjunction in a sensible way when I wasn't completely sure what kind of firm it needed to be. So much depended on the details of my next con but, fortunately, I was very close to knowing what that was. The basic plot was clear and so was the outline of how I'd pull it off. The script was as finished as I could make it until I worked out the final piece of the con: The target. Part of me wanted to use Hollywood's term for the person on the receiving end of a con; the mark, but there was no doubt in this case target was a better word because I had chosen the person to go after and also the person who would be the unwitting accomplice. And there was even a third person who, if the first two people did what I hoped they would do, stood to come out the winner of the con I had named *King of the Trailer Park*.

The normal clattering of the equipment in our printing room was absent when I walked in and I was glad it was the lunch hour. Having the room to myself made me less nervous about having anyone see what I was copying. Over the years I had watched enough documents and presentations get put together and I was comfortable with operating the machines. I took a small, blue thumb drive from my pocket and stuck it into the USB port of our print command computer. A few moments later I was printing out the manual that detailed and scripted my new con. Because it would involve so many people and take an entire year to orchestrate I had to come up with what was essentially an instruction manual for everyone on my team. *King of the Trailer Park* would have to be monitored carefully and in the event of a problem there was a Plan B for every aspect of the con.

Within fifteen minutes the pages, tabbed dividers and cover were printed and collated. I laid the stack of paper on the counter and carefully fed each set, one by one, into a machine that attached a shiny spiral binding and clear plastic cover. The clock above the counter read five minutes to one when the last manual was finished. I gathered them all up, put them into a cardboard box and walked out of the room just as Manny, the printing attendant, walked in. Timing was everything.

Ozzie had just arrived back in the Valley after a long weekend trip to Denver to meet Michelle's parents and sisters. A visit with the parents was farther than any of his post-divorce relationships had ever gotten and I was eager to get a download from him. Right before they had left, he and Michelle had met Delilah and me for dinner at Las Mesas and we had a chance to get to know her. I had been hoping I'd like her because my best friend was totally smitten, but I was also sizing her up as a potential player in my cons. From what I could tell she seemed to be a bit of a tight-ass. She might have potential but I also knew it took a special kind of personality to work a con.

The usual slow start to a Monday was underway when Oz stuck his head in my door. "Hey, man, you can stop pacing the floor, Ozzie's back!"

Well, the traveling man decided to come home, welcome."

Oz dropped into a chair in front of my desk and immediately grabbed the arms, trying to steady himself. "Holy shit, what happened to this chair?" he asked as he stood up again.

"You better use the other one. That one has had too many encounters with Wayne."

"Ah, that explains it," Oz said. As he settled into the second chair I got up and dragged the wobbly one into the far corner of the room where no one else could risk injury from it.

"So you gotta fill me in, how was the big introduction to Mom and Dad?" I asked.

Oz hesitated for a moment, a signal that maybe things hadn't gone as well as he'd hoped. "Oh, okay I guess. Michelle's mother is a real sweetheart and her sisters are both a lot of fun." He hesitated again.

"And her father?" I asked.

"Well, Dad is kind of a handful. He's retired and spends his days watching Fox News and listening to Rush Limbaugh, so that means he's always pissed off at somebody. Need I say more?"

"Oh shit, you must have argued with him all weekend."

"No, I managed to hold my tongue in check, for Michelle's sake, but believe me, it wasn't easy."

Did he find out how disinterested in politics you are?"

"Yeah, I think he had an idea because whenever he made some outrageous comment about the government or gays or who was at fault for every single transgression in the world, it was almost like he was goading me into arguing with him. I just sat there and changed the subject. In fact, I think that pissed him off as much as arguing with him would have. On the way home Michelle thanked me for the way I handled things so I guess that's all over until the next visit. I guess I passed the boyfriend test, at least for now."

And how about Michelle, is she like her father when it comes to politics?"

Ozzie seemed surprised at my question but he answered, "Well, I guess you can't grow up in that kind of family without some of it rubbing off on you." He waited a moment and then added, "Come on, man, there's more to life than politics."

"I'm just checking because you wanted to bring her in on our cons and my next one has politics at its core."

Oh, good, are we going to make another politician fart or what?"

I couldn't help but smile. I was beginning to believe David Pierce's public fart would live forever. "No, not fart, but maybe cry," I answered.

Oz sat up straight in his chair. "Cry; oh goody, tell me the rest of it."

"Not yet, I want to lay this one out to everyone at the same time. It's gonna be a long slog by a much bigger team than we ever needed in the past. And if we're successful a whole lot of people are gonna take notice."

You're killin' me here, man, you gotta fill me in."

"Friday night, eight o'clock at my house, and bring Michelle." As Oz stood up, I added, "I guarantee you, if we all decide to go ahead with this one it will be an absolute thrill ride."

13

Launch Party

The best way to understand something is to experience it first-hand. It's like the old saying, "The only way to know it is to live it." Most people would probably agree with that statement but when it's all said and done few people really want to go that far and actually do it. It's too easy to form opinions based upon things you see on television or read online. Anecdotal evidence becomes fact and that's good enough for most people. I was about to embark on a con of proportions that seemed almost overwhelming and I had to confess that I built the concept largely on other people's observations and opinions. The information we gathered for the trailer park commercials, even though it was solid and accurate from a statistical perspective, was still the result of other people's experiences and not mine. It was time for me to put up or shut up and I was glad that I'd set things in motion so I could do just that.

I had originally planned to keep what I regarded as the launch of *King of the Trailer Park* to myself, Delilah and Oz. I had agreed with some reluctance to include Michelle but a conversation with Wayne when I was walking into the office changed my plan even more. He and his wife Amy had been struggling to keep their marriage together ever since their daughter and only child had graduated from college and moved to Los Angeles. They had grown apart to the point where there wasn't much of a relationship and Amy decided to get away and spend a few weeks visiting her family in Tucson. It was pretty clear that they were headed for a divorce but Wayne seemed to be taking everything in stride. He was going to be a bachelor at least for a while but somehow he managed to keep his spirits up. It was a combination of pity for a man with no domestic skills and my yearning to bring him in on the con that led me to extend an invitation for him to join us at my house.

Ozzie and Michelle arrived right on time and Wayne followed about fifteen minutes later. As usual Delilah was the consummate host with a dining table full of tapas and a refrigerator full of wine and beer. My small bar top displayed an array of bourbon, Scotch and vodka that was certain to help promote open conversation and ideas but it was also there to give me an extra dose of courage when it was time to present my scheme. I was surrounded by friends and loved ones but for some reason I felt oddly alone.

We all went out to the patio and gathered around our large, round coffee table. The plates of appetizers and the multitude of bottles and glasses pretty much filled the table as we all maneuvered our chairs for maximum elbow room. The cardboard box full of the manuals I'd printed was sitting on the patio next to the grille and I decided it would be a good idea to give everyone a little time to eat and drink before I jumped into the discussion of the con. It was a good idea that lasted only about two minutes until Wayne said, "Hey, Linc, how about tellin' us what this big plan of yours is all about."

"Geez," I answered, "I was hoping you'd all drink a little more before I laid it on you. I was thinking you all might need a little softening up.'

Ozzie chimed in, "I'm with you, Wayne. I want to see what kind of con requires this kind of team and all this brain power."

"Okay," I sighed, "but I think we should do this inside where it's more private." After several minutes of picking up plates and glasses and settling into the living room I took a sip of my bourbon, laid the box of manuals on the dining table, counted out five copies and sat down. I looked around at the four eager people who were waiting to know about my scheme and said, "We are about to discuss my newest scheme and before we do I want to welcome Michelle and Wayne to our band of players. Michelle, I know that Oz has told you a little about some of the things we've done in the past and Wayne, you know some of the things we've pulled off around the office." Both of them smiled and I could see the anticipation in their eyes. Ozzie was looking at Michelle and he seemed pleased that she would consider joining in on the fun. Delilah was smiling at me with a look that gently said, "Okay, honey, cut the bullshit and get to the point."

I held up a manual for them to see, with the cover photo and title clearly visible. "Folks, we are about to launch a con called *King of the Trailer Park* and I hope you'll enjoy pulling it off as much as I know I will."

I passed out the manuals to everyone and as they each flipped through the pages I said, "Even though I think this con is going to be a fun adventure, I also want to point out that it will involve us in some serious shit with some serious people, and from this moment on nobody says a word about it to anyone outside of this group. And let's also keep our voices down while we're talking about it now because, you know, we have neighbors."

I must have had a less than light-hearted tone to my voice because Delilah asked, "What do you mean serious shit and serious people?"

This was the moment that I needed a drink to ease my nervousness. I looked at Delilah to see if she'd make a comment about my drinking, hesitated for a moment and put my glass down. Then I said in a voice that I hoped sounded confident, "*King of the Trailer Park* is my plan to help determine who gets elected the next Governor of Arizona."

I was surrounded by raised eyebrows and dropped jaws. One by one each person began reading through the manual, flipping pages and alternately looking up at me. Their voices murmured a string of "Oh mys," "Holy shits" and "Are you serious?" mixed with shaking heads and quiet laughter. The best thing to do, I thought to myself, was to let it play out and wait for one of them to say something. I wasn't surprised that the first comment came from Wayne. "Boss man, this is weird stuff, no, make that very weird stuff, even for you."

Ozzie said, "I haven't read every word and every detail yet, Linc, but from what I see this thing looks kind of scary. Are you sure you haven't gone off the deep end with this one?"

Michelle seemed almost shocked and her nervousness was obvious. "Linc, I've never been involved in this kind of thing before and I don't exactly know how much help I can be." I had just introduced the con and she was already back pedaling on getting involved. Then she looked over at Oz, as if she was looking for support. "And I have to say I agree with Oz. It looks kind of scary."

Not surprisingly Delilah was the last to speak up. She was always my thoughtful, emotional barometer and it was her opinion that mattered most to me even though her hesitation in responding only fed my nervousness. "Honey, I know you love your cons and I have loved being part of them but this one seems to go way, way beyond anything you ever tried before. I agree with Oz and Michelle that it sounds scary and I hope you've thought through all of the things that could go wrong. This all looks like it could lead to trouble and I mean real trouble."

The rest of the group was looking at her when I answered, "Believe me, babe, I have thought about this thing from every angle you can imagine. I'm not taking anything lightly. I know it won't be easy and I'm prepared to see it through to its conclusion."

"Yeah, its conclusion." Oz said, "That's a word that could mean all kinds of things, good and bad."

"Okay," I said, "before we get wrapped up in a lot of speculation and "what ifs," let's open our little instruction manuals to page one and walk through the whole thing together, but first, does anybody need anything?"

There were a few minutes of refilling plates, pouring drinks and a few bathroom breaks before our group was all back in place and ready to dig into the project. Before we began, Delilah, who was sitting beside me, leaned over, kissed me on the cheek and quietly said, "Honey, I'm not trying to be a wet blanket or anything. I just want us all to be very careful because this one looks like it's totally out there on the edge of a cliff." She kissed me again and said, "Like I've said many times before, I have to deal with the fact I'm married to a squirrel and I don't want my squirrel to land in jail." Her words said she was joking but her tone and expression said much more than that.

For the next hour or so we walked through the con, page by page and step by step. I had organized the manual into sections that were intended to make the whole thing easy to grasp. The first section was labeled *Mission Statement* and it declared, in great detail, my feeling that we needed to take steps to ensure the election of a Progressive candidate, a Democrat who would re-engage the fight to get the state back on track. It was a case of acting according to my politics and since I would be the one writing the checks I had to know where everyone on the team stood politically. This was the part of the con that demanded total, unequivocal buy-in from everyone at the table and, at least from that standpoint, that happened easily. I went around the table and asked for comments about the mission and got enthusiastic agreement on it from everyone but Michelle.

The second section, which I had labeled, *Meet the Marks*, was the one that seemed to require the most explanation. My passion for news and for keeping up with what was going on in the world gave me what I believed was a pretty good read on the state's current political landscape. The list of potential candidates for next year's gubernatorial election was already starting to take shape. Arizona was a red state and the list of Democratic candidates was always a short one, while the list of Republican candidates was a much longer one of people climbing all over each other trying to show who was the most conservative and who hated big government more. Occasionally an independent candidate was added to the mix. I had done a lot of research into the polling, the issues du jour, voter turnout and winning margins of the gubernatorial elections since the early 1980s and found that the few times a Democrat had won it had been after a particularly ugly campaign and by a very narrow margin. *King of the Trailer*

Park was my plan to ensure that, in the next election that winning margin would be a sure thing. The ugly part was bound to remain.

I had asked everyone to spend a few minutes reading through that section not knowing how informed any of them might be on the who's who of Arizona politics. It was a very quiet ten minutes or so before Oz spoke up. "Hey, man, it looks like you've done your homework on things but how much of this depends on whether the candidates you have on your list actually make it to the ballot?"

"To be honest, Oz, the "who" of the ballot is almost irrelevant. I listed the people who are already out there, the people whose egos and ambitions are already a matter of public record. The Republicans are so fucking predictable that it almost doesn't matter who they put out there. It'll be someone who claims to hate big government while doing everything they can to be part of one. Arizona's overloaded with people like that so let's not get too hung up on that part just yet. The thing we need to focus on is the given fact that the two parties will trot out the same ideas and the same arguments. It'll be fucking political gridlock as usual. My little plan is to break that two-party gridlock and push the election results in a particular direction, a direction we can live with."

Delilah sat up straight in her chair, her eyes riveted on mine. "Honey, when I hear someone use words like, "a direction we can live with," all I can think is that kind of thing always leads to trouble. I've heard you rant and rave about all the money and outside influence in politics and all I can think is that this is just more of the same, someone trying to game the system for personal benefit."

The rest of the group sat there in uncomfortable silence. Delilah had floated a big challenge to my plan and I had a feeling that everyone at the table was thinking the same thing to one degree or another. I knew I had to respond. I waited a moment and then answered her calmly, "The one thing to remember here and it's really at the core of the con, is that no one, including me, will make one nickel or gain any kind of political favor from this. Like it says in the mission statement this is a plan to even the odds. The Republican leadership has used redistricting to a point where in some districts they simply can't lose. It's like why even bother to have an Election Day when it's a done deal months in advance. *King of the Trailer Park* brings a third candidate into the mix, a dark horse, and that's the guy that can swing the pendulum in the other direction, our direction. And remember, I know, we all know that there is no way in hell we can get our guy elected. That's not our goal here but I don't think we'll have to aim very high to pull five or ten percent of the vote our way."

Before anyone could say anything else I said, "How about looking over the third section, *The Players*, and then we'll pick up the conversation again. I think that'll answer a lot of your questions, and it'll also tell you what your roles in this thing will be."

The group read through the section in complete silence and I interpreted the nodding of their heads as affirmation of the con or at least an understanding of the concept. Wayne was the first to finish reading and he reached for his beer, looked at me and grinned. After a few more minutes the rest of the group finished and I waited for them to get up and stretch and refill their glasses. When everyone was back in place around the table it was Delilah who spoke first

"Okay, I get it now. From what I read there's nothing we'll be involved in that's anything but up front and transparent. On the surface it looks like a pretty straightforward plan but I'm sure it's going to get more and more convoluted as we go forward." She looked at the group and then at me and said, "And it still scares the living hell out of me."

"Of course it's scary and of course it will get convoluted," Oz chimed in, "remember who dreamed it all up, the Master of Deception." He was grinning from ear to ear as he looked at me and added, "And I mean that as a compliment."

"Well, thanks, I guess." I looked around at everyone, trying to read their faces. It was Wayne's broad smile that I noticed first and I just had to hear from him. "Alright, man," I said, "you haven't stopped grinning since we got started so tell me what you're thinking."

Wayne looked like he could barely contain himself. "Boss man, I'm not gonna lie and say it doesn't scare me too, but I love it. It's definitely something I want to be a part of and I confess that I took a quick peek at section four and when I saw how you wanna' work the trailer park research into the thing I thought to myself, "Man, this is really gonna be fun.""

As usual Wayne's enthusiasm for things was infectious and I started to laugh. "I told you at the office, remember? Jethro is a big part of this thing." I glanced over at Michelle and I could tell the whole Jethro thing wasn't registering with her. "Hey, Oz," I said, "I'm guessing Michelle needs to be brought up to speed on who Jethro is. Do you want to do it or should I?"

"No, man, let me." Wayne interrupted, "Jethro is like a buddy of mine." He turned to Michelle and added, "Jethro isn't exactly real, he's more of an amalgam of a bunch of people. We've been workin' on ad campaigns for a bunch of different clients and the one thing the campaigns have in common is that they are really dumbed down so the target audience can understand them without havin' to think much because, well, we know they can't or won't."

Michelle nodded but I could tell she was still a little fuzzy on the concept. Wayne continued, "Okay, think of the trailer park as a place where distracted people live. Not just in trailers but also houses and apartments and condos and hell, even in fuckin' tents for all we know." His smile told me he was having fun spinning his explanation. "They're probably not the most motivated people you'll run across and when I say they're distracted I mean that they aren't payin' attention to the world around them. Nothin'. They just don't give a shit. They have more important things on their minds like next week's football schedule or who's trendin' in Hollywood. And of course, what's on sale at Walmart. To these folks politics don't count for much. While we were workin' on our ad campaigns we learned more about the people in the trailer park than any of us really wanted to. We came up with the name Jethro to define the typical trailer park resident, the guy or even the gal who we had to reach out to and, on behalf of our clients, make them reach for their wallets."

From her expression and nodding head I could tell that Michelle was finally beginning to understand and I felt I had to add something to Wayne's explanation. "Michelle, I'm guessing your first reaction to the trailer park thing was the same as mine and probably the rest of the bunch, that we're making fun of them or looking down our noses at them."

Michelle gave a slight nod and said, "Well, yeah, kind of."

Okay," I replied, "I'm going to say something here and I want everyone to understand it. I think Wayne already does because at least in his head he's been living in this trailer park world for a while now."

Wayne smiled and said, "Oh yeah."

I continued. "Nothing we have done with our ads was meant to be mean or condescending to anyone. We have a small mountain of research that tells us specific things about the particular segment of the population we're talking about here, and we created campaigns based strictly on that information. It's what we do. Wayne, I remember the day you handed me all of the research. You told me to read it if I wanted to get depressed and you were right. The people in all of these places we broadly call the trailer park, Jethro and his family and friends, make you wonder where in the hell this country is going. It's sad, it's scary and yes, it's definitely depressing."

During my explanation I could tell that Delilah wanted to say something and when I paused for a moment she did. "Okay, so we have all this data, we aren't being condescending and Jethro depresses us. How does all of that tie into a political campaign?"

Ozzie chimed in, "I was wondering the same thing."

Even though the answer to Delilah's question was explained in the next section of the manual I was glad to have a chance to answer her aloud. "Here's the deal. In *Section Two* you saw my somewhat hypothetical list of candidates. Our candidate, our mark, will be someone who came from the trailer park, a guy who managed to make it out but not by much and is now a minor figure in the public sector. He's someone that Jethro can relate to."

"And the guy you listed here is the "someone" you have in mind I take it." Delilah said in a matter of fact tone.

"Yep, it's Gabriel Stark. He's currently Assistant Superintendent of Wastewater Management for the City of Phoenix."

Ozzie said with a smile, "So our guy works in the sewer."

"Well, yes, in a manner of speaking."

"So why him? Where did you find this guy?" Wayne asked.

"I found him by doing a long, tedious search through media and government websites, local news websites, social media and of course Google. I found a bunch of people with the right kind of personal background but I needed to find someone with a connection to government work and who showed some kind of indicators for having political ambition."

Wayne grinned and said, "I thought we determined a long time ago that ambition and the trailer park are mutually exclusive ideas."

"Yeah, I know that but we need a guy who likes the idea of being a big shot, a guy who wants to see his name on bumper stickers and his face on television. I went to the City of Phoenix website and watched three videos of Stark speaking at various public meetings. He sounded reasonably well spoken and confident, and I also got the distinct impression that he liked hearing the sound of his own voice."

"What's the rest of his background," Michelle asked.

"He's forty-four years old and he was born and raised in the rural part of Glendale. His father was a truck driver, his mother was a homemaker and he has an older brother who's an unemployed laborer in the masonry business. His parents are still alive and retired, and, get this, they live in Westwood Estates, a mobile home park in Avondale.

"Oh my God, he sounds perfect." Wayne said, "You found us our Jethro."

Ozzie was smiling but I could tell he was skeptical. "I gotta say Linc, I'm having trouble seeing how a low level bureaucrat with no name recognition and no real political experience is going to make a viable candidate for governor."

"You're right," I answered, "but that's kind of the point. It's like I said a few minutes ago, he only has to be viable enough to pull in five or six, maybe ten percent of the votes, maybe even a little more if we're lucky. When you look at the voting history of the state, Independent candidates usually draw votes from the Republican side of the ledger. If the Democratic candidate can keep things close those few extra percentage points should be enough to make the difference. At least that's the plan."

Okay," Oz continued, "let's say you or somebody approaches this guy, Stark, and you say, "Hey mister unknown city employee guy, we think you'd make a great governor and we want to back you." What makes you sure that he'll believe it let alone go along with it?"

"Well, I'm not sure but I think the idea has a real chance. My approach will be to tell him that I represent a group of citizens who have been watching him in action and think he has a future in elected office. I'll say that we have very deep pockets and want to get him out in front of people who will see that he's the real deal. And to clinch things, I'll tell him that we know it will be an uphill battle, the odds are against him but even if he loses, when the election dust settles the entire state of Arizona will know Gabriel Stark and that could be the spring board for launching a run for another office in the future if he wants to try it again."

"So you tap into the guy's ego," Oz said, "and you make him think that no matter what happens on Election Day he still wins."

"Yeah, something like that, and given his background and history of under achievement it should be a fairly easy sell."

"Oh, there you go, boss man," Wayne bellowed, "you sound like you're in the advertising game."

"Yeah," I replied, trying not to sound snarky, "and it won't be the first time that good advertising sold a bad product."

Delilah sat there with a faint smile, shaking her head and then said, "This sounds like the kind of con only you would come up with and it still makes me nervous, really, really nervous, but as long as you promise you'll keep things civil I'm on board or at least I'll do what I can, time permitting." It was a lukewarm offer at best.

One by one the rest of the group chimed in on how they viewed their roles, Wayne with great enthusiasm and Delilah and Ozzie with noticeable timidity. Michelle didn't say much and avoided eye contact with me. I could tell that each of them shared Delilah's concerns and, to be honest, so did I. But for me there was something about the scale and the potential impact of this con that was too enticing to resist. It was an incredible feeling to know I had the money that made the power that made this kind of scheme possible.

I wasn't sure how much more of the plan I should lay out without taking a break or even calling it a night. We hadn't talked about the sections of the manual related to strategy and the section related to campaign funding was one I still wasn't totally comfortable bringing up with Wayne because he wasn't a part of the inner circle of lottery winners. I needed a little more time to think that one over.

Just as I was ready to call an end to the meeting and get on with the party Wayne said, "Hey, man, I've been meanin' to ask you. Where did you get the photo for the cover of the manual? That is one interestin' mobile home there."

I couldn't help but notice Delilah's eye-rolling expression and smirk because she already knew the answer. "That lovely double-wide," I answered, "has been rented in my name and eventually I hope each of you will take the tim to enjoy a little taste of trailer park living."

The wide-eyed expressions that surrounded me were a joy to behold. Ozzie and Michelle kept looking at each other then back at me and for the first time in a long time Wayne was speechless. I smiled and said, "That will be the unofficial campaign headquarters for this little venture and it will be our chance to rub elbows with our target demographic. I want each of us to spend a little time there, hang out on a Saturday night drinking beers with the neighbors, that kind of thing." I looked over at Wayne and said, "And who knows, we all might finally get to meet Jethro."

It seemed like the perfect note to end the meeting on. "Okay," I said as I stood up, "I don't know about the rest of you but I've had enough of the con for one night and I haven't taken much time to eat or drink. How about we all read the rest of the manual over the weekend and, for now, let's just go back out to the patio and relax." There was no disagreement and it seemed that the group shared my desire to stop talking about the con and shift into party mode. With Delilah's approval I poured myself some bourbon and began to unwind, glad that the launch was behind us but still aware that CONjunction had a major challenge ahead of it. My love for pranks and practical jokes was about to become a full time job and a risky one at that.

14

Filling in the Blanks

There's something about sleep that seems to rewire your brain. The stress and problems of the previous day find their way into the little, tiny room in the back of your head where they sit quietly and wait for you to pull them back out when you're ready. And sometimes they go to that room and just disappear. I awoke with thoughts of last night's gathering and with a strange and unfamiliar clarity. Within a matter of hours of the launch of *King of the Trailer Park* I had a much clearer idea of what I was up against. I thought our little gathering had gone reasonably well and that despite the team's obvious fears they seemed interested in being part of the whole thing. Maybe it was because it was a Friday, the end of a work week when everybody started to unwind. Maybe it was the alcohol which flowed freely and lubricated the group of prospective players. Or maybe it was just my wishful thinking. Whatever it was I was feeling good about the con and its chances for success. I leaned over and kissed my sleeping wife and got out of bed. My upbeat mood only lasted a few hours before the cracks in our team unity started to appear.

Around ten o'clock Ozzie called to tell me that he and Michelle had a long conversation on the way home from the party and that she had cold feet about being part of the con. It was an idea so totally new to her that she felt overwhelmed.

Bottom line was she decided to bail out altogether. All things considered it wasn't a total surprise. As for Ozzie, it seemed that his desire to continue his involvement with the con had also softened a bit and he said he preferred to take more of the role of a campaign finance advisor rather than a hands-on participant. I was disappointed to say the least. Oz had been with me on the cons from day one and the idea of going forward with this huge new undertaking without him at my side took some of the fun out of it. I was glad that he'd still be on board to handle the money because I wasn't sure how much of that would be flirting with illegality and Oz could be trusted to help me keep things on the right side of the line. I told him I understood his feelings even though I didn't. The fact was I was disappointed and more than a little pissed off.

Delilah and I were getting ready to go out to lunch when she got an email message from a prospective client and it was great news for her and Terra Nueva. They had been short-listed for a very prestigious project, the redesign and upgrade of the grounds of the Arizona Biltmore Resort. The original design had been the work of Frank Lloyd Wright and his partners, and whoever landed the redesign project would instantly gain national notoriety. It was a huge opportunity for a fledgling firm like hers and Delilah was both flattered and intimidated by the task ahead of her. Given the scale of the project and the timeline for her presentation, she would have to concentrate on it and nothing else. I enjoyed seeing her excitement over the news but I couldn't help but wonder if part of it came from a sense of relief that she wouldn't have to participate in a risky con where her interest was lukewarm at best. In a way I was glad that I wouldn't have to find out.

So now it would be just Wayne, me and whatever additional talent we brought on board who would have to complete the con. Even with all of the jokes and pranks and cons I had pulled off in the past I suddenly felt alone on this one.

On Monday morning while I was pulling into my parking space at the office I saw Wayne getting out of his car a few spaces down the row. He stood and waited for me and when I reached him he was wearing his usual grin. "Mornin', boss, how was your weekend?" We started walking toward the entrance.

"Oh, okay I guess, except that since I last saw you our little cast of characters shrank some."

What do you mean, did somebody bail on us?"

Yeah, Michelle got cold feet, Ozzie decided to be a part timer and just work from the sidelines on the accounting part and Delilah found out she has a chance to win a huge project and it's going to fill her calendar for the next three months or so."

Ever the optimist, Wayne shrugged and said, "Guess it's up to you and me now."

Yeah, you, me and whoever we can find to round out the team. Did you read the section of the manual about the skill sets we have to find?"

"Yep, and I have a few ideas on people we can talk to." He hesitated and then added, "I'm not sure how to replace Oz or Delilah because I don't know how they fit into your other cons. Is it okay to use that word?"

"Hell yes, let's call it what it is. And as for Oz and Delilah, I'll have to give that some thought. How about sitting down with me after your staff meeting and let's see what the two of us can do to kick start things?"

"I wouldn't miss it for the world. See yah' around ten."

Wayne's unfailing enthusiasm lifted my spirits a little. Somehow I knew things would move forward the way it said in the manual or at least reasonably close to it. The next few hours were filled with e-mails and knocks on my door. Now that the con was launching I felt the first pangs of sadness that I'd have to turn over the reins of Carr Creative for a while, at least on the operational side. It had become obvious that CONjunction couldn't operate solely on its own. Carr Creative would have to be a partner and the engine of talent and experience that moved the con forward. And somehow I'd have to keep a low profile while I juggled my roles in both of them.

When Wayne stood in my doorway fifteen minutes early and smiling from ear to ear I knew I'd better get our meeting started and take advantage of his energy. "Close the door." I said, "We better get used to the fact this is going to be a clandestine operation right smack in the middle of the company."

Wayne walked toward my desk and said, "Hey, man, you got new chairs."

"Yeah, it seems that the old ones broke prematurely," I answered, preferring to say nothing more on the subject.

During the course of creating the concept and writing the script for the con I had built a sizeable pile of material and it was sitting on my desk in front of Wayne's chair. He noticed it but before he could ask about it I said, "This stuff is for you. It's a couple of CDs with the manual and all of my notes on the script for the con on them. I also have hard copies of every bit of the data we got on the trailer park and some additional stuff I dug up on my own. The red binder is information on Gabriel Stark."

Wayne picked up that binder first and thumbed through it. "Geez, boss, where did you find all of this shit?"

"Well, as creepy as it might sound I went trolling online and found all kinds of stuff about him, I felt like a damned stalker. It's scary how much information is out there on pretty much everyone and our friend Gabriel seems to enjoy talking, sharing and posting all kinds of things about himself."

"Big ego, huh?"

"Very big, and that's what I'm hoping will be the key to *King of the Trailer Park's* success. Everyone has a special little button that when it's pushed makes them do things. My gut feeling is that Gabriel Stark has one that will make him very, shall we say "cooperative" when we push it."

"So have you contacted him yet?"

"Not yet, except to ask to connect with him on Linked In and then like his Facebook page. Just call it laying the groundwork."

"Sounds good, what happens next?" Wayne had no sooner asked his question when he leaned sideways in his chair and I heard the all too familiar groan of a stressed frame.

"There's a regularly scheduled public meeting on Wednesday night down at City Hall, I answered. "It's one of those "meet your government and complain to them" kind of gatherings. I'm planning to show up, sit and listen and try to stay awake and then when it's over I'm going to introduce myself, tell him that I'd like to discuss an idea related to his political future and find out if and when he's available to meet formally."

"Shouldn't we wait to see if he likes your idea before we go any further with things?"

"No, I have a strong feeling that when I dangle the carrot of political notoriety in front of him he'll grab it with both hands. He'll see it as his path out of the sewer." It was a smart-ass remark to make but it was based in truth. "And I have a Plan B and C ready if necessary, two other people we can consider talking to if Stark says no, but I'm telling you I don't think that will happen.

Wayne leaned forward and my brand new chair again squeaked noticeably. "Okay, so that's just two days from now. Assumin' he says yes we'll have to get somethin' rollin' right away, some kind of an announcement to the press, right?"

"Right, and I already drafted a statement for him to read. I've also got an appointment to meet with a company that does ballot access petitioning but our first order of business, for you and me, will be to build a campaign staff. Our part of that is the media team, including the ad buying, writing, blogs and internet stuff, production and everything else. Our product is Gabriel Stark and we have to identify the market of voters who might actually vote for the guy, and I think that market starts in the trailer park."

Boss man, you actually said that with a straight face."

Of course his comment made me break into a smile. "That's going to be the biggest challenge we'll face with this con," I said. "We, every single one of us on the team, will have to act like we really believe that Gabriel Stark is a real candidate, that he's qualified and capable of being Governor. We can't joke around about it in case anyone's listening. We have to keep a straight face and a controlled voice at all times. The ads and materials we produce have to be the best in the race, first class all the way and believable to everyone who sees them. We're going to be outspent from both sides of the competition but we can't let

Stark think for one second that we aren't totally committed and positive."

"Don't you think he's goin' to realize right from the get-go that he can't possibly win?"

"Well, that's where my, make that our skills at selling stuff to people who don't think they need it will come into play. Our goal, the one we don't talk about openly, isn't to guarantee him a victory. Our goal is to make him think he has a shot to be competitive and that no matter what happens the day after the election the people of Arizona will know who the hell Gabriel Stark is."

"And you think that's his hot button?"

"Yep, and we're going to push it long, hard, and often!"

For the next two and a half hours we focused our conversation on the people and skills we would need to build a campaign and marketing team. We assumed that Stark would want some input on his campaign staff and that was fine with us as long as he knew that we would be totally in charge of the message and working with the media. Slowly, one position at a time, our little CONjunction team was coming together. I typed it out as we talked and when we had a list of job titles that we both felt met the challenge I sent it to my printer and then handed a copy to Wayne.

"Geez, boss," Wayne said, his expression more serious than when we first sat down, "This is quite a list of people. Who's gonna' pay all of them?"

I take it you looked over the *Campaign Funding* section in the manual," I replied.

"Yeah, I looked it over real good and I saw a lot of what and when but not a lot of who."

It was a moment I knew was coming and I had rehearsed it a dozen times in my head but somehow it still made me nervous as I chose my words. "Well as you can probably guess, the total amount we might need is kind of a moving target. I think my projections on media buys are pretty close. I came up with monthly allowances for things like printing and I did some digging and got a handle on the cost of hiring petition circulators and the number of signatures we'll need on the ballot access petitions. Then we'll have a ton of miscellaneous costs like filing fees, sign permits, legal and consultant fees, getting someone to write the blog and internet content, stuff like that."

"Yeah, and I got that much from the manual but I still don't get who's gonna be throwin' in the money to get this guy elected. From what you told us his family doesn't have two nickels to rub together and I'm guessin' the City of Phoenix doesn't pay the Assistant Superintendent of Waste Water Management a whole lotta' dough. So where do you see the money comin' from?"

"Well, my friend, this is something else to add to the list of things you're not allowed to talk about. Most of the money will be coming from CONjunction."

Wayne's eyes widened. "So it'll be coming from your company that doesn't have clients and doesn't make any money, which means it'll be coming from you."

"That's right." I waited for his reaction.

He sat there, his body perfectly still, his arms folded across his broad girth and his head nodding slowly. His usual grin was more like a smirk. "What did you do, rob a fuckin' bank?"

"Nope, nothing illegal." I paused and then said, "Again, man, this is something you simply can't talk about and I mean with anyone, okay?"

"Sure, man, come on, let's hear it."

Well, last Spring Delilah, Ozzie and I got a case of lottery fever and we pitched in on twenty bucks worth of state lottery tickets, you know, like everybody does once in a while. I picked up the tickets a few at a time at a Circle K while I was getting some gas and never really thought much about it and then lo and behold, we won some money. Not a fortune but enough to split equally and all have some fun with."

Wayne's smirk slowly grew into a smile and he leaned forward. "Holy shit, man, so that means you guys are millionaires!"

"Yeah, don't blow it out of proportion but I guess we are, not crazy rich or anything like that, but like I said it's enough to have some fun." I felt bad having to lie about the amount but it was the strategy Delilah, Oz and I had agreed to and it still seemed like the best way to handle things.

"Okay, so now things are all startin' to make sense. Ozzie's pullin' back on his hours at the office and Delilah startin' her own business overnight. And you, you crazy son of a bitch, want to elect the next governor with your piece of the dough." He paused and then bellowed, "I fuckin' love it!"

"Then I take it I have your word that you won't breathe a word of this to anyone, Amy included. My role in this whole thing has to be kept in the background."

"Don't worry man, everythin's cool here, there's no reason for me to tell her about it." He paused for a moment, looked down at the floor and said, "I was gonna' tell ya' this soon. We decided that it's over, time for a D-I-V-O-R-C-E." What should have been a totally serious and melancholy moment changed instantly when he added, "You know that was an old Tammy Wynette song and I fuckin' loved it."

Despite his omnipresent light hearted attitude I knew Wayne had to be hurting at least a little and it bothered me to ask him to keep secrets from his wife. "Hey man, sorry about all that." I said, "No matter what the circumstances might be it's always a bummer when two people split up." I waited a moment to let the mood lighten at least a little bit. "But I also have to tell you that I really appreciate your loyalty. When this thing gets rolling I'm going to need a lot more from you besides secrecy and it'll mean splitting your time between Carr and CONjunction. Both of us are going to get very good at wearing a lot of different hats by the time the election is over."

I was hoping for an easy way to get off the subject of divorce and Wayne handed it to me on a platter. "Okay, man, no problem. This seems like a good time to talk about our little list of accomplices here," he interrupted, "because I had some ideas on a couple of people we should think about bringin' into the mix."

I felt in immediate sense of relief. "Are you thinking people from the Garage or new blood?"

"Actually both. Since you're thinkin' of tappin' into the trailer park stuff I think we should make Jeremy Kyle the lead artistic guy on this. He has such an amazin' read on the people we've been goin' after and the stuff he comes up with is like music to their ears. I swear he knows Jethro as well as I do, maybe better. I asked him one day if he was born in a trailer and he just laughed but he didn't say no!"

Yeah, I remember his piece of the first presentation for ProInsure. He sounded like he'd known the trailer park folks his whole life. But if we bring him on board here what kind of a hole does that create in the team at Carr?"

"I think we'll be okay. Jeremy has created templates for every one of the ad campaigns and the rest of the crew understands the mission. I'll be able to keep enough of an eye on things to make sure we stay on track."

"Okay," I said, my comfort level improving by the minute, let's put his name down and then fill in the rest of the blanks."

Okay, but real quick, Ben Autry is one of those blanks. I'm guessin' this campaign is gonna' involve more TV than internet and Ben knows everybody at all the stations. He also has this strange fuckin' gift for knowin' when and where to put the ads, like he knows exactly who's sittin' in front of the tube at any given time."

"Maybe he was one of those kids whose parents parked him in front of the TV instead of actually dealing with him."

"Hey, to one degree or another weren't we all?"

I was starting to feel like we had things pointed in the right direction. "So how about the internet piece? I know we need to be strong on television but online content has got to be a big part of how we get our unknown guy in front of the people. There's some interesting stuff, actually you could call it scary stuff going on out there called Native Advertising. Have you heard of it?"

"Yeah, a little. Isn't it like making an advertisement look like a real news story?"

"Yep, the people who do it spin the whole dirty game and call it "sponsored content" but what it boils down to is the wall between news and advertising is crumbling away and the viewers can't tell the difference. Who do you think we should put in charge of the internet part of the campaign?"

"Linc, to be honest, I don't think we have anyone who could actually create the content. That sounds like someone with experience writing about politics and the best I could come up with would be someone to run the campaign website and not much else."

"I kind of figured that might be the case. Let me scout around for someone who can write the blog and then you and your team can take it and make sure the ad looks and smells like a legitimate piece of news. Sound okay?

Wayne hesitated for a few seconds and I couldn't help but wonder if I was asking him to take part in something underhanded but then it also occurred to me that the word "underhanded" was probably the perfect label for my entire con. Finally he answered, "Yeah, it sounds like we can make it work." He made a tapping sound on my desk with his big hand and said, "Remember that sound, it's the ticking of the clock as the advertising world we know slips away."

"I know what you mean. Nothing is black and white anymore. We're living in a very gray world. And let me just add something that will make things look even grayer. I just read the results of a *Pew Research Center* poll that showed millennials rely on social media for most of their political news. To them, Facebook and Instagram are the go-to sources for news."

"Boss man, that is scary on so many levels. I've been on Facebook, albeit reluctantly, for almost two years and I gotta tell you, it's ninety percent bullshit and ten percent drivel."

"Well, I'm not sure I agree with you totally but it's a force we'll have to deal with. Like it or not we're going to have a *Stark for Governor* Facebook page so we can attract whatever people, young, old and in-between that we can find who have even a slight interest in actually voting."

Wayne smiled and nodded. "I wonder how many millennials live in the trailer park."

"Yeah, and of those how many will bother to stand in line on election day or mail it in."

It seemed like a good point to take a quick break so I took a few minutes to order sandwiches and salads for delivery so we wouldn't lose our momentum. By the time they arrived we had the core campaign team put together. It would be a mix of Carr people working part-time alongside some full time production people that both Wayne and I would find through his industry sources. By the time we finished eating we also had a list of job titles and skill sets that would be needed to form the political side of the campaign team. That was the group that I wasn't real clear on and I figured that Gabriel Stark would want to share in choosing the people. That would be the big variable in running the campaign; herding a group of strangers and making sure they didn't try to wrest control of anything from my side of the team. I knew I'd have to make Stark think we were all one big, happy family when I knew full well that would be impossible. *King of the Trailer Park* was my creation, my child and I would be in charge of feeding and raising it, and no one was going to get in my way. No one, not even Stark himself.

15

Meeting the King

It's always an interesting experience when you spend any amount of time in a government building. If you can momentarily forget about whatever agenda brought you through the front door and just look around and see things strictly through the eyes of a taxpayer you get a totally different perspective on the way things work in the public sector. Passing through a security gate staffed by people who look like they'd fall over from a stroke if they ever actually had to perform a physical act related to security. Waiting in a sterile, impersonal feeling lobby furnished with long rows of tightly spaced metal and vinyl chairs separated by large potted, artificial plants. Sitting and watching the constant flow of public employees, access cards on lanyards around their necks, on their way to the restroom, the lunchroom, the coffee kiosk and, hopefully, on occasion their desks.

It was my second consecutive day with a visit to this mecca of minimal effort. As my plan had called for, I attended the previous evening's meeting to observe the workings of the Waste Water Authority and to observe Gabriel Stark in action. Like the three previous videotaped meetings I had watched, Stark was in charge of the agenda, controlled the questions and answers and generally talked to, at and over everyone in the large meeting room. The moment the meeting adjourned I walked up to him, introduced myself and told him word for word what I had carefully scripted in advance: I was representing a group of people who wanted to see a fresh, new face in government and were impressed with Stark's way of dealing with the public. He listened, just politely at first, but when I reached the point in my little pitch where I said we wanted to introduce the people of Arizona to a rising star his demeanor changed noticeably. And when I told him that our group was very well funded I could almost feel the hook sinking in.

Sitting in the Water Department waiting area, I had just finished checking my email messages on my phone when a painfully thin young woman with long, black hair and a distracting over-bite approached me. "Good morning, are you Mr. Carr?"

"Yep, Lincoln Carr, and you are?"

"I'm Fawn, I'm Mr. Stark's assistant. Please follow me, Mr. Stark is ready for you."

I followed the Assistant to the Assistant down a long corridor and then through a maze of beige cubicles, most of which were unoccupied. When we reached Stark's office Fawn smiled and asked, "Can I get you some coffee or water?"

"No thanks, I'm good," I answered, assuming that the coffee had probably been in the pot and thickening on the burner since the workday began two hours earlier.

"Mr. Carr, good morning, nice to see you again," Stark said, extending his hand toward me. I shook it and noticed his skin felt clammy and sweaty just like the handshake we'd exchanged the night before. "Here, please have a seat," he said, motioning toward one of the same uncomfortable chairs that filled the lobby.

"Call me Linc," I said, "and may I call you Gabriel?"

"Make it Gabe," he answered as he sat down in his chair. "So, I have to admit our short conversation last evening kept me awake all night." I was glad he was smiling when he said it. As I settled into my chair I noticed something I had observed at last night's meeting, the faint signs of underarm wetness on his light blue shirt. I made a mental note that if a campaign actually came out of this conversation I'd recommend that he wore only white shirts.

"Yeah, I should probably apologize for laying something like that on you and then leaving but I wanted to make sure I got your attention." I laid one of my business cards on his desk and slid it toward him.

He glanced at it and said, "Oh, don't worry, you definitely got my attention." His smile was growing and it was obvious I had a receptive listener for what I was about to lay out. When I had studied him during the previous night's meeting, looking for clues to the things that made him tick, I couldn't help but notice that he colored his hair. Stark was forty-four years old yet ever strand of hair on his head, every single one was the exact same unnatural shade of light reddish-brown, combed and arranged with great precision to hide, or at least try to hide a very large bald spot on the top of his head. Since he was over six feet tall it probably worked well enough to fool most people, at least the short ones. And his closely-cropped goatee and mustache shared the same perfectly uniform color.

Fawn reentered the room and placed a steaming coffee cup on Stark's desk. "Thanks, Fawn. Please close the door on your way out and hold my calls until Linc and I are finished here, okay?" She smiled, nodded and left the room.

"Okay, so how do we start this conversation?" Stark asked, leaning on his elbows and folding his hands.

"Well," I began, "since I don't want you to lose another night's sleep why don't I just lay things out for you step by step?" Stark nodded and I continued. "As I told you last night I'm part of a group of people who'd like to see things get better in Arizona, I mean from a political point of view and we don't see that happening with the people who are holding office right now. For the most part it's the same, tired old group of well-heeled hacks and hangers-on who we've suffered through for the past two or three election cycles. We think it's time for new faces, new blood and a new direction."

Stark unclenched his hands and leaned back in his chair. "And you and your group somehow think I'm one of those new faces."

We definitely think you could be one of them. We know it'll take more than one person to turn the wheel in another direction but we decided to start with you, that is, if any of this interests you."

"It definitely interests me but I've had like, what, twelve hours to think about it?"

"Believe me, Gabe, we aren't taking this lightly and we don't expect you to either. This is a big decision, huge, and it will affect you, your family and every single part of your life."

Stark sat still and silent for a moment and then said, "Let's kind of shift gears here for a minute. You keep using the word *we*. Who are *we*?"

"That's a good question and believe me I understand your curiosity about who would want to back a total stranger for political office. But let me just ask you to please be patient for a little while, at least until we get your agreement on things and we know you're on board with this. Some of the people I'm in on this thing with want to stay in the background in the event you say no and we have to look elsewhere."

"Understood," Stark replied, "these days of wide open campaign financing and PACs and that kind of stuff, man, it's like a big mystery of who and what and why people are throwing their money around." He hesitated and I could tell from his expression that he was still receptive but also noticeably nervous. "Okay, Linc, for the moment let's just say that I'm interested in hearing more. While I was lying in bed last night staring at the ceiling the biggest thing I wondered about was which office you were thinking of, like City Council or some County office or what." He left his comment hanging there in front of me like a piñata that I needed to hit and break open so the answer would spill all over him.

I straightened up in my chair, looked him in the eye and said in a very matter-of-fact way, "Gabe, we want to make you the next Governor of Arizona."

I studied Stark's face knowing that, despite his ego, the very word Governor probably had him wetting his pants or at the very least his armpits. He looked back at me but his eyes were blank, like he didn't even see me sitting in front of him and his brain was struggling to process my words. Finally he said, "Governor, oh my God, you've got to be kidding." Another pause and he said, "Governor, that's ridiculous. I'm not qualified for that."

"Why do you say that? I've done my research on you and I like what I see. You've been working in government for over eleven years, you deal every day with the people and help them solve their problems and you know how to handle yourself in a public setting. And you also seem to be great at thinking on your feet"

"Yeah, well thank you, but I deal with waste water. You know, sewers, flooded streets and small stuff like that, nothing big, nothing on the scale of what a Governor has to deal with."

So far everything Stark had said was following my script exactly. I fully expected him to be surprised and even shocked and I knew he would be skeptical of the idea to the nth degree. "Yes, but when you break it down you're really dealing with the same things as any office holder has to face; budgets, setting goals, management of staff, allocating time and energy to solve problems, getting stuff done, all of that." I leaned forward, trying hard to look serious and concerned. "Gabe, I know it sounds, well, preposterous, is that word too strong? But when my friends and I started talking about this whole thing, about the kind of person we needed, well, about you, we all agreed that we needed to shake things up, that real change won't happen unless we found a guy with no ties to party politics, to lobbyists and all of the usual bullshit that has infected our government. We knew we needed to find a candidate who could connect with the average guy, the guy in the office, the guy on the assembly line, hell, the guy in the trailer park." When I said that last part I hoped that I hadn't sounded condescending but Stark seemed to understand.

He sat there, staring at something over my right shoulder and I couldn't help but turn to see what it was. "See that picture there on top of the bookcase, the big one in the brass frame?" he asked. "That's my Dad and my Mom, John and Madelyn Stark." I turned and looked at the somewhat faded color photograph of a slender man in a 1970s-looking green, plaid leisure suit. The man bore a strong resemblance to Gomer Pyle and standing beside him a smiling woman with bright red-orange hair in an equally stylish yellow and green flowered dress. I had no clue how to respond so I just said, "Nice, happy looking couple."

"Dad always told me to reach for the stars and Mom used to tell me there was nothing I couldn't do once I put my mind to it." He showed a slight, almost wistful smile.

"That's great advice," I said. "So what do your Mom and Dad do?"

"Well, Dad drove a truck, mostly cross country stuff for almost thirty years. He's retired now but he's the head of the Owner's Association for the trailer park they live in. He works really hard for his neighbors. Mom, she's just a housewife but she was always active in things like the PTA when my brother and I were in school."

"Good, solid, hard-working folks," I replied. "You must be really proud." I immediately cautioned myself not to lay it on too thick or too soon.

"Yep, the best kind of people, the kind they don't make any more."

For just a few seconds I let his comment wait for a reply and then said, "Gabe, who in the hell is representing those kind of folks these days? Republicans cater to the rich people, the people of privilege and the Democrats are focused on protecting the unions and the whole freaking planet. But the little people, the people like your Mom and Dad and their neighbors in the trailer park and all the other average Arizonans who just get out of bed every morning and try to make their town and their neighborhood a better place to live, they get run over by the big money and the high rollers. They're invisible. They aren't important enough for politicians to even notice. It's time we changed that."

"This is just too much to think about all at once. I have a full-time job and a family to feed so I can't afford to just drop everything and go out on the campaign trail."

"We realize that and what we'd suggest is that you take a leave of absence, as long of a stretch as you can qualify for, and our campaign team will pay you the same amount you're making now, a check every week."

"Is that legal?"

"Well, it's sort of a gray area but we feel confident we're on solid ground with it. As long as we keep a low profile I'm sure we'll be okay." I was making it up as I went along.

Stark was nodding very slowly but he didn't say another word and I couldn't tell whether or not my little sales pitch had registered with him. Finally he said, "Okay, Linc, I hear what you're saying and I have to say that my mind is racing like crazy but let's just say for a minute that I decide to run. How do I get past all of the other candidates? I'm a registered Democrat like a lot of the other city workers are and most everybody else I know outside of work is a Republican. Politics is the favorite topic of conversation around the office and I already know from the City Hall buzz that there's going to be a long list of people trying to get on the ballot. How would we overcome that?"

Again, Stark seemed to be following my script almost as though he had rehearsed it. I was feeling a sense of power, of control over the situation and it felt good, but I knew I had to stay focused on the con and not on myself. "That'll be good for us. Let both parties throw up as many candidates as they want and it'll turn into a feeding frenzy. They'll all spend a bundle trying to muscle their way to the front of the line and when the dust settles the two guys still standing will have spent a boatload of their campaign funds and will limp into the general election scrounging for support. You won't have to go through that." I paused for a moment to let everything settle in to Stark's thoughts and then I said, "Gabe, I have spent my entire career in the media and advertising field. My job has always been to sell something, a product, a service and now, in your case a person, to people who need to know what's out there and can be of value to them."

"And you think I'm valuable to people, is that it?"

"Absolutely, and we also think the best approach for you is to run as an Independent. You'll be the new, fresh face, the new guy with a new approach and new ideas. The guy who they feel they can sit and have a beer with and talk about their problems. Screw the Scottsdale and Biltmore Republican crowd and screw the

Democrats who want to fix the world but not the people down the street. You'll be the populist, an independent voice that calls out to people who have been ignored and under-appreciated. There's a lot of anger out there and it's directed against both parties, and we'll tap into that anger and make it work in our, well, your favor." I stood up, turned and pointed at the photograph of his parents and said, "You'll be the candidate that cares about John and Madelyn and everyone in that trailer park." I was proud that I said that with a completely straight face.

"Okay, so I run as an Independent, with no party machinery to help me and any help I get will probably be from people with no experience in this sort of thing."

"Yeah, you're right to a point, Gabe and I know that sounds like a very big hill to climb. I can tell you that we would bring in some experienced people, people who have worked on successful campaigns in the past and they would make sure that everything and everyone gets pointed in the right direction. But just keep in mind that politics takes a lot of hard work and a lot of time. Nothing happens overnight. And I, we, want you to remember one thing most of all and that's how ever this race turns out, when it's all said and done Gabriel Stark won't be a political unknown. He'll be a familiar face that people will know and trust and if you decide to run for office again you'll have a base, people who'll help you and support you. You'll hit the ground running." I knew from the very beginning that that little bit of ego stroking was the key to convincing him to buy into my con and I hoped I had made my point.

Stark stared at the picture of his Dad and Mom and didn't say a word. His silence lasted long enough that I was starting to feel a little uncomfortable, like I might have overplayed my hand. Then he got up from behind his desk, slowly walked over to the bookcase and picked up the photograph. He held it tightly in his left hand and ran the fingers of his right hand over the smiling faces under the glass, staring at them with an expression that I couldn't quite read. Then he pressed the frame tightly against his chest, looked at me and said, "I need to talk with my wife and my kids about this first but, all things considered, I just have to say, "Let's do this."

We shook hands and a word suddenly popped into my head, a word that Wayne liked to use when he talked about the people in the trailer park, *gullible.* "That's great, Gabe, really great. Talk to your family and take some time because we want you to be sure about this. Once we start there will be no turning back. Think it over while I lay the groundwork for the ballot application and the petition work."

"I'll let you know for sure by tomorrow but I know that my family will be one hundred percent behind me."

I turned and pointed to the photograph of his smiling, polyester-clad parents and said in a very well-rehearsed tone, "Remember, Gabe, you're doing this, no, we are doing this for good folks like John and Madelyn.

16

A Brief Stop Back in the Real World

A trip along the entrance drive to the Arizona Biltmore Resort is like a trip back in time, a time of elegance and style. A time when creating a luxurious oasis in the hot Arizona climate seemed like an impossible feat. The genius of Frank Lloyd Wright and Albert Chase McArthur had created "The Jewel of the Desert" and its magnificent design had inspired Presidents, movie stars and people from around the world for eight decades. The long colonnade of towering palm trees interspersed with mounds of lush flowers led to the imposing building façade that looked like something out of an old movie. As many times as I had been there for conferences and dinners with Delilah, I still felt awe struck every time I visited the place. And now Delilah's involvement in the landscape re-design competition gave me another chance to savor its unique beauty.

I pulled up to the entrance portico and had no sooner stopped my car when a lanky, young man in the typical black and white parking valet outfit came to my door. "Good evening, sir." he said sounding somewhat out of breath, "Will you be dining with us this evening?"

"No, not tonight," I answered, wishing it were otherwise, "just a quick drink then home, so don't park me too deep."

"Got it. Have a nice time, sir."

The sun was just setting and a few lights had already come on under the large portico. The amber sunlight bathed the famously artistic concrete blocks of the building, highlighting their sculptural beauty and making the walk toward the tall, grand entrance doors even more special. As Delilah and I had planned, she was to meet me at seven o'clock when she got a break from her early evening photo session. I headed through the main lobby and turned toward The Wright Bar, possibly the most elegant lobby bar anywhere in the country. It was a warm, inviting atmosphere inside and the views outside to the courtyards were nothing short of spectacular. All in all it was hard to imagine a better place to drink and kill time.

I grabbed a stool at the corner of the bar, ordered a double shot of bourbon and settled in for a few minutes of people watching. It was easy to relax even though I felt a little guilty since I was there only because Delilah had to work on getting some night time photographs of the grounds. Her presentation to the Wright Foundation and Waldorf Properties ownership team would be a computer-generated, photo-realistic walk-through of the entire Biltmore property from sunrise, through sunset and into the night, complete with Terra Nueva's redesign concept fully envisioned and integrated into the video. The only good way to achieve that was to get video and still images of key areas as the day progressed into night. It had been a long, stressful couple of days for her and I was eager to help her unwind even if it would only be for a little while. And to make sure there was nothing else to add to her stress I had decided not to tell her about another heart rhythm episode I'd had earlier in the day.

My cellphone was sitting on the bar in front of me and it was less than a minute before the screen lit up and the text message signal rang. "On way see you in 5" was Delilah's shorthand text conversation style. Fifteen minutes went by, then twenty, then thirty and then I finally saw her walking down the lobby concourse toward me. Her laptop bag was slung over her shoulder along with her purse and she was carrying a stack of what looked to be large format magazines. She looked exhausted.

"Sorry, honey, I had a hell of a time breaking away from the meeting," she said as she leaned in to kiss me. "What a day. The next part is to get the shots in darkness and this guy is still quibbling over the shots we took at sunrise."

"Is this the high-priced videographer from Chicago, the one who claims to be the best in the business?"

"Yep, that's the one. He really does great work and has a great reputation but he's also a total asshole with an ego the size of Lake Michigan." When our server, a young woman with impossibly red hair, came over to the table to take Delilah's drink order I leaned back and gave her a moment to discuss the alcohol options.

When she was finished and was walking away I leaned over and quietly said, "You know, babe, you've been working twelve hour days for the last month and there's gotta' be some way that Mia or Tom or someone else from the office can fill in for you tonight."

"Believe me, I've been thinking that all day long but this last part of the shoot is the tough one. Besides Mr. Chicago Superstar I've got the lighting engineer on the clock, my computer rendering consultant plus a set designer with a crew of guys to move things around when we need to clean up the backgrounds or make the scene look better. And since I'm the one who signs their checks they insist that I'm there to okay every freaking little thing."

"Sounds like this competition is gonna' cost you a bundle."

"Yeah, it's really starting to add up but we have some amazing ideas and I think we have a real shot at winning the project." She paused while our server set her glass of white wine in front of her. When we were alone again she added, "And, honey, thanks to your generosity and good luck I can afford to pay all of those high priced people, and if everything goes as planned and Waldorf awards the work to us my new, little company will be on the map by the next day." Her pride and enthusiasm showed clearly through her fatigue.

I hoisted my almost-empty glass of bourbon and clinked it against her still full glass of wine. "Well, let's just hope there's still a little bit more good luck floating around us. Here's to Terra Nueva."

We spent about half an hour trying to relax and catch up with each other and talk about our revived efforts to look for a new house but it was next to impossible with the constant ringing and beeping of her smartphone. I tried hard to be the understanding husband but it wasn't easy to keep myself from complaining. Somehow I managed to restrict my actions to sighing and rolling my eyes. Finally, after at least a dozen electronic interruptions she sighed and said "Honey, I'm sorry but Chicago guy needs some direction and it has to come from me so I have to leave." She read my facial expression for what it was, frustration at the fact she was hardly ever with me lately except to grab five or six hours of sleep each night before leaving again for the office. "Come on," she said, her own frustration as obvious as mine, "you knew this competition was going to tie me up for a while."

"Yeah, I realize that but knowing it doesn't make it any easier to take."

She gathered up her computer bag and the rest of her load. "Honey, things will be back to normal in a couple of weeks, I promise. Maybe we can take a long weekend jaunt to Vegas or someplace, just kick back and catch our breath." I reached out and hugged her as best as I could with her armload of work paraphernalia between us. "I love you," she said, smiling.

"I love you too, Babe. Have a good shoot and knock em' dead. See you what, around ten or eleven?"

"Yeah, but probably closer to eleven. I'm just glad it's Friday so I can sleep in a little in the morning." She leaned in, we kissed and I watched her hurry back toward the main lobby exit. I was proud of her, her creative energy and how far she had come in so little time. Delilah was an artist in every way, with a sensitivity and vision that never ceased to amaze me. But I knew that winning the competition would be a double edged sword; instant national recognition that would undoubtedly lead to a huge workload that would increase exponentially over time. I couldn't help but feel the irony of the situation. My lottery winnings had made the good part of the situation possible and the bad part probably unavoidable. I remembered Jon Aiken's advice, to be prepared to be surprised. The money had created a situation where Delilah's ambition was given a chance to grow with almost no boundaries and I couldn't decide if I was surprised.

That Sunday when I first won the lottery all I could think about was maintaining control of myself and here I was watching my wife struggling to keep her own kind of control on things. It brought to mind again the symbol of the theater, the smiling mask beside the sad mask, the constant interplay of comedy and tragedy, of taking the good with the bad. My life had become one with some uncomfortable trade-offs and I just hoped those trade-offs would turn out to be worth it for both of us.

17

Baby Steps

Most people remember how they felt the first time they voted. Maybe it was the cold November weather or the long lines of people ahead of them. They might have remembered the day because the candidates were local people they knew and trusted. Or they might have felt the first little head-rush that can come from being a citizen actively engaged in the political process. For me it was a feeling of obligation to my college *Principles of Marketing* professor who had spent much of his time in class trying to convince me and my fellow seniors that choosing the right candidates would have a positive impact on the economy and that it was critical for us to show up at the polls. Had it not been for my deep respect for him I might not have bothered to vote that year. Somehow that first Election Day set a tone for how I felt about politics after that. When Ozzie and I sat in our apartment on election night watching the returns with our beer drinking friends I felt like I had crossed some kind of threshold into adulthood.

People remember things like that and they see all of the red, white and blue that candidates wrap themselves in. People see the signs, the bright lights and the perfectly choreographed movements of the people who run for office. What they don't see are all of the mind-numbing tasks and hard work that go into creating and operating a political campaign. I was only a few weeks into the Stark for Governor Campaign and I was already overwhelmed with the minutiae of it all. In a way the candidates have the easy part, the smiles and speeches and handshakes. But before any of that could happen for Gabriel Stark a very large machine had to be built around him.

It was clear that the time had come to deal with a situation that I had been avoiding for quite some time and I knew we couldn't move ahead with the con until I got things squared away at Carr Creative. Ozzie's desire to cut back on his time at the office had somehow turned into a situation much more like his retirement. All of the things that I had wondered about, mainly how the money would affect him, had pretty much played out right in front of me. My old friend was enjoying his renaissance as a man with a soul mate, a beard and a song in his heart. It was obvious that he had turned a page in his life's story, the next chapter was just beginning to be written, and being my partner at the office just wasn't going to continue as a part of the storyline. A guy who started out as a bearded, pot smoking student, garage band guitarist turned accountant had become a former accountant turned bearded, pot smoking guitarist looking for a band. As happy as I was for Oz I was feeling just as sorry for myself. Our lives had been so intertwined for so long it was almost as though we were dependent upon each other, and now he was breaking away to live a new life of his own. I comforted myself with the thought that he was just a late bloomer and that I got to share both parts of his life. But I also couldn't shake the feeling that my friend had baled out on me at a time when I really needed him.

To make things work at Carr Creative and to ensure that CONjunction and the con would endure, Ozzie and I met with Jon Aiken and arranged a plan for Wayne to buy out Oz as a full partner in the firm. When I presented the idea and the details to Wayne over a drink at Las Mesas I was afraid my big, rowdy friend was going to start crying right then and there. Tears welled up in his eyes, he looked me straight on and his voice trembled as he said, "Thanks, boss man, you are one fantastic and generous son of a bitch." Strange as it sounded, it was one of the nicest compliments I'd ever received. Delilah and I took Wayne to dinner at the Biltmore to celebrate and seal the deal and I felt as though Carr Creative and CONjunction had somehow strangely merged.

We put the formation of the campaign committee as our second priority. The first task was actually a two-pronged effort of filing our campaign financing plan and getting Gabriel Stark's name legally on the ballot. The financing part was the tricky one and the one that would be closely scrutinized during the entire election cycle. It was also the part that made me squirm when I first revealed my involvement in the campaign to Jon Aiken. He never said it in so many words but I could tell he was surprised and more than a little curious why I was so willing to spend my money on an obviously bad investment.

Ozzie and Jon helped me navigate the financial and legal waters and we decided to create a conventional PAC rather than a Super PAC because it didn't require that we have five hundred individual donors. This was going to be a somewhat clandestine operation despite its public nature. We named our PAC "Arizonans for Tomorrow," as vague and trite a name as we could come up with and one that didn't suggest any lofty goals or call attention to any one person or issue. The registered donors were Mr. Oswald John Hanson and Ms. Delilah Anne Samuels Carr. The PAC was our one concession to openness and transparency in campaign contributions.

Our other finance entity gave me chills and was the single-most questionable idea I had for the entire con but I had to keep my direct financing of the scheme totally under the radar. Without involving Jon and with the help of Jim McShane, an old lawyer friend in San Diego I formed a non-profit organization named *The Bright Future Group*. Who wouldn't love a name like that? We established a 501c4 with California as its legal home and Lincoln Alan Carr listed as its Executive Director and sole Board member. With the non-profit status we were not required to disclose other donors or reveal much about our expenditures. Dark money had become a shadowy part of most large political races in the country and I was sure that the Republicans and Democrats we'd be opposing were already working on their own plans to do the same thing. The trailer park had just gotten a whole lot dirtier.

The process for getting Stark on the ballot wasn't a challenge to my conscience but it had its own set of daunting issues. Because he would be running as an Independent there was no party machinery to assist him and no automatic registration rolls that guaranteed him a place on the ballot. To get ballot access we had to work on a county by county basis and get the valid signatures of three percent of the registered voters who weren't already registered with another party. Once our newly-created campaign committee was formed we could hire a firm to circulate voter petitions throughout the state and begin the arduous task of introducing Gabriel Stark to thousands and thousands of people who more than likely couldn't care less. It must take a whole lot of balls to knock on a stranger's door and tell him or her why they should sign the petition. It was almost as though I'd be giving those petitioners combat pay.

Between us, Wayne and I had put together what we felt would be a strong team of media and message people. Two of them were Carr Creative people and would have to split their time with CONjunction but the rest of them were people I'd found from talking to veterans of local campaigns and who had the campaign skills and savvy that we lacked. After several days of meetings the core team and expenses were established. Much to my relief Stark hadn't given us a long list of his family and friends to run things. That had been my biggest fear. Since his out of work brother wasn't interested in getting involved all Gabe asked for was that his out of work cousin, Albert, be given some position related to his experience with setting up sound systems for a local rock band. I couldn't help but think that this team would have a definite trailer park feel to it.

In the first two weeks of our efforts a ballot signature firm had been hired and was in full operation knocking on doors throughout the state. I was sure that those thick skinned people were encountering all kinds of negativity from people who didn't want a stranger standing on their front porch asking them to sign on with their support for another stranger. The process is a throwback to the early days of our democracy but somehow it still works and it did for us as well. After three arduous weeks Gabriel Stark got the number of signatures needed to make it to the ballot plus a comfortable margin of error. The petitions were filed, verified and registered with the Secretary of State's office and we received the official notification to proceed with our election activities. Our King of the Trailer Park scheme, whatever it would involve going forward, was finally legitimate, sort of.

The next few months were filled with completing the list of players and our campaign staff. With the help of a friend of a friend in the Legislature we found John Claridge, a recently retired old hand at running local campaigns in Arizona, to be Campaign Chairman and he quickly helped us put together the rest of the team. I made it clear to Claridge that CONjunction would have control of all media and that Ozzie would be in charge of every nickel that the campaign brought in or spent. He didn't question either condition and I got the impression he was just glad to be able to coast along and supplement his retirement income. When the team and all assignments were clear we began a series of planning meetings and strategy sessions. Both Wayne and I were surprised at how similar the process was to building campaigns for our Carr Creative clients. We were selling a product, albeit one we didn't know much about and we knew we probably wouldn't sell very many units. Part of me felt a little guilty for taking a man's identity and life so lightly but a bigger part of me enjoyed what the sales pitch could accomplish if we did it right.

The first meeting with the entire team was without a doubt the strangest business gathering I had ever been a part of. Besides assembling a large group of people, most of whom had never met each other, there was the undeniable feeling that nobody in the room actually believed what we were doing could be successful. Wayne and I were the only ones who knew the real mission; to grab a few percentage points of voters from the Republican to help elect the Democrat. We both knew if that little tidbit ever got out there would be no one who'd want to continue the campaign. In large part everyone was working for the fees the campaign committee was paying them and since I was the entire funding mechanism I knew I had to keep the team happy, at least as far as their wallets were concerned.

We had arranged the furniture in CONjunction's big, new conference room into separate areas where each individual team could gather together yet still be able to see and hear the other teams. The walls of the room were covered with large Arizona state maps depicting county-by county voter registration numbers, population breakdowns and even a breakdown of every major ethnic group. Thanks to Ben Autry's expertise we had an array of four large, flat-screen TVs on the front wall that would give us the ability to tie into the main local stations when needed as well as do video conferencing from anywhere in the state. And also on the front wall, flanking the TV array, were two identical poster-size portraits of a smiling Gabriel Reese. Despite his desire to buy new suits and ties I was able to convince him that his current look was more real and more appealing to our demographic. "Let the other guys look like Wall Street," I said, "you're going to be the candidate who looks like the voters." When I thought back to some of the people I'd seen at Sunset Estates mobile home park it dawned on me that I wasn't setting the bar very high for him.

John Claridge was the first to enter the room and the others trickled in over the next fifteen or twenty minutes, picking up their name badges and coffee while Wayne and I quietly talked in the far back corner of the room.

"You nervous, boss man?" Wayne asked. He seemed a bit distracted and less energetic than usual.

"Yeah, a little, maybe a lot. Before we can convince the voters of Arizona that we have a real, honest-to-God candidate we have to convince the people in this room and we have to do it with a straight face."

"I know what you mean, man, but we've been sellin' Jethro for so long we can probably do it in our sleep. It's like you always say, good advertisin' can sell a bad product so just stand up there and make your pitch." After a pause he added, "Hey, man, I need to let you in on a little somethin' and please keep it to yourself, okay?"

I studied his face and answered, "Sure thing, what's up?"

"Well, since Amy and I finally decided to pull the plug on the marriage there's no way we can stay under the same roof so I'm gonna' find a place for a while and she'll stay at the house until things get wrapped up legally."

"Have you talked to a lawyer yet?"

"Not yet. I was thinkin' of Jon Aiken if I can afford him."

You can afford him, believe me, I'll make sure of it. Give him a call and he'll do right by you. I know that first-hand."

"Okay, I'll call him from the car when this little bash is over."

The curiosity was killing me. "So where are you going to stay in the meantime?"

I saw what on anyone else's face would pass for sheepishness but I knew Wayne better than that. "Well, actually, I had a strange idea about that. I was thinkin' that if it's okay with you I'd stay at the trailer for a while. It's actually about the same distance from the office as my house but from another direction." He paused, grinned and added, "You know, from the other side of the tracks."

I couldn't have held back a smile if my life had depended on it. I nodded and said, "Man, I had a feeling you were trailer park material."

"So it's okay then?"

A sudden feeling, almost like big brotherly love came over me. Wayne didn't really work for me, he worked with me and he was as loyal and decent a friend as anyone I'd ever known. "Your damn right it's okay. Consider it your new home for as long as you want it."

Wayne's eyes glistened a little and I could tell that, despite his usual good humor he was hurting. "Thanks, boss man."

I pulled my key ring from my pocket and carefully slid off the key to the big, tan double-wide that would be Wayne's temporary home. "Here you go, and let me know if you need any help moving in your shit."

You'd actually help me move furniture?"

"Fuck no, but I'd help you find a cheap mover." He reached for my hand to shake but I didn't give him the chance. I wrapped my arms around my big, strapping friend and said, "Good luck, buddy."

We had no sooner finished our hug when John Claridge walked over and shook our hands. "Well, are we ready to launch this rocket?" he asked in a voice that sounded tired and burned out.

I smiled, looked at Wayne and answered, "Yep, we're ready at our end and we hope you're just as excited as we are about this thing."

"Yeah, John, Wayne added, "you're the political campaign expert here. We're countin' on you to steer things in the right direction while we do our thing on the media side." Probably because of his personal circumstances Wayne kept his usually ebullient demeanor in check but his wide grin was still telegraphing his sense of humor. I could only hope that Claridge would see it as honest enthusiasm for the campaign and not what it really was.

We were interrupted by a murmur of voices and some minor applause at the door into the room. Gubernatorial candidate Gabriel Stark had entered the building. He had taken my advice and switched to a white shirt that wouldn't show his armpit wetness quite as much as a colored shirt. I was hoping he wouldn't notice that we'd Photo Shopped his poster photo to give him a sprinkling of gray hair mixed into his cheesy drugstore reddish-brown hair dye. He was smiling broadly as he introduced himself to the mildly enthusiastic throng near the door and he finally worked his way over to us.

"Good morning, Linc, John, nice to see you." He turned toward Wayne. "We haven't met, I'm Gabe Stark, and you are?"

Wayne smiled, squeezed Stark's hand and said, "I'm Wayne Hartzell, a partner of Linc's and the guy who's gonna' make sure your name and face are plastered all over Arizona." It was an answer in true Wayne style. I couldn't help but notice that when their handshake ended Wayne subtly wiped his hand on his slacks.

I looked at Claridge and said, "Well, John, we should get things started."

"Let's go," he replied and gave a waving signal to his assistant, Annie, who then began to herd the crowd toward their respective tables. "Linc, this is your show today so how about you getting up there and kicking things off."

That was my plan all along but I let Claridge think I was taking his advice. "Sounds good, John." I walked up to the front of the room and stepped up on to the small riser we had installed so the person speaking could be seen from the back of the room. Most of the people had settled into their seats and I looked around the room while Stark's cousin Albert finished his tinkering with the sound system. Finally, when the din of voices had died down a bit I stepped to the microphone and said, "Welcome everyone." I had to stop with those two words because Cousin Albert had set the volume level of the system to a rock concert level and my voice practically shook the walls. I put my hand over the mike and said to Albert, "Hey, man, I think we need an adjustment here." Albert looked embarrassed as he knelt down and tweaked the controls of the main sound panel. "Sorry, man," he said, "it should be okay now."

Hoping that the settings were now correct for the room but still not totally confident in Albert's skills I leaned toward the mike and said quietly, "Welcome, everyone." The sound level seemed right and I nodded to Albert and then continued. "This is a big day for all of us and for the State of Arizona. I know we're all here because we share the same hope and vision, that we can make a difference and that we can bring about a break in the political gridlock that has handcuffed this state." I paused and looked at Stark. "I know we share the belief that the right man with the right plan can turn things around." I paused for what I expected to be dramatic effect and hopefully some validating applause but none came. I looked around the room for a few seconds and then said, "Ladies and gentlemen, we are here to launch the campaign of an Independent candidate, a candidate with no ties to an entrenched, unyielding political base, a candidate who knows the concerns of the average man and woman because he has walked in their shoes. He's a man who was raised to believe in the value of hard work and the love of community and family. A man who gets up every morning and goes to work to make his contribution to his neighbors and earn his way in life."

I paused again, looked around and noticed that I finally had the attention of everyone in the room. I glanced over at Wayne who was grinning and giving me a thumbs-up. It seemed like the time to drive it all home. "Ladies and gentlemen, we are here to give Gabriel Stark the opportunity to show the good people of Arizona that he is not tied to big corporations, that he does not rely on lobbyists to set his agenda and that he will listen to the people who need his help." With a brief dramatic pause that I learned in a college drama class I turned toward Stark and said, "Please help me in introducing the next Governor of Arizona, Mr. Gabriel Stark!"

The applause started slowly but built to a steady din as Stark walked to the podium and waved to the crowded room. Even though almost everyone in the place was a paid employee of the campaign, Stark's beaming smile made him look as though he was basking in sincere adulation. We shook hands as I stepped aside and let him have the limelight to himself. I studied his expression and saw what looked to be the face of a man who truly believed in the sham that was his campaign. For a brief moment I felt a twinge of guilt but fortunately it passed quickly when Stark began to speak. "Thank you, everyone, thank you so much for the warm welcome and thank you for coming here this morning."

I looked around the room and wondered what was going through the heads of the people sitting in the dim light. I wondered if they believed even a little bit in the man, in the campaign or were just grateful that for the next few months they would be receiving regular paychecks.

I watched and listened as Stark began his speech and I saw the same non-stop, never come up for air style I had seen in the videos of the Water Department meetings. He rambled on and on, veering in many directions on many topics and after about five minutes I saw the glazed eyes of the audience. When he glanced over at me I held up one finger as a signal to wrap things up and then made a mental note to talk with him about staying on point in future speeches. The voters in the trailer park would have to be spoken to in short simple bursts and Stark would have to learn how to do that.

There was more polite applause when Stark wrapped up his remarks and I stepped back up to the mike and suggested that everyone take a short break. John Claridge walked up to us and extended his hand to Gabe. "Nice work, nice work," he said almost convincingly. "You came across very natural and very sincere and that's what people want to see."

"Thanks, John," Stark replied with a grin, still seeming to believe the crowd adored him When two women approached him he turned away from us to talk to them and Claridge took it as a cue to pull away. He turned to me and tossed his head sideways, a signal that he wanted to talk with me in private.

We walked to the corner of the room farthest from the coffee and snacks and checked to make sure we were out of earshot of the crowd. Claridge took a quick glance to his left and right then looked straight at me and said, "Mr. Carr, Linc, I have to tell you this is going to be one fucking big hill to climb with this candidate."

I wasn't surprised at the comment or the frustration in his voice. I tried hard not to look at the prodigious crop of gray nose hair showing in both of his nostrils and answered, "Yeah, I know but I think it will be worth the effort. Stranger things have happened in politics."

"I agree. I've seen a lot in my day but this one feels different, more like it smells different." His expression and tone seemed more than skeptical, they were almost confrontational. "When you asked me to run this campaign I knew it was a longshot but I agreed because I've been away from things for a while and I missed the high you get from a good campaign. Now that I've been aboard for a while and had a chance to find out more about Stark I just have to be blunt with you." He paused, took a breath, looked from side to side and said, "This guy not only doesn't stand a snowball's chance in hell but he also might be the most embarrassing guy who ever ran for Governor of any state."

I fully expected that, sooner or later, Claridge would reach the conclusion that Stark wasn't even close to being Governor material, no one in his right mind would, but I'd been hoping he wouldn't get to that point until a bit closer to Election Day. "John, I know you have a lot more experience in politics than I do and that's why we sought you out for this campaign. Gabe is green as grass, I know that and so does everyone else in this room." Claridge had moved to a stiff, ramrod straight position, his arms folded across his expansive stomach. *Body Language 101* would tell anyone that he was taking the hard line posture of a non-believer. I took a deep breath and said, "You have to keep in mind that what led me into this campaign was what I've learned in the past few years about the people in this country and in particular this state. There has been so much research, so many studies trying to pinpoint what makes people tick in today's world. When you look at the statistics of who votes and why, the first thing you see is that it isn't these people."

Claridge's forehead wrinkled, his right eyebrow curled up and he asked, "What people, who are you talking about?"

"John, I'm talking about the huge segment of the population that every candidate writes off, the invisible people that nobody notices. I'm talking about the people who happily live their lives under the radar of the rest of the world." I could tell by Claridge's blank expression that he didn't get what I was saying. I glanced around and then leaned in and said, "I'm talking about what I refer to as the trailer park."

The expression on Claridge's face changed so quickly it caught me off guard. His eyes seemed as big as saucers and his jaw was dropped to the knot of his tie. "The what? Are you kidding me?"

I didn't want to go into too much detail or tell him how the trailer park had become an inside joke based upon an undeniable reality but I knew it was time to explain, at least partially, what was going on. "Well, maybe trailer park isn't exactly the right term to use but what I mean is we are going to reach out to the people who basically haven't been paying attention, the ones who get by day after day without noticing most of what's going on around them."

I had done my homework on John Claridge and I knew he was nobody's fool. When I first approached him about coming out of retirement to help with the campaign I knew two things for certain; one, he would relish the chance to get a paycheck to get back into the political arena and two, he would eventually see the Stark for Governor campaign as the farce it was. What I wasn't sure about was how he'd respond when that finally dawned on him. "John, you've been on successful campaigns and losing ones and you've done the post-election "Come to Jesus" analysis that tells you the "what and why" of the results." He was nodding but still looked strangely confused. "Look, you know as well as I do that in this fucking Red State there will be voters who'll pull the lever for anyone with a capital "R" beside their name and the same goes for the Democrats with a capital "D" in their column. There are Independents who'll hold their noses while they vote for the less awful candidate but what I want to do, or what we want to do is put up a candidate who they'll see as the "not an "R" or "D" guy and pull that lever accordingly."

Claridge had taken on a more relaxed posture and dropped his arms to his sides. He was looking at me with a very slight smile and said, "So you see Gabriel Stark as "none of the above," is that it? That's not exactly a resounding statement of support."

"Well I wouldn't put it in those exact terms but that's essentially the meaning. Gabe will be the guy who hasn't pissed off anyone and who hasn't made political enemies. If we craft the right image and the right message he'll be the candidate for all of those people who have dropped out of the election process."

"And that would be the people in the trailer park," Claridge said, spitting out the words as if they were obscene.

"Look, don't get too hung up on that term," I said, trying to get back to my point. "Just stay focused on the fact that there are a whole lot of people out there who'd vote for "none of the above" if it was on the ballot and we'll make them realize that in this election "none of the above" means Gabriel Stark."

Claridge seemed to nod in agreement even though he didn't look even close to being convinced. His expression and body language also seemed to say that he didn't totally understand or trust me. I knew I'd have to keep an eye on him, keep working on him and that there was a very good chance I would never make him a believer. He would be going through the campaign thinking he was trying to elect a governor and I'd be going through it trying to scratch for five or six or ten percent of the votes. It would be essential that he never found out that we had totally different goals.

The morning's events brought back a big handful of memories of things like my college drama classes, my experiences with practical jokes and all of the things I had studied about con men and their schemes. I was facing an enormous juggling act of propping up an inept, unqualified candidate, a savvy and suspicious campaign manager, a skeptical campaign staff and a state full of potential voters who, at this point, didn't really give a shit about this or any election. It was not exactly another day at the office.

18

And Now for a Short Break

Advertising has been called an "artful form of persuasion" and that is undoubtedly true in many cases. It might be beautiful photography, memorable music or an idea or image that just stays in your mind. That was what we always strived for at Carr Creative. But at the other end of the spectrum is real estate advertising and it's far from being artful. Several months of searching online and in the newspaper had driven home that point for me. I knew the process of creating good, compelling advertising but the people in the real estate profession obviously did not.

Over the previous few months Delilah and I had looked at hundreds of photos, read dozens of ads and had even done almost daily drive-bys looking for a new home. We both had reached the same conclusion; real estate people should not be allowed to write their own ads. I envisioned their process as being a roomful of latte-fueled agents, clad in yellow blazers, gathered around a large table and sharing a giant thesaurus as they wrote their copy. The stuff that made it to the ads was so adjective-heavy and pretentious it boggled the mind. As I sat in the driveway of the house we were interested in touring, waiting for both Delilah and the realtor, I pulled the two-page property description brochure from my folio and read through it again.

Simple facts, square footage and a few good photographs were all anyone really needed to see to get a good feel for a property but I was holding two pages of some of the worst drivel I had ever seen. The house "boasted" five bedrooms. Really, this house is boastful? And "the central staircase, with the sensuous curves of its railing leading to a master bedroom suite that offers romantic space and many seductive details" sounded like it belonged in a sinful getaway in Las Vegas. Maybe the worst phrase was the one describing the backyard, "You'll be the envy of your family and friends when they see the luxurious zero-edge pool, eclipsed only by the alluring call of the intimate, stone-trimmed spa." It sounded as though the house had a sex life of its own. Was I man enough to live here? Would this house just set up Delilah for disappointment in me? I crumbled the brochure and tossed it on to the passenger-side floor.

A few minutes went by and then the realtor pulled up in her white BMW and parked beside me. Delilah was late, which had unfortunately become a regular part of our routine over the last few months. Winning the Biltmore project had brought Terra Nueva huge recognition, both locally and nationally. Suddenly their office phones were ringing off the hook with requests to plan and design the landscaping for all kinds of projects. Delilah had to hire four more people just to meet the needs of the new clients and the calls continued to come in. I had known from the day I met her that she had enormous talent and that she just needed the chance to show people what she could do. Then along came that rainy Sunday and all of that money and all of that worry about how it might change our lives. With Ozzie missing in action with his guitar and his new love and Delilah buried in her new-found success it was getting easier for me to decide if those changes had been good or bad.

The realtor, who had told me on the phone that her name was Marnie, had walked to the front entrance portico and waited for me there. I texted a quick message to Delilah before I got out of my car and walked across the brick-pavered driveway to the sidewalk. I noticed Marnie was looking at my gently aged Explorer as it sat beside her seven hundred series Beamer and I had a hunch she was wondering if a guy who drove a nearly six year old car could afford a four and a half million dollar home. That kind of dichotomy had become a real source of amusement to me lately and I enjoyed knowing that people couldn't quite figure out how I could afford to do some of the things I had been doing.

"Hello, Mr. Carr, I'm Marnie Simon, we spoke on the phone." She was everything I'd expected and nothing more. Mid-fifties, straight hair cut short below her ears, yellow blazer, white blouse, black skirt and a practiced smile. She fit the realtor specification to a tee.

"Hi, Marnie, Lincoln Carr, please call me Linc," I said, as we shook hands. Before I could apologize for Delilah's tardiness my cellphone vibrated with a message from her. "Few minutes away get started sorry." I tucked my phone back into my pocket and said, "That was my wife. She's still a couple minutes out but said for us to start the tour."

Marnie turned and unlocked the tall, wood paneled front door and I followed her inside. The house was even more impressive in person than it was in the website photographs. Stone and hardwood floors, twelve foot high beamed ceilings, tall windows with muntin bars and dark metal frames, and the views from every one of them were amazing. It was the house's location on the side of a mountain overlooking Paradise Valley and Phoenix that first attracted us. The lot was an acre and a half and Delilah was excited about the planting possibilities. I was taken by the Santa Barbara style architecture. Between the two of us we thought we had found a house we could grow old in and, in a very real way, finally stop hiding the fact that we had a little bit of money.

I glanced around the place as Marnie delivered a rehearsed listing of the amenities. When we reached the large, central staircase I couldn't resist running my hand over the massive wood handrail and saying, "Geez, this thing is so sensuous." Marnie raised an eyebrow but said nothing.

We were standing in the large dining room when the front door opened and I heard Delilah call out, "Hello, Linc, Marnie?"

"In here, babe," I shouted. Delilah came around the corner, walked up and kissed me then smiled and said to Marnie, "I'm so sorry I'm late, things are so crazy at the office."

"It's fine," Marnie answered, "we really were just getting started.

It took us about half an hour to tour the two floors and talk about the history and details of the place. It had been built in 1997 by a hedge fund manager from Los Angeles who wanted to move his family out of the big city stress and congestion. A number of upgrades had been made in 2005 and the house was put on the market about six months ago when the owner died. It was obvious that the place had been well maintained and it was immaculate top to bottom. When we finally stepped out on to the patio Delilah said, "Oh, honey, this is so beautiful"

"It sure is," I said, and with a straight face I added, "We're going to be the envy of our family and friends." Delilah knew what I was doing and threw me a disapproving look. Marnie gave me the same raised eyebrow and I had a strange feeling she knew what I meant.

When Marnie's cellphone rang and she stopped to check the call Delilah leaned close to me and whispered, "Geez, honey, do you have to be such a dick?"

"I held my smile to just a slight grin and answered, "Sorry, I couldn't resist. I'll behave."

When we had finished the tour we gathered around the kitchen island and Marnie answered our questions about what we had seen. When we told her we liked the place but needed to go home and talk with each other she said, "And please talk to me about financing because I have some people who can get you a great rate."

I looked at Delilah, then turned to Marnie and said, "So do we."

Over dinner that evening Delilah and I made the decision to buy the house. Months earlier I had met with Jon Aiken and worked out a cash purchase plan for whatever house we decided to buy. That would cut way down on the waiting period for a move-in date. Now, after months and months of foot dragging and casual house shopping we suddenly felt the pressure of uprooting our life in our small, urban bungalow and moving to a home way larger than either of us had ever imagined owning. For so long we had been pretending that everything was normal, that we were living an ordinary middle class life and working hard to get ahead. Moving into a house that looked like it was built for a Hollywood star, that was perched on the side of a mountain with breathtaking views and that loudly screamed "affluence" would for once and for all announce the fact that Delilah and I had money and a lot of it. We were both prepared for some kind of fallout but neither of us knew exactly what it would be. After today it would take more than driving my old Explorer to fool people.

19

The Plot Thickens

Being part of any political campaign is a mix of excitement, hope and drudgery. We were three months into things and it was hard not to get high on the energy that constant advertising and public appearances create. Officially it was the Stark for Governor Campaign but within the campaign committee it was "Gabe for Guv" and to me it had always been and still was Operation King of the Trailer Park.

There was also a strange vibe to the campaign so far, like we were sitting on the sidelines watching the real campaign unfold beyond us. Since Gabriel Stark was an Independent candidate there was no need to run in the primary so we all got to sit back and watch the Republicans and Democrats beat the crap out of each other on the run-up to the primary. Now that the primary was over and the other faces in the race had been determined, the *Arizona Republic* editorial pages had been full of articles about the main party candidates with almost no meaningful conversation about Stark.

The Republican candidate was Mark Laughlin, a former Phoenix attorney and current second term member of the state legislature. He was well known, well financed and well connected. The Democratic candidate was John Leone, a former accountant, former state auditor and currently in his first term in the state senate. I had met John a few years back at a fundraiser for the Phoenix Art Museum and took an instant liking to him. He was the kind of man I wanted to see in the Governor's chair and I hoped my con would make that happen.

Knowing who Stark's competition would be helped us focus on the details of his campaign. Besides his new *Facebook* page and *Twitter* feed we had run just enough campaign ads on television and the newspaper to keep his name in play but it was obvious that not enough people seemed to be taking him seriously and that was something we'd have to overcome. We had also hired Carol McAdams, an experienced freelance editorial writer and Jared Toobin, a young, talented internet geek. Together they created and managed our campaign blog. We titled it *Stark Reality* and it was an ongoing masterpiece of native advertising; The two of them crafted slick commercials masquerading as news stories, all targeting, along with the trailer park, the millennials. We hoped they didn't realize that they were being stroked and manipulated. The blog was going to be critical to our tapping into potential young voters who hadn't yet committed to the same old party ideologies. It was more than likely a small number of voters but hopefully enough to get us the percentage points we were after.

I had been keeping a close watch on John Claridge. Even though he had worked on numerous campaigns during his career most of them had involved Republican candidates. In a red state like Arizona he had known his fair share of victories and I could tell that he was very uncomfortable with the lack of progress we were making on Stark's campaign in capturing the public's attention. Claridge was used to having an easy flow of campaign funds from people who voted Republican simply out of habit. I wondered how long it had been since he had actually had to craft a message or define clear positions to his crowd of older people who only cared about party loyalty and a political ideology that never seemed to change with the times.

Something else that made the strange vibe even stranger was the fact that Claridge had been focused on getting Stark's polling numbers up into the twenty-five to thirty percent range so it would be a competitive race among the final three candidates. While he'd been tearing out his hair trying to get the polling into double digits I'd been thinking about the five to ten percentage points that could send the Democrat to the Governor's mansion. Obviously it was something I couldn't reveal to Claridge or anyone on the committee. To them it was a campaign and to me it was a con and our goals couldn't have been more different.

I still met with my Carr Creative team every Monday morning just like I had been doing for years. There was a lot of curiosity about why the owner was never around the office but so far Wayne had managed to maintain control of the situation and nobody had asked any questions. When the main meeting was finished Wayne and I met privately to talk about the work CONjunction was doing for the campaign. So far the advertising side of the campaign was way ahead of the political side in getting Stark's name and face in front of the voters. But a name and a face don't necessarily add up to a message and that was by far our biggest struggle. Wayne and I had continually reminded each other that good advertising can sell a bad product but we knew it was time for Stark's message to be heard. The problem was he didn't yet have one.

Our weekly campaign staff meetings, held every Tuesday morning at 10:00 AM, had become increasingly awkward. John Claridge had been struggling to work with Stark to create a platform or at the very least a list of talking points that voters could relate to. Stark's lack of vision on things like tax policy and job growth had become glaringly clear and it had been painful sitting in on the discussions with the two of them. The looks that Claridge sent my way during those meetings seem to say "What the fuck were you thinking?" and "What did I get myself into?" Trying to look and act like a true believer in Stark was one of the hardest parts of the con and here, three months into it, I wasn't sure if my act would keep Claridge on board. He had been strangely aloof for over a month, even more than usual. I had a hunch the meeting we were about to sit down to could be a pivotal moment in the campaign and that I'd have to muster every ounce of bullshit I had in me.

When the entire team had settled into their chairs, coffee cups near at hand and iPads and laptops in front of them I said, "Okay, everyone, it's time to hit the accelerator and play catch-up to the big party guys. We have less than ten weeks to go and that might sound like a lot of time but it isn't." I turned toward Claridge and said, "John, I believe you have something you wanted to say to start things off."

Claridge had been scrolling through something on his laptop that I couldn't see from my position and whatever it was it seemed to upset him. He glanced at me over the top of his glasses and nodded. Then he looked down to the end of the table where Stark was seated, tilted back the screen of his laptop and sighed heavily. He stared at the screen for a moment and I couldn't help but wonder what was coming. Finally, he cleared his throat, looked straight at me and said, "Linc, I need you or Gabe or Wayne or somebody to tell me where the fuck this campaign is going." He seemed to immediately catch his slip of the tongue and looked around the table at the other members of the team. "Pardon my French, folks, but I am one very confused son of a bitch this morning."

I had an inkling of what Claridge was looking for and when I looked across the table at Wayne he nodded slightly and ran his hand over his beard. "John," I said, "that's a pretty broad request, how about focusing it a little."

"Well, to be blunt, I see a lot of time and money has been spent on media of all kinds, print, internet and television, and most of it has been spent in Districts One and Four where practically nobody lives. I have seen ads that seem to be, well, almost simple-minded, like they're talking down to the voters, like a bunch of print ads that look more like the covers of supermarket tabloids. I see a list here of planned speeches and "meet-the-candidate" events, none of which is planned to be held in an urban venue, just places out in the boondocks. And I also see, and this is what really troubles me, I see that Gabe has signed on for a candidate's roundtable in about three weeks and we still don't have one god-damned position statement in place."

He left that comment hanging in the air, leaned back in his chair and stared at me, waiting for a response with an expression on his face that seemed to say he had just drawn a line in the sand. I had known from the very beginning that it would be hard to fool Claridge for too long. He was kind of a hard-nosed personality who had too much experience working in the trenches to not know when something didn't smell right. I looked at Wayne again for no particular reason other than he was the only one at the table who was in on the con with me but he was looking down at his own iPad. I looked over at Stark and his blank expression told me that I'd be getting no input from him. I knew it was time for me to either duck, dodge or step over that line in the sand.

I did a quick scan of the faces around the table and saw the same blank expression on every one of them. It was obvious that Stark's lack of credentials had become clear to the people who'd been working every day to create a viable campaign for a not so viable candidate. I needed to buy myself a little time, even if it was just minutes, to come up with a response that would sound plausible. Claridge had been a concern from the beginning and I had known all along there was a chance he would just bolt and leave the campaign in the lurch. That was the biggest point of control I demanded and got when Jon Aiken helped me write Claridge's employment contract. There were nine other people at the table who probably felt the same way and I had to gamble on the fact their need for a paycheck would outweigh their obvious disregard for the candidate. I had the power of the money on my side and couldn't help but wonder if that would be enough to hold everything together. I took a breath, looked at Claridge and said "Okay, John, let's address your concerns. I'll get to the media spending and marketing plan in a minute because, as we agreed up front, that's my piece of this campaign. As far as the ads being simple-minded, you know exactly what we're trying here. Wayne and his team know how to find their way through the state's demographic breakdown and at least for now they have targeted the, shall we say, low information voter, the guy who we know isn't really paying attention."

Claridge was looking at his laptop screen during my comments and when I finished he again looked at me over the top of his glasses and said in his usual hoarse voice, "And from what I've seen in the ads there isn't much information being given to voters who you say need it."

"No, John, that's not what I'm saying. These people aren't low information voters because the information isn't available to them, they're low information voters because they're too lazy or distracted to go out and find it."

"Hey, man," Wayne interrupted, looking right at Claridge, "you gotta' remember what we're doing here. I know you've worked on like a bazillion campaigns but, with all due respect, you were workin' for fat-ass Republicans who don't like to venture outside of Scottsdale or Ahwatukee. If our ads look different or strange to you it's because they are different and hell, maybe strange too. Hell I sure hope so." Nearly everyone at the table was trying to stifle a smile and Wayne was on a roll. "My guys have worked on advertisin' for all kinds of shit and that has made us familiar, I mean very familiar, with the kind of people we want to introduce Gabe to." He turned and made a sort of saluting motion to Gabe and said, "Gabe, my man, we're tryin' to find you the folks who mean well but don't always take the time to, well, think. No disrespect intended but with you being brand new to politics and hell, let's be honest, green as grass, we need to grab on to the folks who are never gonna' make it to Scottsdale in a million years." Stark sat there with an expression that seemed to indicate he was trying to decide if he had just been insulted or praised.

It was all I could do to contain my glee over the way Wayne had seen the challenge that Claridge had laid before us and then proceeded to stuff it back in his face. Claridge's expression seemed to be a combination of anger and total confusion. The man was clearly out of his usual comfort zone. It seemed clear to me that the campaign had reached a point, maybe a breaking point as far as Claridge was concerned, and I had a feeling things were playing out to a logical conclusion. Despite my best efforts I had never been able to connect with the man on any level and something inside me knew it was time to draw my own line in the sand.

"Well, Mr. Hartzell, Wayne, thank you for that rather graphic explanation. I think I understand your point. I have to admit this campaign isn't like any campaign I have ever been involved with. I'm not the media expert in this group that much is true, so for now I'll defer to your experience and just wait to see what unfolds going forward."

I could tell that Claridge was completely rattled and it left me with mixed feelings. I knew that his experience was valuable to a group that had none but I also knew he had become a clear adversary and an obstacle to the con. Whatever this meeting would lead to I knew it was time for me to put Claridge into a box. "Okay," I said, trying hard to sound conciliatory when I wanted to go into full smack down mode, "Let's all just let the advertising message work its way through the process over the next few weeks." I waited a few seconds and then asked, "Now getting back to your original comments and to put things into similar terms as you made a few minutes ago, John, why the fuck haven't you helped Gabe come up with a platform?"

Claridge looked stunned, not expecting me to be so confrontational. This entire campaign, this con had been my creation and mine to control. If this pompous old man wanted to play hardball then it was time for me to throw him the pitch high and inside. I took a quick look around the table and the staff, to a person, shared Claridge's surprised look. Only Wayne showed the slightest sign of a smile. Stark seemed to be in a fog.

Claridge seemed flustered and hesitated for a moment before he answered,. "Well, that's an interesting question and the short and sweet answer is that Mr. Stark, Gabe, doesn't seem to have a clear personal or political position on anything related to this campaign. Tweeting an occasional comment on a Twitter account or having someone write things in a blog doesn't constitute a platform as far as I'm concerned."

It was hard to tell whether Claridge had hit the ball back to me or to Stark but it was obvious that he wasn't about to back down or accept any blame for the impasse. Stark was tugging at the knot of his tie and his face had turned red. I couldn't tell if it was from anger or embarrassment. It was obvious that this was a moment where I could lose control of the entire con or, for once and for all, get Claridge to realize that despite his years of experience he wasn't really in charge of one damned thing. I could feel my adrenaline kicking in and my heartbeat accelerating. "Okay, I can see this whole meeting is close to imploding on all of us," I said as calmly as possible, "and maybe we need to take a little break." I turned toward Claridge and said, "John, Gabe, let's go to my office and talk for a few minutes, okay?"

Claridge sat perfectly still for a moment, then slowly closed his laptop, stood up and answered, "Yes, let's do that."

I motioned to Wayne to join us and the four of us left the big room full of silent people. My office was right off the conference room and I hoped the adjoining door was heavy enough to buffer the sound of a conversation that had all the chances of being a loud one. I plopped down into my chair and laid my iPad on my desk while Wayne sat in one of the visitor chairs. Stark sat down in the chair beside him, Claridge laid his laptop on my desk but remained standing. I knew if he started to speak first the rest of us would be following his lead so I didn't give him the chance. "John," I said, "it's been obvious to me, probably to everyone in that room, that you haven't been happy with this campaign for a long time. Wayne and I have built ad campaigns and promotions for years and we're used to having people question our ideas so challenging us in front of the team, well, we can roll with it. But you sitting there and calling Gabe's abilities into question and that's something we can't have, no matter what. It's a morale killer that could doom this campaign."

Claridge stood there rigidly, his arms folded and his face showing his displeasure at my comments. I half expected Stark to jump in to defend himself but he sat there silently, staring at Claridge. Finally Claridge growled, "Look, when you hired me it was to take hold of this inexperienced bunch and turn it into something resembling a political campaign. I didn't question your thinking on the advertising even though now I think most of it has been bullshit aimed at people who, from what I can tell neither of the other candidates have been wasting their time on."

"You still don't get what we're trying to do here," I said, trying to keep my voice down to a controlled, professional level.

"What, you mean all that trailer park bullshit you've been spewing from day one? No, sorry, I don't get that. What I get is what I read in this morning's *Republic*, that Laughlin is holding the usual Republican lead at forty-two percent, Leone, like the Democrats usually do is trailing back at thirty-one, Gabe has a whopping three percent and the other twenty-four percent either don't know or don't care. Shit, three percent is just the "none of the above" vote. So given all that, how about enlightening me about what we or I should say you are trying to do here."

I didn't like Claridge's sarcastic tone and I also didn't like the fact he was standing while we sat. It was as though he was talking down to naughty children. Wayne must have felt it too because he stood up, turned toward Claridge and put his hands on his hips. He was twice the other man's size and I noticed Claridge lean back slightly. "Okay, John," Wayne began, "let me explain things to you one last time." He turned back toward Stark and said, "And, Gabe, if you want in on this, man, feel free to jump in." The smile on Stark's face couldn't have been more welcome. "So here's the deal," Wayne continued. "The key to this campaign is that Gabe is a new face, no old party baggage, no debts to pay back to rich supporters and none of the" party-first, people-second bullshit" that was probably part of every fuckin' campaign you ever worked on. To me, that's a really simple message that anyone includin' the folks in the trailer park can understand."

"Yeah, but," Claridge started, but Wayne cut him off. "Let me finish, man." One thing I had come to know about Wayne was that his trademark jovial nature could, when the situation called for it, give way to a no holds barred style of arguing his position. I sat and watched him work. "There is no fuckin' way that Gabe Stark's campaign is going to look, feel or smell like the ones the other guys are runnin' because flat out, Gabe isn't like the other guys."

Wayne had given Stark a pretty obvious opening and much to my relief Gabe finally joined the fray. "John," he said, more forcefully than I had expected, "from the first time you and I sat down and talked about my positions and my ideas I couldn't get a word in edgewise. You wanted me to be "Republican-light" because it was all you knew. I know we have to steal some votes from those guys but I can't do that simply by being one of them." It was obvious that, without him knowing it the message of the con had quietly seeped into Stark's thinking and it was just as obvious he had finally grown a pair of testicles.

Claridge looked more than angry, he looked desperate. "So tell me then, Mr. Stark, if being your own man is only worth three percentage points is this race really worth running?" The question was harsh, condescending and typical old-school politics. Stark wasn't prepared for it and was clearly rattled. Maybe his newly found testicles still needed to grow a bit more.

I stood up, leaned toward Claridge and snarled, "You're god-damned right it's worth it."

It was clear to me that the conversation had reached the point of no return. Claridge looked at Stark, then at Wayne and then turned to me and asked, "Can we speak in private?"

Wayne turned to Stark and said, "Hey, man, let's go grab some of Linc's expensive coffee in the other room." The two of them left and closed the door behind them.

Claridge didn't wait one second to comment. "Alright, that's it. I knew this whole campaign smelled funny from the start and god-dammit I want out."

When the idea for the con had first popped into my head I had felt like an actor playing a part in a very strange play and this moment brought that home to me more vividly than anything that had happened so far. I looked at Claridge and said, "Then it's out you shall be."

The silence in the room lingered for a moment and only added to the tension. Claridge looked surprised, as though he expected me to beg him to stay with the campaign and he seemed to be struggling to make a response. "So that's it then?" he asked weakly.

"Yep, that's it. I thank you for all of your help getting us to this point but we will somehow manage to keep things moving forward." I made sure to keep any kind of emotion from my voice and maintained a straight, stoic expression on my face.

In what seemed like an attempt to cling to whatever bargaining position he thought he still might have, Claridge said, "You know this kind of thing, a campaign manager leaving in the middle of a campaign, well it's the kind of thing that can sink the whole damned effort."

Still presenting a totally emotionless demeanor I answered, "That might have been the way it worked for you in the past, John, but let me remind you of the terms of your employment with *Stark for Governor*. Upon leaving your position for whatever reason, all fees, salary and reimbursable expenses owed to you will be held by the committee until ninety days after the election. I don't know how comfortable your retirement has been but I'm guessing the high five figure amount we will owe you will turn out to be very valuable to your future situation." I paused and then added, "And remember that if there is any indication that you have shared information about the campaign or made derogatory or damaging remarks, whatever they might be, all moneys owed will be held and you will be forced to seek them in court."

Claridge looked like a beaten man. I had called his bluff and there was nothing for him to do but walk out the door. He picked up his laptop and when he turned toward me I did what I thought was the gentlemanly thing and extended my right hand. It was a very brief and awkward handshake and then he turned and walked out the door. A moment later Wayne and Stark walked back into the room and sat down. Stark was wearing a surprisingly relaxed expression and Wayne was looking at me as though he was waiting for the punchline of a joke. "Well, guys," I said, looks like it's all up to us now."

Wayne turned to face Stark and leaned toward him. "You ready, my man?"

Stark nodded. "Yeah, I guess so, but I sure didn't think something like this would happen when I signed on. It's kind of, oh I don't know, scary almost."

"Don't worry," I said, addressing his nervousness. "We have things moving in the right direction and I have a feeling things are going to run a lot smoother from now on." I looked at him and added, "And a whole lot of the smoother part is going to have to come from you, Gabe. This roundtable is a really big deal and it will be our chance, make that your chance to show the people what you're made of." The words were a challenge to Stark and a reminder to me of the huge task that lay ahead of us, namely strengthening his very weak personal sales pitch. As glad as I was that Claridge was gone I knew that his frustration with Stark had been legitimate.

"Okay, boss," Wayne interrupted, "there's a room full of people in there squirmin' in their chairs and dying to know what's goin' on in here. How do you want to handle it?"

As much as I wanted to maintain my tight grip on the situation I knew the best way to settle the nerves of the staff was to show that Stark and the campaign wouldn't be damaged by Claridge's departure. "Gabe," I said, "it seems like this is your moment."

"Stark looked at me, swallowed hard and said, "Well, okay."

Despite his perspiration-inducing nervousness Stark managed to do a fairly good job of announcing the news about Claridge. He even told Annie Kolchik, who had been Claridge's assistant on the campaign, that he wanted her to stay on and help him out. When I leaned over and assured her it would mean an upward bump in her salary she was all smiles and told the group she was looking forward to the challenge.

The next week and a half were the most intense since the beginning of the con and the campaign. Wayne and the media crew ramped up the frequency of television ads and created a number of new postings on Stark's *Facebook* page. *Stark Reality* also increased the number of its postings and even though I knew what was going on I had to struggle to separate the commercial from the news content. Annie and I spent hours and hours working with Gabe to define his positions on everything from taxes to immigration to education. At times he seemed overwhelmed with all of the things he had to know and memorize but after one particularly intense session he leaned back in his chair and said, "You know, I think I can do this." I hoped he was talking about the roundtable and not being the Governor.

When there were just two days to go before the big night I gathered Wayne and Ozzie at the new house for an update on the spending we'd been doing. Even though Delilah and I had been moved in and settled for a couple of months it was the first time either of the guys had been to our big house on the side of a big mountain. I felt very sheepish when they walked through the front door together, wondering what they were thinking about my owning a home that looked like it belonged to a rock star instead of an ad man. Wayne put an end to my concern the moment I opened the front door. He looked up, down and all around and asked, "Holy shit, boss man, will you adopt me?"

I started to laugh and Ozzie added, "Yeah, me too, you can tell people I'm Wayne's little brother."

I was glad that Delilah was home for the gathering and after hugs and handshakes we filled our glasses and did a quick tour of the house and grounds. It felt good to have us all together again. Ozzie had been spending a lot of time in Nashville working with a songwriter and a studio band and with his now shoulder length hair and full beard he looked more like my old college buddy than my former business partner. Delilah was more relaxed than I'd seen her in months and was back to being my beautiful, Bohemian wife and friend. And Wayne, well he was Wayne.

We decided to have our meeting on the patio even though it was almost dark and I knew the lights of the Valley spread out below us would be a distraction. Between the efforts of Delilah and the people at *Whole Foods* there were plenty of small and tasty things to eat. I knew that with the view, the wine and the usual chemistry of our group it would be a bit of a struggle to stay focused on the matters at hand.

To no one's surprise Wayne started things off. "Hey, man," he said to me, "I hope you're enjoying your new home as much as I'm enjoying mine."

It was an odd thing to say, and Delilah replied, "So I take it you're not still living in the trailer."

Wayne grinned and said, "Oh, I'm still in the trailer and I'm enjoying the hell out of it."

Suddenly it felt like a mile-wide chasm had opened up between Wayne and me with my big house and his little, rented trailer sitting on opposite sides. "Geez," I stammered, "I thought that was just a temporary thing for you."

"Well, it was and is just a short term deal as far as I'm concerned. The divorce is all wrapped up and I'll be looking for a place to buy just as soon as the election is over but for now I gotta admit I've sort of blended in with the locals."

"So what does that mean?" Oz joked, "Are you putting down roots among the trailers?"

Wayne hesitated and then answered, "Not exactly, let's just say that I made a new friend, a lady friend, and she's been makin' it a lot easier for me to adapt to life in the trailer park."

Ozzie crowed, "You old dog, it didn't take you long to get back in the hunt, did it?"

Before Wayne could answer him, Delilah said, "Well, good for you, Wayne, tell us about her."

It was obvious that part of Wayne wanted to fill us in on the details of his new romance while another part was nervous about facing the jokes and teasing. "Okay," he said, I won't bore you with the whole damn story." One by one he looked at all three of us and then stood up and fished his cellphone from his pocket. He touched the screen and opened a bunch of selfies he had taken and handed the phone to Delilah before he continued. "Her name is Luanne, she's divorced too and she's really cool. And I think you all know how much I like redheads, just like you do, Oz. We both like Country music, Mexican food and dogs and let's face it, that's a hell of a lot more than some couples have."

Delilah was scrolling through the photographs on Wayne's phone and she said, "Oh, Wayne, she's really pretty. You guys look like you're having a lot of fun together." She handed the phone to

Ozzie and added, "So I guess Linc's renting the trailer turned out to be a good thing."

"Yeah, maybe," Oz interrupted, "but we've been expensing that trailer as a satellite campaign headquarters and now you turned it into a damn love nest. We might be on thin ice here with the auditors." His smirk made it clear that he was just kidding and Wayne seemed relieved that his little secret was out in the open.

"When do we get to meet her," I asked.

"Well, I was thinkin' of bringin' her to the candidate's roundtable, you know, just so Gabe has a few warm bodies in the seats."

"That sounds fine with me," I said, "but I have to ask, is she okay with our whole trailer park thing? I don't want her to feel offended by the things we're saying and doing here."

"Oh don't worry about Luanne, she's cool with things. When she first got wind of what we were doin' with the campaign she got her back up at first but I filled her in and now she totally gets what's goin' on.'"

"Great," Ozzie chimed in," and I don't want to break the mood here but since it was me that brought up the subject of the auditors I think we better get started on our little financial review. I only have about an hour before I have to pick up Michelle at the airport and I have to file our expenditures report by the end of the day on Friday."

I agree," I said, feeling glad that my friend the wandering musician was, at least for a while, back to being my friend the accountant.

Delilah went back into the house and Ozzie, Wayne and I went over the draft report that Oz had prepared. When Wayne got up to use the bathroom Oz took advantage of the opportunity to tell me about the finances and what the con had cost me so far. He leaned forward and said quietly, "Well, my friend, so far you have spent, or should I say the *Bright Future Group* has spent nearly five hundred thousand dollars and Gabe is still stuck at three percent. It's gotta be up to you to decide if it's worth it. And that doesn't even include the cost of the upcoming roundtable."

Well," I answered, "I'd be lying if I said I wasn't disappointed. A half a million is a lot of dough but at least the cost of the roundtable will be split equally among the candidates. Calendarwise we still have a ways to go."

"Yeah, a long way to go and a short time to get there," Oz answered. "We have about a month to add another six or eight percent to Gabe's numbers. Judging by the poll numbers I saw yesterday Leone is going to need to have at least that amount taken away from Laughlin."

I knew Oz was right and for the first time since the con started I was getting nervous about the chances for success. When Wayne came back into the room I quickly changed the subject and asked him, "Any ideas on what we can do with the advertising that we aren't already doing?"

"That's a good question," he said, as he plopped on to the sofa and reached for his glass of beer. "The TV spots have just been introductory stuff so far but after this damn roundtable we're gonna' have to get specific about shit. People are gonna' want to know what the guy stands for."

"Yeah, don't we all?" Oz said in a tone dripping with sarcasm.

"We've done everything we can to get him ready for Wednesday night," I said. "He's as prepared as we can make him. Now all we can do is turn him loose and hold our breath." They weren't exactly words that instilled confidence in Oz and Wayne but it was all I could come up with. Holding our breath seemed to be our new strategy and it was anybody's guess when we'd all be able to exhale.

20

Maybe There is a God

Standing on the stage of an auditorium that seats nearly two-thousand people is more than a little intimidating even when you're not the person who has to speak to the crowd. A cavernous space full of lighting gantries, speaker arrays and recording equipment seems to demand that everything that happens there must be important and well done. With the house lights up I could see that most of the seats were already filled and I couldn't help but wonder if at least three percent of them were filled with Stark supporters. This roundtable discussion would be Gabe's only opportunity to present himself and his ideas in a format that was live and not carefully staged and controlled by friendly faces the way his advertising had been.

Workers representing all three campaigns were scurrying around making last minute checks on everything from the angle of the lights to making sure there was a bottle of water at every podium, and when I saw them leave the stage I knew that I had to as well. The three candidate's podiums were arranged in an arc along the right side of the stage and the moderator's desk was placed on the left, angled to face both the candidates and the crowd. Stark was standing at the center podium and I shook hands with him, wished him luck. As I walked off stage to find a place where I could watch everything from the darkness I nodded and smiled at John Leone. He was already standing behind his podium on the left side of the array looking through his notes. Moments later Mark Laughlin and one of his aides walked on to the stage and as they reached the right side podium I heard Laughlin say to the aide, "So that's Leone's deal and the only people Stark has are trailer trash."

The reason I heard what he said, along with every person in the auditorium and in the media booth, was because the microphones were all live and cranked way up in volume. I knew immediately that once again Cousin Albert must have had a hand in the sound system set-up. The shock and embarrassment on Laughlin's face were matched only be the same expression on Stark's. Leone had turned to stare at Laughlin and the buzz that ran through the audience quickly turned to a ruckus. Laughlin's aide put his hand over their mike and angrily shouted at someone off stage. A moment later Cousin Albert trotted out and went from mike to mike, making volume adjustments at each one. While he worked at Laughlin's podium the aide, still covering the mike, seemed to be cursing at Albert who seemed to be cursing right back at him. It was a bizarre start to what was expected to be a night of intelligent political discourse.

David Miranda, an editorial writer for the *Arizona Republic* and moderator of the evening's discussion, hurried on to the stage went from podium to podium, each time covering the microphone with his hand. I couldn't tell what he was saying to the candidates but he seemed to be speaking loudly to be heard over the noise from the audience. His stop at John Leone's podium was brief and Leone just seemed to be listening and nodding. When he got to Stark's podium the conversation lasted longer. Gabe was red faced although I couldn't tell if it was from anger or embarrassment, and as usual he was glistening from perspiration When Miranda finally got to Laughlin the aide had left the stage and Miranda seemed to be lecturing Laughlin, or maybe scolding him. Whatever was being said Laughlin was nodding contritely.

Finally, Miranda walked over to his desk, sat down and pulled the microphone close to his face. He looked down at his notes and then out at the crowd and said, "Ladies and gentlemen, we'd like to get things started." His face showed his frustration with the still-rowdy crowd. "Ladies and gentlemen, please, let's quiet down, please." It took a few minutes before the crowd finally settled into their seats and seemed ready for the event to begin although the huge room was still far from silent. "Alright, I'd like to thank you all for coming tonight for the first and only Candidate's Roundtable for this year's gubernatorial election. This will be your chance to hear from all three candidates and to learn where each of them stands on the important issues you care about and the issues affecting our state."

After introducing each of the candidates Miranda started in on the list of prepared questions, all of which had been approved by the three campaigns and the *Arizona Republic* editorial board. In addition to answering the questions each candidate would have a chance to make a three minute long statement at the end of the roundtable. That was the portion of the event that had me the most concerned.

For the next forty-five minutes Miranda asked each candidate the same list of questions. Laughlin's demeanor was almost cocky and his answers were right out of the same old Republican playbook of lower taxes, fewer regulations and smaller government. Whenever he spoke there was a murmur in the audience that at times delayed his ability to answer. Leone's answers were just as predictable but definitely more in line with my own thinking, with calls for an improved school system, job creation programs and sensible tax reform. His words were a reminder to me that it was his election I was really working for and not Stark's, and that I was willingly working both sides of the fence to make it happen.

Gabe did an adequate but underwhelming job of handling the questions. As in the case of Laughlin, when he was called upon to answer a question the crowd noise often slowed his response but to his credit he managed to maintain his composure. If Laughlin's "trailer trash" comment had rattled Gabe it didn't show while he was responding to Miranda's questions. The glare of the overhead lights accentuating the shine on his face was the only major negative for me and I hoped it wasn't a big deal for the people watching him.

Miranda did an excellent job of controlling the clock but he had a little more trouble when it came to maintaining control of the audience. Since the questions had been prepared in advance he couldn't change their wording, so when he asked the candidates a question that included terms like "average Arizonan" or "first-time homebuyers" a handful of people in the audience would respond with raucous shouts or applause. When Miranda presented a question that mentioned the fact Arizona schools were "trailing" the rest of the country someone shouted, "We're trailers!" It was obvious that Laughlin's crude remark had made an impact on the crowd.

Leone was the last to present his closing statement and when he had finished Miranda thanked the candidates and the audience, the house lights went up and the still animated crowd began its slow crawl toward the exits. As I walked toward Stark I saw the candidates exchanging insincere smiles and handshakes and when Gabe grasped Laughlin's hand I was glad he had his perspiration problem. I was just coming within earshot when I heard Laughlin say, "… and that wasn't meant to insult you." I stopped a few feet away and Stark asked him, "Then who was it meant to insult?" Yep, Gabe had definitely grown a pair.

The next morning, I got up earlier than usual so I'd have time to read the *Republic's* report on the roundtable as well as flip through the news on the local television stations. There was plenty of news about the candidate's individual comments but the dominant story was Mark Laughlin's mean and sarcastic trailer trash remark. It was being called everything from insulting to deplorable to vicious. Laughlin's handlers had issued a statement to the press saying that "Mr. Laughlin misspoke and his comment wasn't meant to offend anyone." It was the same old politician ass-covering. I never understood how lies, insults and slander could be so easily dismissed with the word *misspoke*.

Stark seemed to be out in front of events. Less than an hour after the roundtable he had tweeted "#StarkforGovernor, "Couldn't believe my ears at the event tonight. Didn't know a candidate could think so little of Arizona voters. Calling them trash, disgusting." His *Facebook* page showed a list of friend comments too long to read and they ranged in tone from irritation to outrage. The campaign committee had already scheduled a meeting for 10:00 AM to follow up on the roundtable event and whatever agenda I had anticipated had flown out the window after Laughlin made his arrogant comment.

"You're up early," I heard from behind me and before I could turn around Delilah's arms encircled me. She bent down and kissed the back of my neck and asked, "So is the media as upset as you were when you got home last night?"

"Yeah, from what I've seen so far Laughlin really stepped in it and he's going to have a tough time cleaning his shoes."

"What do you think is going to happen, can he explain it all away?"

"Oh, I'm sure he'll try. They're already using the old "he misspoke" bullshit but I have a feeling this one is going to be a real problem for him."

Delilah leaned back against the kitchen counter, looking right at me with a bemused expression.

"What?" I asked.

She shook her head, still smiling. "Oh come on, honey, I can't believe the irony of this whole thing escapes you." I didn't immediately respond and she said, "You created the whole trailer park ad concept. You identified these people, studied them, dissected them and catered to them. They made you curious, they pissed you off, you laughed at them and they totally got under your skin. This whole con of yours required their involvement and now this Republican asshole has unknowingly called you out."

"What do you mean, he called me out?"

"I mean this campaign you and Wayne have created hasn't exactly been flying under the radar. It's pretty strange and even if Gabe Stark isn't bright enough to see what's really going on Laughlin and his cronies seem to be sniffing around the edges of it. When he let his nasty little comment slip out it was proof that he knows those people are out there, that you're going after them and he doesn't think they amount to much. He said it out loud and in public and if I was working on Stark's campaign I'd say you can't just let Laughlin's words pass. You have to respond somehow."

Once again Delilah saw things through the fog and helped me see them too. When Laughlin stood by that microphone and spoke the words "trailer trash" he told the entire state of Arizona that Gabriel Stark, for some reason, appealed to a part of the population that everyone else dismissed. From now on, all the way to Election Day, Stark would be linked to Jethro and his trailer park pals. From the very beginning of the con I had figured we'd need about five or ten percent of the vote to hurt Laughlin and help Leone, and the under-achieving, distracted denizens of the trailer park would be our means to that end. And now one of our opponents seemed to say that he was on to us and our little scheme and that troubled me.

I took a moment to absorb what Delilah had said and then answered, "Babe, you're right, "you're absolutely right. Judging by what I've been reading and watching this morning this is the biggest news in the State and we have to figure out what it all means and how we can use it. We have a meeting at ten o'clock so I guess I better get to thinking about some kind of magic answer to Laughlin's snarky slip of the tongue."

Delilah hugged me again and said. "Remember, honey, your cons are like your children and you always seem to know what they need when there's a problem."

I tilted my head back and we kissed. "Yeah, and this one just gave Daddy a major pain in the ass."

I skipped breakfast, hurried through my shower, gave Delilah a less than lingering goodbye kiss and headed downtown. When I pulled into my parking space at the CONjunction offices half an hour earlier than normal I was surprised to see that I wasn't the first to arrive. Wayne's car was there along with four other cars whose owners I had never bothered to determine. The lights in the lobby were still on the nighttime setting but the corridor and offices were lit up like a normal workday and I could hear voices coming from the conference room. I walked down the hallway and pulled open the door to find Wayne and his creative team, along with Annie Kolchik, gathered at the conference table. The morning newspaper and piles of notes were spread across the table, a taped replay of the roundtable was beaming from the large flat screen TV on the wall and two smaller sets were showing the morning news reports from *Channel 12* and *Channel 15*.

As I stood in the doorway taking in the scene, Wayne looked up and bellowed, "Hey, boss man, welcome to the party!"

"Wow, I'm impressed by your dusk to dawn work ethic." I answered, "What's going on?"

"Well, I looked for you last night after the thing was over and I couldn't find you so on the way home I called everyone and told them to be here early 'cause we had a lot of work to do. Gabe called me a few minutes ago and said he's comin' but he's gonna be a little late."

I laid my laptop bag on the table and walked over to Wayne. "Okay, bring me up to speed."

He fidgeted with a remote control to turn down the volume on all of the screens and then said, "Well, man, I don't have to tell you what happened last night. Luanne and I were sittin' right in the middle of things when that asshole Laughlin said what he said. I was surprised, hell, I was shocked, but Luanne, man, she was pissed! There I was, sittin' next to a woman I'm hopin' will understand and approve of what the fuck I do for a livin' so I bring her to this event that I helped put together and this idiot Laughlin gets up there and calls her trailer trash. I was like, "What the fuck, man?""

It was interesting to see Wayne be so wound up so early in the morning and judging from the noise level of the rest of the team he had already gotten them wound up just as tightly. He turned and tapped Jeremy Kyle on the shoulder. "Hey J-man, tell Linc your idea." Wayne looked at me with a huge grin and said, "Remember when I told you that Jeremy knows Jethro better than I do? Well, listen to his idea."

Despite what Jeremy lacked in years I had always thought he had a very old soul. His ideas seemed to come from the deep reservoir of a stranger, much older person and when he turned and stood up in front of me I found myself almost holding my breath. "Hey, Linc, good morning," he said, looking like he had just gotten out of bed.

"Okay, you guys," Wayne shouted, "listen up. Jeremy came up with somethin' you all gotta hear."

The group of five people, Annie Kolchik in particular, quickly turned toward us, silent and looking like they all needed someone to guide them out of the confusion of the morning's headlines.

"Okay, Jeremy," Wayne said, "tell the folks your idea."

The tall, skinny young man with the shoulder length blonde hair and the perpetual distant look in his blue eyes took a deep breath and said, "Hey, guys, I don't know if this idea of mine will mean anything to the campaign but here it is." He turned to look at me and then at Wayne, who was grinning from ear to ear. "So, last night this Laughlin guy walks out on the stage and he says that Gabe has the trailer trash vote, and I'm thinking, yeah, so what the fuck else is new? But then I get to thinking, yeah, he's got the trailer people and this guy thinks that's nothing but then I think, fuck you, man, the trailer park rules! I mean, we all know these people have been kind of sitting on the sidelines but then I'm thinking, wait, man, what if we come up with something that says, "Yeah, we live in the trailer park, and fuck you!"

I watched Jeremy's quiet, rambling message quickly turn into a rant and despite his colorful choice of words I liked where it was going.

"So this guy, Laughlin, thinks the people in the trailer park are trash, and I say, "Fuck you, Laughlin, we might be trash to you but we still vote and guess what, we aren't voting for an asshole like you!"

Wayne was standing there with his arms folded, smiling broadly and looking like he was giving approval to a son who was struggling through a rite of passage. He looked at me and I gave him a thumbs-up. Jeremy had momentarily stopped his little speech, the group was standing there with a collective look of astonishment, and I asked, "So Jeremy, where do you see this thing going?"

The young man who had just offered what was probably his first original advertising concept looked at me, then the group and said, "Okay, picture billboards, picture bumper stickers, picture fucking TV and internet ads and they all say, "I'm trash, and I vote." With that, Jeremy tapped a few keys on his laptop and a large image appeared on the projection screen. It was Wayne standing at the door to his temporary home in the trailer park. His arms were folded across his chest and he had a proud and defiant look on his face. Under the photo were the words, "I'm Wayne, I'm trash and I vote."

The silence in the room was deafening. The team members were looking at each other and no one seemed to know how to respond. The concept was so off-the-wall, so different from any kind of political ads anyone had ever produced before I figured they didn't know if it was a real idea or another one of Wayne's outlandish ideas.

I remembered what Delilah had said to me over breakfast and this bizarre ad idea seemed to echo her words perfectly. It was a direct, in-your-face response to Laughlin and his snotty Republican handlers. The group was still silent and I looked over at Annie and asked, "Annie, you're the campaign manager. What do you think?"

She sat rigidly in her chair as if she couldn't move, looking at me through her round, red-framed glasses with an expression that was nothing less than panic. "I, I don't know what to say. It's like, what, that we're saying we're all trash?"

"No, Annie," Wayne interrupted, "it's not that, not exactly. It's all a big, tongue in cheek, sarcastic answer to Laughlin. What we're sayin is, "Hey, man, if you think Gabe's people are trash then you're not only disprespectin' Gabe but you're also disrespectin' a hell of a lot of good people and we're not gonna' let you get away with that."

Annie nodded but the uncertainty and panic on her face were still obvious. "Maybe," she said softly, "maybe we should see what Gabe thinks first."

I felt like I needed to step in and get a grip on things so I stood up, looked around the table and said, "Look, folks, this trailer trash comment is the hottest topic in the local news and we all know it will only last a short time before the next hot topic comes along and knocks it off the front page. Whatever we do, whether it's this idea or something else, we have to get it up and running today. I repeat, today!"

I had no sooner finished speaking when Stark finally walked through the door. He looked as though he hadn't slept all night and he seemed nervous and confused. "Good morning, everyone," he mumbled as he stood and laid his laptop case at the end of the table.

I was sure that everyone in the room had been wondering the same thing I had been; Was Stark feeling embarrassed, angry or even regretting that he'd ever gotten involved in the race? I knew we'd have to handle this crazy idea very carefully when we presented it to him or we'd risk him losing whatever remained of his self-confidence.

"Gabe, good morning," I said, trying to look welcoming and upbeat. Before I could say anything more I saw him looking at the image on the projection screen. He stood and stared at in in silence then turned toward Wayne and then to me. "Geez," he said, "looks like I missed something."

Suddenly the members of the team, with the exception of Wayne and Jeremy, looked down as though they were fascinated by their notes and iPads as they all ignored Stark's comment. "Gabe," I said, "I don't have to tell you that last night was kind of strange to say the least." Stark nodded and turned again to look at the screen as I continued. "Well, last night, when some of us were in that auditorium and the rest of us were watching at home, we weren't aware of the fact that one of our opponents, Mr. Laughlin, had just handed us a gift." Wayne was looking at me knowing that I was in full-on bullshit mode.

Stark finally sat down, a confused look on his face. "What do mean a gift, what gift?"

225

"Gabe, do you remember our conversation that first day in your office when I first proposed the idea of you running for Governor?"

"Yeah, what about it?"

"Well, I told you that people were looking for a different kind of candidate, a different kind of person. And remember when I said how a lot of people feel that they've been ignored and unappreciated?" Stark nodded as I continued. "There's a lot of voter anger out there and this morning there's even more of it and we have to tap into it. Last night Mark Laughlin slapped your supporters in the face. Hell, he even slapped your mom and dad in the face." I paused for a moment hoping that last statement would get his attention.

Stark leaned back in his chair, looked up again at the screen and then at everyone around the table. "You know," he said softly, "last night when I was standing there, like six feet away from Laughlin and I heard those words come out of his mouth, I wanted, I wanted to reach over and punch that smug son of a bitch right in the mouth."

"Me too, Gabe!" Wayne bellowed.

So did I," Annie said, surprising everyone in the room with the departure from her normally meek, all business demeanor.

Wayne stood up and slowly walked to the screen at the front of the room. "Gabe, we all feel the same way. We're all fuckin' pissed off. This picture up here on the screen was Jeremy's idea and I think it's fantastic." He took a deep breath and looked at me. I nodded my approval of what I knew he was going to say. "Gabe," he said, "Laughlin doesn't like you and he doesn't like your supporters. Hell, that might only be three percent of the voters right now but that's still a whole hell of a lot of people who don't deserve to be treated like shit." He pointed up at the image on the screen and said, "So how about you go out there and show him what you're made of."

Stark still looked confused but I was hoping his anger and bruised ego would be enough to sell him on our idea. "Gabe," I said, somehow keeping a straight face, "We need you to trust us on this one. Let us get rolling on the concept now, right now because we have to move fast. Believe me, I think this will get us out of the three percent hole within a matter of days."

I looked over at Annie and she nodded, raised her hands as if it was a sign of capitulation and said, "Just go and do what you think you have to do."

Stark looked at me and I could tell that his ego had finally caught up with his anger. "Okay, just tell me what you need from me

21

Uncaging the Beast

Despite the months it took to create the con, all of the meticulous planning and the many more months of working on the campaign I never imagined that it would lead to something like this. We were literally starting over. Jeremy's basic idea that he described off the record as "trashy people coming out of the closet" had quickly become a fully developed concept. We had a print campaign that included everything from bumper stickers to billboards to newspaper ads. We had purchased television slots for fifteen and thirty second ads on every station in the state and Carol had already written an in-your-face article for the blog. Because Wayne wore both the hats for Carr Creative and CONjunction he was able to finagle some additional time and talent to totally retool the campaign website and develop new internet ads that had already been uploaded. And in a matter of two hours Jeremy had redesigned Stark's *Facebook* page and sent him half a dozen comments to Tweet under his own name. By mid-afternoon the team had created a whole new multimedia campaign that I was certain was unlike anything anyone had ever tried before. Two things made me feel that way. One, in all of my years in advertising and media I had never seen anything close to it and two, the wide eyed, almost terrified looks on the faces of the rest of the team only reinforced my notion.

Wayne, Jeremy and I sat in my CONjunction office with the door closed, enjoying beers from my mini-fridge, trying to catch our breath and take a few moments to comprehend what in the hell it was we had just done. For a few minutes none of us spoke and then finally Wayne asked, "So boss, are you feelin' the same way I am about all this?"

"Hell, I don't know how to answer that because I'm trying to figure out exactly what it is we just did." I looked at them both and added, "And I have to be honest, part of me wants to take a shower."

Jeremy nodded. "I know what you mean, Linc, it's like all this time I've been working on all of the trailer park and Jethro shit and I knew the whole damn thing was kind of tongue in cheek, like an inside joke around the office and we were all kind of laughing. Hell, not kind of laughing, we were definitely fucking laughing at these people and then this Laughlin guy who's our competition comes out with his trash talking and now I'm thinking, hey you asshole, you can't talk about my people like that!"

Wayne let out a huge laugh and said, "*My people*, I love it, man, *my people!*"

Immediately, Delilah's comment over breakfast popped into my head. "Man, you are so right." I said, "You are so on the money. This morning Delilah told me that she thought the trailer park people had gotten under my skin and she was absolutely right. Carr Creative has made a ton of money catering to people that we did all of this research on and we lived and breathed what we thought they wanted. But when it comes right down to it we sort of know them but none of us really cares much about them."

Wayne chimed in with a smirk on his face, "Hey boss man, I'm startin' to care a whole lot for one of them, Luanne."

"Okay, my friend, you got me there and if all that caring helps you learn more about trailer park behavior just please be careful and judicious in what you reveal." Wayne's booming laugh told me that he got my point. Then I added, "But you have to admit, this new "I'm Trash" bit is kind of, what, snarky, insulting, what's the right word?"

"Honest," Wayne said without any hesitation. I didn't immediately respond and he said, "Linc, you read that entire mountain of research and the studies and shit just like I did and you know damn well the kind of folks that we're talkin' about here. Shit, I remember back when you were all worried that we were bein' condescendin' and you didn't want to offend anyone." I nodded and looked over at Jeremy who seemed to be waiting eagerly for my response.

"So," I asked Wayne, "do you think that Laughlin was right when he called them trash?"

Wayne leaned forward and looked me square in the eye. "Boss man, you've always told me, "Don't ignore the data." You said that a campaign should always talk to the target in his own language and that he had to feel the ad was talkin' to him personally."

"So, again, I have to ask, was Laughlin right?"

I noticed Jeremy looking over at Wayne and then down at the table, almost as though he was embarrassed at the answer he knew was coming. "Boss," Wayne said, "let's not forget everything we've learned and let's not forget our mission here." He paused for a moment and then said with an odd little grin, "With the exception of Luanne the guy is absolutely right."

Jeremy had a guilty-looking smile on his face and I knew that we had reached a sort of moment of truth with the campaign. "Okay," I said, "let's go find out if the trailer park is everything we think it is. Let's see if we can get away with this, and let's see if Jethro and his friends can get us all the way to ten percent."

The next twenty-four hours were a non-stop thrill ride over a political landscape that had literally been transformed from what it had been just a day before. Our campaign had become a news story unto itself and judging from the commentary by the local news anchors the public wasn't quite sure if it was for real or just payback for Laughlin's comment. The online chatter on *Facebook* and *Twitter* suggested that there was a sudden ground swell of support for Stark, and whether that support was rooted in sincere political agreement or just jumping on the "I'm trash" bandwagon out of pity or for the fun of it, the number of people getting involved was rapidly growing and it was coming from all over the state. Urban, suburban and rural folks seemed to be united in their ability to identify with the campaign. It was a reminder that from everything we had learned about the behavior, tastes and attitudes of the average consumer the trailer park was far bigger than just places where mobile homes were sitting. Annie Kolchik had called me to say the campaign staff couldn't keep up with the requests for bumper stickers and lapel pins. There was even demand for them from outside of Arizona. It was as though it was suddenly cool to call yourself trash. I gave her the okay to order more.

While I was packing up my files and laptop bag so I could make my commute home in time to catch the local evening news shows, Wayne walked into my office. "Hey, Linc, do you fuckin' believe what's goin' on out there? This trash thing has taken on a life of its own." He dropped down into a squeaking chair in front of my desk, then noticed me doing my end of the day ritual and stood up again. "Oh, looks like I'm slowin' down your exit."

"Yeah," I answered, "I want to get home in time to catch *Channel 12*. Annie said they called her this afternoon and they're going to do a segment on the phone interview she did this afternoon. It'll be on at six o'clock. And she also told me she's been getting requests for yard signs but only if they say "I'm Trash" on them. I don't know what's going on with this strange, new campaign but, if nothing else, Gabe's name is finally getting out there."

"I know, I talked to Luanne about an hour ago and she said some of her friends at work want to help with the campaign. She said these are people who never talk about politics or votin' and all of a sudden they want to get involved." He walked out into the hallway with me and said, "And before you leave, here's a little idea Luanne had, somethin' for you to think about tonight." I waited, half afraid of what was coming. "Luanne has some girlfriends who are, shall we say, smokin' hot, and she has this idea of gettin' them together in some tiny little red, white and blue outfits, boots and cowgirl hats and making them part of the events when Gabe gives speeches and stuff. And here's the best part, they'd be called, "Gabe's Babes."

On any other day, in any other place, under any other circumstances I would have laughed and dismissed the idea as one of Wayne's crazy brain farts, but not on this day. After seeing what was going on with the campaign and how being "trash" was suddenly trending all over the media I just saw it as the next logical step in a very illogical plan. I smiled and said, "I love it. Help Luanne set things in motion."

Wayne nodded and said, "Just one more thing, man. I have a feelin' Annie's gonna shit a brick when she hears the idea. She's kind of prim and proper about some stuff."

"Don't worry, I'll talk to her in the morning. After all, once you take that step and adopt an "I'm trash" mindset it's only one more, short step to scantily clad women."

On the drive home I scanned the local radio stations looking for any kind of news or commentary about the gubernatorial race in general and Stark's campaign in particular. I was rewarded with numerous reports on what had become known locally as "Trashgate" and the story that people couldn't seem to get enough of. Even though the reporters and talking heads tried hard to present the story in a professional manner it was obvious from their tone that our campaign was still being viewed as little more than a very amusing sidelight in an otherwise mundane election year. The entire situation was nothing I had ever expected when I first came up with the con but I knew I had to stay focused on getting Stark's polling numbers up to ten percent or even a few points more so John Leone and the Democrats would have a shot at overcoming the Republican registration advantage. I was nervous because it didn't seem as though I still had control of things. My con, my child wasn't behaving the way I wanted but I knew that our goal hadn't changed even if everything else had.

Pulling into an empty garage and walking into an empty house was getting to be routine for me. Delilah's hours at work hadn't loosened up at all. She didn't like practically living at her office any more than I did but we had just finished converting one of the five bedrooms into a very well equipped home office for her and she said she was ready to start doing more work from there. It meant she'd be handcuffed to a computer in the house instead of the one at her office but at least we'd be under the same roof. Ozzie had his music, Delilah had her work and I had my cons. The lottery money had made it possible for all three of us to feed our addictions.

After thumbing through the day's mail, letting Bowser out into the backyard and feeding Otto I turned on the televisions in the kitchen, living room and bedroom. I poured myself some bourbon and walked from room to room, changing my clothes, munching on pretzels and trying to take in multiple reports on the election campaign. The news anchors and reporters presented their stories with straight faces and in matter-of-fact tones but the occasional smirks and near giggles told me that our campaign was already woven into the fabric of the race for Governor. In a strange and dark way I took great pride in the media's fascination with the word "trash" and my role in creating the arena in which they could use it. With a second glass of bourbon in hand I sat down in the living room and watched the news play out on my big screen TV. I was feeling mellow and smug until the anchor on *Channel 12* announced something that jarred me back into focus. He showed a graphic of polling results, compiled earlier in the day, that showed Laughlin had dropped to thirty-two percent, Leone had moved up to thirty-three, Stark had grabbed a twenty-three percent piece and the Undecideds had dropped down to just twelve percent. I stared at the screen, stunned. Our goal had always been to use Stark to steal around ten percent from Laughlin and hope that Leone could build his numbers from the other side. Now, forty-eight hours after Laughlin's roundtable faux pas we had accomplished our goal and then some.

I was sitting there trying to absorb what it all meant when my cellphone rang. Wayne's name came up on the screen and I had a feeling I knew what was coming next. I put the phone to my ear, took a breath and said, "So I take it you saw the poll results."

Wayne's voice was so loud I had to pull the phone away from my ear. "Holy shit, man, do you believe those fuckin' numbers?" He sounded like he was out of breath. "Twenty-three percent, man, twenty-three fuckin percent! And Leone is up on Laughlin by a point!"

"Yeah, I'm sitting here watching *Channel 12* and trying to figure out what it all means."

"What it means, man, is we did it. We got our ten and even more!"

"The ten percent was a vague number and I was hoping for a little more but this isn't just a little."

"I know, boss man, but it's good news and we, mainly you, should be proud."

"Okay, relax, big guy, you know what they say in sports about peaking too soon. We still have a few weeks to go and a lot can happen." I knew that my comment was logical but I also knew that logic in this campaign had pretty much disappeared. "With numbers like this, what we have to concentrate on now is making sure that we don't do anything to turn this trend around or see our numbers fall and hurt Leone."

It had always been a difficult task to turn off Wayne once something got him turned on and this situation was no different. "I hear what you're sayin', boss, but the way I see it we finally got our man on the radar and we just gotta' keep things rollin' along and, like you said, make sure he doesn't slide backwards."

Our conversation was interrupted by the beep of an incoming call on my phone. I looked at the screen and saw it was Stark. "Hey, man," I said to Wayne, "Gabe's calling in and I better take it."

"Go, boss man, and let me know what you wanna' do next."

I touched my phone to end Wayne's call and touched it again to answer Stark's. "Hey, Gabe, I was just going to call you. Can I assume you've heard the news?"

Stark's voice sounded different than I'd ever heard it before. His usual nervous, tentative tone had become noticeably more confident. "Yeah, I heard the news and I have to say, I'm kind of in a daze. What in the hell happened? Is this just from the trailer trash thing?"

I wished I would have had some time to think about everything before Stark and I had a conversation but I was caught in a position now where I had to shoot from the hip. "Well," I answered slowly, trying to choose my words carefully, "It's really hard to say, Gabe. I think people just needed a chance to see who you are and what you're all about and this trash thing kind of, well, it opened the door." I had been conning Stark for so long I should have gotten used to doing it but I was still struggling to sound sincere.

"When I heard we're at twenty-three percent I just about shit. My wife and kids are going nuts and my dad called and he was practically in tears. It's like, so hard to imagine gaining twenty points in a few days."

"Yeah, I agree. It's like nothing I've ever heard of before but let's not look a gift horse in the mouth here." I paused and then added, "I have a call into Annie. I want to meet with her tomorrow afternoon to go over the stuff we have coming up. I want to make a big push in the final couple of weeks. I saw your schedule this morning and it looks like a speech at a senior center, one at an elementary school, a tour of the casino construction and a couple of meet and greets at a Walmart and a K-mart."

"Yeah, I saw that too. Doesn't it seem like I should be busier, you know, seeing more people?"

Before the latest poll numbers had come out I had put together a plan that would keep Stark in the public eye just enough that they wouldn't forget him and enough to keep his number at around the ten percent mark I had been figuring on. But it was a totally different race now and I was facing a juggling act to keep Stark's numbers from sinking as fast as they had risen. Despite what I had told him earlier about finally being on the voter's radar I knew it was the "I'm Trash" campaign that had pumped up the numbers and not his ideas and policies. "Gabe," I said, trying to sound like I was in agreement with him, "I think I'll sit in on your meeting with Annie and help her put together enough stuff to keep you busy in the home stretch."

We talked for a few more minutes and after we hung up I called Wayne back. He agreed that we needed to keep a lid on

Stark without letting him realize it. We couldn't let him screw up and risk dropping back down to three percent.

The final few weeks of the race showed that the public seemed to have an endless appetite for our cheap, tawdry campaign. Gabe's Babes were a huge hit with the male voters and we even scheduled a couple of events where they appeared without Stark. He appeared at what we thought were safe venues where he couldn't talk too long or say too much. There were "I'm Trash" signs everywhere and people were proudly wearing their lapel pins in offices, stores and restaurants. The TV spots had migrated from television screens to being shared on *Facebook* and had over three hundred thousand views on *You Tube*. To the media and the general public it was seen as a pop culture phenomenon and that should have been something that ad men like Wayne and I could be excited about. But there was a totally unexpected side to the campaign and we were both getting more and more nervous about it. Despite his lackluster performance Stark's poll numbers had continued to grow. Two days before the election the numbers stood at Laughlin 30, Leone 31, Stark 25 and Undecided 14. Those undecided voters, if they actually showed up to vote, would make or break the election and now all we could do was sit back and watch. All we needed now was for Laughlin's numbers to stay put or shrink, for Stark to avoid saying anything stupid and lose points to Laughlin and for a few more percentage points to move over into John Leone's column and get him elected. It looked like my con had a very good shot at working.

22

Losing CONtrol

The first sign that things weren't exactly going according to plan came just before ten o'clock. When the details of our election night event had been planned two months earlier Wayne and I had envisioned a quiet gathering at the downtown Sheraton with the proper mix of enthusiasm and concession. I had written a speech for Stark to give, one that would thank his staff, congratulate the winner and mention that he was grateful to the voters who came out in support of him. The number of those voters was hoped to be high enough to do two things; swing the election toward John Leone and make Stark think he actually had some kind of a future in elected office. That was what the script for the con had called for but, strangely, that's not what seemed to be playing out.

The large room we had rented included a small portable stage with a podium and we had mounted three large, flat screen televisions on the wall behind it so we could watch the local news coverage at polling stations throughout the state. The crowd noise in the room made it impossible to hear the talking heads on the screens but, starting around nine o'clock it seemed that every time I'd glance up at one of them a piece of video was playing that showed Gabriel Stark at some earlier campaign event. It seemed odd that the guy who was in last place in the polls was the focus of the coverage. All I could figure was that the news story was still focused on Stark's *Trash Campaign.*

This went on for nearly an hour and it was when I saw Annie Kolchik standing off to the right side of the stage, a hand over one ear while she held her cellphone tightly to the other that I began to get a strange feeling. I watched her face closely and when I saw her eyes widen and her mouth drop open I knew what had happened. She had no sooner pulled her phone away from her ear when it rang again and it brought the same reaction. She stood in that spot, staring down at the floor and not moving a muscle. Then she turned and hurried over to Stark and shouted into his ear over the noise of the crowd. Stark's face became the same wide-eyed expression as Annie's. Neither of them moved for a moment and then she walked to the microphone but before she said anything I saw her look across the stage at Cousin Albert. She nodded toward the mike and he gave her a thumbs-up sign. She appeared to be shaking in her shoes. Then she cleared her throat, took a deep breath and in a voice that sounded more astonished than happy or triumphant she announced to the crowd that both Mark Laughlin and John Leone had called to concede the race to Gabriel Stark. At that same moment images of their unhappy concession speeches flashed on to the television screens with a text trailer stating that both men had, in fact, conceded the race to Stark.

I sat at the front table in the banquet room, with Delilah, Ozzie, Michelle, Wayne and Luanne around me. While the staff applauded, while Stark hugged his wife and kids, while his father and mother waved to the crowd, while Gabe's Babes wiggled and cheered, the mood at our table was decidedly different. My *King of the Trailer Park* con had sadly and unintentionally made Gabriel Stark the official Governor of Arizona. I actually began to feel sick.

"Jesus H. Christ, how did we fuck this one up?" Wayne muttered as he leaned back and stared blankly at the ceiling.

"Oh my God," Delilah said, exhaling and shaking her head, "is this even possible?"

Ozzie leaned toward me, looking angry and stated the obvious, "God dammit, Linc, this wasn't supposed to be what happened."

Michelle looked at me as though she was in shock then turned and put her arm around Oz like she was trying to console him.

From head to toe I was a mass of mixed emotions; shock over Stark's victory, a sense of dread for what it meant to the state and a faint but real feeling that I needed to laugh. I sat there in silence, trying to grasp what had happened, looking first at Delilah and then at the rest of my little team. I could feel my heartbeat pick up its pace and I tried to keep my mind on the election instead of my pulse. I looked up at Stark standing on the stage. Despite the clear look of elation on his face he also looked like a deer caught in the headlights.

Wayne broke into my thoughts when he said, "Boss man, this is about the craziest fuckin' thing I ever heard of. This just can't be happenin'."

It had been my idea, my con and my money and I knew that everyone at the table was expecting me to offer some words of wisdom, some kind of apology or explanation for what went wrong. I thought about it a few moments longer and was starting to feel less ill. Then, finally, it dawned on me me. I reached for my glass of bourbon but my racing heart suggested that I should set it back down. I paused, took a deep breath and said, "You know, what happened was exactly what was supposed to happen. It was inevitable."

"Now just how in the hell do you figure that?" Oz asked with the anger in his voice obvious.

Delilah told me later that I was smiling the entire time I was answering Ozzie's question. "Look, the entire campaign was based upon research that we had already done for someone else. Even if I had never come up with the con we knew that what we called the trailer park was something real, something that could be measured and something that could be manipulated. That's what advertisers do and that's what we did. We set about on a specific plan with a specific goal and in the process we awakened a sleeping giant that more than likely will fall back to sleep in a matter of days."

"You're probably right about that, boss," Wayne chimed in, "but it still didn't go according to our specific plan."

"Wrong, my large friend, it went exactly the way we scripted it, we just misread where the end point was. All of our advertising concepts, all of the campaigns for whatever product it might have been, they all have had sales targets or some kind of goal. So here we are, watching the results of a campaign that we created end up selling three or four times the number of units we expected."

Delilah was quick to respond. "Yeah, honey but people aren't units. Instead of helping the people of Arizona we just screwed them over."

I glanced at all of them one by one, their expressions seeming to agree with Delilah's comment, and then I looked back at her and said, "Nope, I disagree." I had no idea if my argument would make a difference in what they were thinking but it was slowly starting to make perfect sense to me. "Stop for a minute and think about the mess the last three or four governors have made. A billion dollar deficit, a horrible reputation for intolerance in the national media, selling off government buildings to raise cash, a school system that's almost at the bottom of the list and what were we trying to do? We were trying to squeeze out a few lousy percentage points so John Leone could somehow turn everything around." I waited a few seconds and no one said a word so I backed off a little. "Look, this was my con and I will admit that I might have been a little naïve in thinking it might actually make things better but I felt I had to try something."

Oz nodded and looked at me. "Well, I agree that your heart was in the right place even if the plan didn't work exactly the way you expected. But in hindsight, John Leone losing to Mark Laughlin still would have been way better than turning the state over to Gabe Stark."

Would it really?" I answered sharply. "Would it have ended the gridlock at the Capital? Would it have lessened the bigotry or balanced the budget? Would it really have made one fucking bit of difference?"

"So, man," Wayne asked, "what's your point?"

"My point is this. There's an old saying that "people get the government they deserve" and when you get right down to it that's just what they got. The poll results we saw a few days ago said twenty-five percent of the voters wanted Stark and that number obviously went up because he won. So that adds up to a whole hell of a lot of people. We didn't pull the lever for them, they did it on their own. Stark didn't lie or mislead anyone. He was out there straight up in all his polyester and dyed-hair glory for everyone to see."

"Sorry, honey, no matter how you spin it or want to look at this there's just no way you can say the people of Arizona deserve this mess." Delilah said. It was a blunt statement that I knew was meant to cut right through what they all considered the bullshit I was spewing.

I took a deep breath and answered, "Honestly, babe, it might be a mess but I'll guarantee one thing. Gabriel Stark will be the most watched, analyzed, scrutinized and criticized governor this state or maybe any state has ever had. And that just might make people realize what happens when you don't take the time to vote or don't think about the consequences when you do. I looked over at Luanne and said, "With all due respect to our new friend here, we have to remember what all of our trailer park research told us, that those people don't pay attention and they don't care? Well look what happened when a guy called them trash and they started paying attention and caring real fast. There's a lesson to be learned here and maybe after a month or two of soul searching I'll know what the hell it is." I hoped my words sounded sincere as I struggled with my very guilty conscience.

The rest of the evening was an interesting challenge for all of us; pretending to be happy over the victory, trying not to look worried about the future, trying to keep a straight face when Stark gave his acceptance speech and, most of all acting like the outcome was what we had planned all along. Later, when the party started to die down I invited my little team of accomplices to slip away and join me in the lobby bar. It was late and the place had all but emptied out. We sat at a corner table and watched as the last television crew walked out the front door. It might have been the late hour or the alcohol or maybe the relief that the campaign and the con were finally over, but a surprisingly happy feeling came over me. I raised my nearly empty glass. "Okay folks, it's time for a toast. Here's to our new Perspirer-in-Chief." The uncomfortable laughter and the clinking of our glasses probably appeared to anyone who was watching to be a normal victory celebration. If only they knew.

Ozzie, still looking upset, sat quietly for a moment and then offered his own toast. "Here's to a day that will live on in history and will always be known as *The Great Arizona Train Wreck.*"

More awkward laughter and more clinking of glasses followed until Delilah put things into perspective. "I guess it's good that we can find something to laugh about in all this, kind of like we're whistling past the graveyard." It was a great metaphor for the situation.

When things around us seemed to be reaching some kind of finish I waved to our server for the check.

"Well, Linc," Wayne said, his voice sounding tired, "before we wrap up this little party I just wanna' say it's been an interestin' year and a really weird night but in spite of the fact we probably created a four-year long disaster movie, thanks for the adventure." He raised his glass and the others followed, albeit half-heartedly.

"Thanks, I appreciate your hard work and everything you all gave up to get us here."

"And where is here?" Oz asked.

I couldn't help but smile. "When one of you figures it out please let the rest of us know."

Wayne leaned toward me with a devilish grin on his face. "So what happens now, boss, now that we've got CONjunction runnin' like a well-oiled machine?"

"Yeah, we do," I answered, "and if we're not careful some other political hack will ask us to run his campaign."

"But seriously, any ideas for your next con, cause' we all know damn well one is gonna' come sooner or later."

I had a dozen ideas for future cons and wanted to see them happen if the future would allow. I looked at Wayne with a smirk.

"Well, as a matter of fact, since you asked I do have an idea that I think might be fun."

Delilah grabbed my arm, kissed me on the cheek and said, "Oh please don't say that. Those are the words that got us here and we need a break."

"Relax, it won't involve getting anyone elected. It'll be more for the pure entertainment value." I looked at the curious faces around me. "This one will take some time and it needs some more thought but here it is in a nutshell. Remember awhile back when a bunch of anti-government rednecks in Texas was talking about launching a move to secede from the United States? Well, what if some creative, well funded and experienced con artists were to get involved and offer to help them do it?

"Shit, we know Texas is like the epicenter of crazy but do you mean really help them secede?" Wayne asked.

"No, not really, that will never happen but think about how the rest of the country will look at it. Hell, we'll have a wild redneck, trailer park comedy playing every night on the national news."

Oz laughed. "Sounds exactly like something you'd come up with. Got a name for the con yet?"

"Yep, I'm calling it *Forget the Alamo*."

The End